Pioneer Girl

Also by Bich Minh Nguyen

Stealing Buddha's Dinner: A Memoir

Short Girls: A Novel

Pioneer Girl

Girl

BICH MINH NGUYEN

VIKING

VIKING
Published by the Penguin Group
Penguin Group (USA) LLC
375 Hudson Street
New York, New York 10014

USA | Canada | UK | Ireland | Australia | New Zealand | India | South Africa | China
penguin.com
A Penguin Random House Company

First published by Viking Penguin, a member of Penguin Group (USA) LLC, 2014

LIBRARY OF CONGRESS CATALOGING-IN-PUBLICATION DATA

Nguyen, Bich Minh.
Pioneer girl : a novel / Bich Minh Nguyen.
pages cm
ISBN 978-0-670-02509-1
1. Vietnamese Americans—Fiction.   2. Immigrants—Fiction.
3. Women Journalist—Vietnam—Fiction.   4. Bracelets—Fiction.
5. Vietnam War, 1961–1975—Fiction.   I. Title.
PS3614.G84P56 2013
813'.6—dc23   2013018403

Printed in the United States of America
1   3   5   7   9   10   8   6   4   2

Set in Carre Noir Std
Designed by Alissa Amell

For Po, Henry, and Julian

Pioneer
Girl

PROLOGUE

In August 1965 a woman named Rose walked into my grandfather's café in Saigon. That much is known. My grandfather would say that's the beginning of this story. My mother would say I should have left it at that.

Back then, my mother and grandfather lived in the rooms above the café. She was twelve, an only child whose own mother had died the year before. In the evenings my grandfather taught her English from a friend's borrowed textbook. He had a feeling, he used to say, that it was the language of the future. On that day when an American woman sat down at one of his teak tables, looked around at the blue-trimmed doorways and the ceiling fans that had paddles shaped like gingko leaves, he took it as a sign. She asked for coffee or tea, whichever was freshest, and he brought her a cup of French roast with condensed milk and half a baguette, using his most careful pronunciation to ask if she needed any kind of help. It was monsoon season, the part of the year when heat and steam were the same, unrelenting. The traffic of bicycles and mopeds and pedicabs crisscrossed the windows, and the woman seemed glad to be free of it. There weren't many American women in Vietnam, and she didn't seem like a nurse or aid worker. She was old, surprisingly so, hair a silver sweep beneath a straw hat.

Oh, I don't need help, she said. I need conversation.

She was a reporter, on assignment for a magazine that wanted her to write about the war in Vietnam from a woman's point of view. She was supposed to spend a month getting a sense of the country, the people, the culture, and distill it all into an article. My grandfather, always interested in other people's stories, sat and talked with her, while my mother watched from the kitchen. I have imagined the languorous way Rose might have sat, the way her dress folded around her, making her seem protected, somehow, as if she knew the war would not touch her.

Rose stopped by the café often during her week in Saigon, and though she and my grandfather talked for hours, he remembered little about her history. If Rose revealed her full name, if she spoke about her own mother and father, or anything about the roots of her family, he didn't remember. He recalled, instead, her lively voice, her many questions about Vietnam; he remembered her largeness, how she always wore a hat. In anticipation of her visits, he reserved pineapple and lychees for her. He offered her delicacies usually eaten on holidays—sticky rice buns stuffed with sweet sausage, candied ginger snacks, curls of dried coconut. She ate them heartily. He gave her advice about lodgings in Da Lat and Hue and, whenever she bade farewell, he helped her cross the street. One day, when Rose complained of a cramp in her leg, he had my mother run out to fetch some balm that Rose later said cured her instantly. *You are lovely*, my mother remembered Rose saying. *The loveliest little family.*

Ten years later, when my mother and grandfather fled Saigon for America, one of the few things they took with them was a small gold pin, engraved with a picture of a house, that had belonged to Rose. She had dropped it, perhaps, forgotten it. Left it sitting on the table where a plate would be. They had kept the pin safe, but Rose never came back.

When I was growing up my grandfather liked to tell these stories about Rose. Once in a while my mother joined in too. *That big white lady with a purse and a notebook*, she would say. *All by herself, in Saigon, in a war.* Her voice would take on a kind of tenderness, wonder, that I rarely heard otherwise.

We would usually be packed in the car when they got to remembering like this, but I didn't pay much attention until the time we moved from a town in southern Wisconsin to a town in central Illinois. I was eight years old and book-crazy, could read for stretches in the car without getting sick, while my brother, Sam, listened to the same music on his Discman over and over. Even then, at age nine, he had the ability to close himself down to everyone around him. That year, my obsession was the *Little House on the Prairie* box set my grandfather had given me for my birthday. As we drove toward our new town I imagined every farm we passed was Laura Ingalls Wilder's and that I could see her, calico-bonneted, walking in wheat. I'd been following her, book to book, from childhood to adulthood when, one Christmas, her new fiancé Almanzo gave her a present.

There in a nest of white cotton lay a gold bar pin. On its flat surface was etched a little house, and before it along the bar lay a tiny lake, and a spray of grasses and leaves.

It sounded just like Rose's pin, the narrow shape and delicate weight I'd known from helping my mother clean her jewelry.

Outside, wildflowers along the road blurred together as my mother accelerated to pass a minivan. She was a faster driver than my grandfather, who liked to point out the semis ahead and keep a watch for police cars.

Ong Hai, I said, which was what we all called him. Listen to this. I read the description aloud.

How funny, he said. Isn't that funny?

You read too much, my mother said to me.

I say Rose's pin was a gift too, my grandfather went on. Even if by accident. Can't refuse something like that.

My mother said nothing more, but I figured it must have meant the same for her. Why else would they have kept the pin, brought it to America?

We drove on, all of us confined together in the old Mercury. We were, if nothing else, accounted for and heading in the same direction. A new restaurant. A new town. A new apartment. My mother and grandfather would take turns behind the wheel, fiddling with the temperature controls. The urn that carried my father's ashes rode up front with them. In the back, Sam and I stared out the windows at the electric wires leading us deeper into the big Midwest that was the only landscape we knew.

I decided to pretend that the two pins were the same, that Almanzo's gift to Laura was not just based on a true story, but a real treasure now hidden away in my mother's jewelry box. In books, characters were always keeping secrets. This would be one of mine. I didn't know it would stay that way for years, waiting to be brought out into the light.

I went back to my books. My mother gripped the steering wheel; my grandfather searched the radio for weather and news. Sam leaned against his door, eyes closed, arms tucked beneath the marled blanket our mother had knitted the previous winter. Outside, the afternoon had long given in to clouds. We drove on, together, toward our next new home.

ONE

always thought when I left my mother's house there'd be no looking back. That the restaurant life my family had followed for so long would not figure into mine. If there was one thing Sam and I had always agreed on, it was that. In college I'd majored in English, then kept on for a PhD that my mother called a waste, meaningless compared to dentistry, engineering, or at the very least, accounting. So when I had to move back to Franklin after grad school, nowhere else to go, I said it was because I'd lost the lease on my apartment in Madison. I wasn't about to admit that I'd struck out on the academic job market.

My mother put me to work right away at the coffee-slash-noodle shop that she owned with Ong Hai. Within days I was fixing summer rolls, chopping up onions and herbs, learning how to blend dark-roast coffee and condensed milk into a perfect cafe sua. At first there was something soothing about the routine, the symmetry of a shrimp sliced lengthwise onto a bed of rice noodles. But soon the panic crept in. I'd seen girls like me before. Sullen daughters, stringy-haired and oily-faced, wearing stained aprons and shuffling around their parents' restaurants, all hope lost for lives of their own. They were like a modern-day version of the docile spinster daughters who had always terrified me in the books of my childhood.

Then there was the name of the café: the Lotus Leaf. When I said out loud that it sounded excessively exotic, my mother told me that proved I had no sense. Too much education for my own good. *We been running this place two years and everyone else likes it just fine.* Ong Hai's Vietnamese coffees and lunchtime pho had generated good reviews on Yelp and a small mention in the suburb section of the *Chicago Reader*. But I knew that business was thinning and that he was worried. I told myself that these were matters that Sam was supposed to inherit—my mother had taken on the café in the first place for him. But Sam had flouted all of us by leaving, dropping out of contact two Christmases before. They'd argued, that much I knew, though I never learned about what.

So when, three weeks after my own return, Sam called my phone and hung up without leaving a message, my mother cleaned the whole house down to the window blinds. I told her the missed call was probably a mistake but she believed it meant he was coming home.

It turned out she was right.

A couple of days after the phone call I left the café early, taking a long route back to the rental house my mother and Ong Hai had claimed as home. The space between their neighborhood and the Lotus Leaf was a soul-numbing continuum of chain restaurants and local efforts with names like Itemz and If It's Baskets. You wouldn't even know Chicago was less than twenty miles to the east.

I wanted to forget about the long summer, or more, that stretched ahead of me. My brother was far from my mind.

So when I saw him on the cement stoop I wondered, for half a second, if he was the ghost—sounds crazy to say now—of our father. A spirit in the way of Vietnamese belief. And then I realized I was thinking the way my mother probably would. And then I realized that she was right, that Sam's call had been a signal. A long time later, I would understand that the signal wasn't for her but for me.

In a burst of fury, my mother had changed all the locks after Sam left. So he was just sitting there, hanging around waiting for someone to open the door. I parked in front of the black SUV that must have been his and as I walked toward him I wondered who would speak first. What were you supposed to say to someone who had reappeared after more than a year of silence?

Sam cast his gaze around me as if checking out the neighborhood. In warm weather, the old couple across the street liked to set up lawn chairs just inside their open garage, where they would wait for their grandkids to come visit and wave to anyone who happened to walk by. Their chairs were empty at the moment but two drink cozies were sitting on the garage floor.

A city bus stopped at the corner, exhaled, then heaved its way onward again.

"How long have you been here?" I finally said.

Sam shrugged at the question. He had started doing that in high school—a practiced, careless shrug, full of dismissal, hinting at derision. He looked older, just as thin, but more gaunt in the face, as if his skin were doing extra work to pull itself around his fine features.

"I need your help with something," he said.

As we walked into the house Sam glanced at the corner of the living room where our mother kept the shrine to the dead: our father's urn, a small statue of Buddha, candles, incense, a plate of fruit, and a photograph from the eighties, turning sepia-toned in the glass frame. Our father was perpetually starting to smile. He was outside somewhere, blue sky and stilled clouds behind him.

Instead of heading to the kitchen, where I always went first, Sam went down the narrow hall to our mother's room.

"Hey," I said, following. "What are you doing?"

He opened her closet and started checking pockets, the insides of shoes, the insides of shoe boxes. She had a few old purses lined up and he looked in those too.

"Where do you think she keeps it?" he asked.

"Keeps what?"

"The money. Jesus."

I was so surprised I laughed a little. "Seriously?" When he didn't reply, I said, "Sam. What money?"

Finished with the closet, he went over to the old mahogany dresser that our mother had gotten for twenty bucks at a garage sale because it had a cloudy water stain on its top. I didn't stop him. Maybe a part of me was curious too if he would find anything.

He was messing up her clothes, I told him. And besides, was he really going to look through her underwear and bras?

He hesitated, then shut the top drawer. "I'm talking about Hieu's money." Hieu. It was a name I hadn't heard in a long time. He and our father had been best friends back when we lived in La Porte, Indiana, where I'd been born. They had talked about starting a restaurant together. Later Hieu had moved with us to Battle Creek, then back to La Porte. He had persuaded my father to go on a weekend trip with him, up to Michigan to fish the St. Joseph River, where my father had drowned.

When I told Sam I didn't know what he was talking about he studied my face for a moment, deciding whether or not to believe me. Then he said, "Hieu gives her money. She's been guilting him into it for years, ever since Dad died. I thought I was the only one who hadn't known."

11

My immediate reaction was distance. "That's ridiculous," I said. "Are you on something?"

He turned to the bed, lifted up the top mattress, and stuck an arm in there, looking for holes in the box spring.

"If you don't know about that, then I guess you don't know about the money that's yours. Or was yours."

I didn't want to know what he was going to say next, already disbelieving him. At the same time, I thought: *Of course.* Of course my mother would have done this, whatever this was—the crazier the better. "All right," I said. I straightened the bedspread. "Tell me."

He said that years back, Hieu had set up accounts for us, to help pay for college. Our mother had taken the money instead and used it to open the Lotus Leaf. "Last year, I followed her and saw her with him. Then she saw me. You can imagine how she reacted. I confronted her about it and told her I wanted my share of the money. She said that *you* wanted the money to go to the café."

"No," I said, too stunned to say anything else. *College* accounts?

"Didn't think so."

"What makes you think he's still giving her money?"

"You don't need a fucking PhD to figure things out. The guy is loaded. He drives a Mercedes. I asked Ong Hai about it and he didn't deny it. He wouldn't talk about it, but he didn't deny it."

I watched Sam go back to the dresser, open the middle drawer, and pat down the sweaters and shirts. "What's wrong with you?" he said. "Aren't you pissed?"

"This is what you guys argued about last year, then. At Christmas."

"Yeah, remember what a fun holiday that was? A couple of days before you got here I found out her secret. That money is blood money, Lee. It belongs to me, or you, just as much."

"It's not blood money. Don't be so melodramatic."

"Dad would never have gone fishing if Hieu hadn't made him."

We'd never talked like this before, broken into plain speech about our father. Sam's words echoed thoughts I'd had thousands of times. But still I said, "It was an accident."

"The money is no accident."

"What makes you think she'd even keep any of it here? She's not an idiot."

"You know how old-school she can be."

The bottom dresser drawer held my mother's winter scarves, a couple of old Vietnamese magazines, some Christmas gifts she'd never used: a bottle of Calvin Klein Eternity, still in its packaging, an empty leather photo frame, a Mylar space blanket.

"Look at all this crap," Sam said. He touched the blanket, which was supposed to be one of those emergency items to keep in the trunk of a car. Ong Hai had bought it at a kiosk at the mall.

Sam eyed our mother's ballerina jewelry box, which no longer had a ballerina and no longer played music. In it she kept the four gold and jade necklaces that had been her grandmother's, the jade bracelet I'd been made to wear as a toddler, and the double-strand gold chain bracelet my mother used to wear before deciding it got in the way of work. And the little gold piece, engraved with a faint image of a house, that the American woman, Rose, had left in Ong Hai's café in Saigon. I hadn't seen the jewelry in years, not since high school. As far as I knew, my mother never had occasions for dressing up.

I picked up Rose's pin. "Remember this?"

"Not that stupid story again."

"It was a big deal to them."

"Their first white American customer. Wowee."

"I'm pretty sure it was more than that." Not that I could have explained what. I almost started telling him how, as a kid, I'd imagined the pin to be an heirloom from Laura Ingalls Wilder. But it seemed silly, a faraway thought, so I put the pin back with the rest of the jewelry, closed the box, closed the drawer.

Sam stood up, glancing around the room once more. I fixed the wrinkles in my mother's nubbly yellow comforter. She always made her bed: the slight hill of one flat pillow, the sheets tucked tight. She had no patience for decoration, and the room showed it. Nothing had ever hung on the putty-colored walls, here or anywhere else she'd lived.

"You know Ong Hai would give you money, if he has it. Or

just ask Mom. She went nuts cleaning this whole place after you called."

"Whatever I found wouldn't be stealing. It would be my money too. Hell, it'd be yours too."

"They're going to be home any minute."

At that, he seemed to waver. I wondered if he was thinking of escaping to his car and driving away, so I said, "Come on. Let's get something to eat and you can figure out the money later."

He relented, but I knew he was far from done with the pursuit.

In the kitchen, Sam helped himself to one of Ong Hai's Corona beers. The fridge was crammed as always, plastic-wrapped bowls and plates balanced on each other. Like me, my mother and grandfather had this compulsion to hang on to even the smallest amount of leftovers. Then we'd forget how long something had been there.

Sam said again, "How is it you're not pissed?"

"I *am*," I said, though I sounded calm, felt it, even. There wasn't much I'd put past my mother.

"She mentioned that you'd moved back." Sam said that easily, conversationally, like he hadn't just been scouring her room for money.

I didn't know they'd communicated at all since that day he had stormed out, over a year ago.

Sam must have read as much on my face. "She sends me these texts," he said. "Every once in a while."

"Do you reply?"

The answer was no, of course. He didn't reply. Just let her keep texting into the void.

"So why'd you move back?" he asked.

I gave him my standard lie—in between semesters, waiting to see where I'd end up in the fall.

"Does that mean you're staying here?"

"Are you?"

I'd been away in Urbana, in my last year of undergrad, when my mother and Ong Hai and Sam moved into this rental house. Sam had halfheartedly enrolled in a few classes at the nearby community college but soon dropped out. For a while the name of their new street, Durango Road, gave us something to joke about. When I came home during winter break we'd whistle Wild West tunes and talk in cowboy accents about our home on the range. *What's Ma Kettle a-cookin' for supper?* I'd say. *I best be moseying*, Sam would say. *It's just about high noon at this semi-OK corral.*

It was a three-bedroom, larger than what we were used to, and since Sam claimed the basement my mother left the last bedroom for me, certain that I'd come back home after graduation. She didn't know that, in high school, I'd counted down the days to the start of college, that I couldn't get to the dorms fast enough. Back then I went home as little as possible; summers, I took extra classes and worked retail on campus. Of course I had to go to grad school right away.

Sam drank his beer and said, "Everything looks the same

here on Durango Road. Except we got ourselves some problems." He spoke with a cowboy twang, but I couldn't keep it going. I was thinking about my mother and Hieu.

Then she was there, at the kitchen door, she and Ong Hai, and I felt as nervous as Sam seemed to be, setting the beer bottle down too quickly. Would she notice that we'd been in her room? Did she really have a stockpile of money extorted from my father's best friend?

"Hey, Sam!" Ong Hai called out, as though Sam had only been away for a semester at college.

"Hey." Sam gave his first genuine smile, and Ong Hai reached forward and grabbed at his forearm.

"Too skinny," he said. "You working?"

"Sure."

"Then work less, eat more. That your SUV too? It's nice."

To me, Ong Hai never aged. His hair had always been a floaty sheen of gray and he'd always worn the same round glasses. He favored old-man short-sleeved button-downs with patch pockets, yet he was as quick as my mother, could stand all day making pho and spring rolls.

My mother paused before setting a plastic bag of café leftovers on the counter. She didn't acknowledge Sam by voice—she wasn't going to make it *that* easy—but glanced at him while getting some plates from the cupboard. I took out the shrimp and tofu summer rolls, banana bread, containers of pho that were our dinner.

"Where you working?" Ong Hai asked Sam as I put the soup in the microwave.

"I've got a friend who has a computer business."

"Lots of money with computers."

"It's just selling them."

"You tell your friend to feed you more food. Tomorrow, you come to the café. Maybe you'll eat more."

The dining area next to the kitchen had the same oval wood table, the same candlestick-spindled chairs, that Sam and I had sat at throughout our childhood. Ong Hai brought forth chopsticks and paper napkins and my mother and I set out the dishes and food. This was the way we ate. Always had. Eating without talking, not bothering to cover up the sounds of our chewing. We ate with a swiftness that would have alarmed any non-Asian. Though my mother and Ong Hai knew to eat in a quiet American style out in public, at home they ate the old way, bringing their bowls close to their chins and sweeping food into their mouths. The sight was a strange comfort to me, as much as it was just to gather at the same table, the Lien family of Durango Road. This had never been a normal occurrence, not with restaurant schedules to keep.

As soon as we were done my mother jumped up to clean. I helped her, as was my eternal duty, while Ong Hai and Sam went to the living room TV. I could hear Ong Hai asking Sam if he liked the computer work.

"Sure," Sam said. "It's all right."

"Downtown Chicago?"

"Sort of. Nearby."

I rinsed my mother's old coral-pink Fiestaware dishes. When I set the plates in the drying rack she rearranged them. She wiped down the counter, the sink, even the rice cooker, faintly printed with flowers, that we'd had for probably fifteen years. She didn't say anything and I wondered what would happen if I blurted out Hieu's name. If I had the nerve. Which I didn't.

In the living room the guys were watching a *Seinfeld* re-run. There almost wasn't enough space for all of us, suddenly packed in as if it were a holiday. I pulled up an ottoman near Ong Hai, and my mother brought her knitting bag to the re-cliner. We watched the same television, lifeblood and anchor of our household, beloved distraction and focal point. The room still had these giant, formal-looking window swags that a previous tenant, or maybe the owner, had installed. They were heavy, poly-satin burgundy edged with golden tassels, at once pompous and sad, and they seemed to lord themselves over us.

Ong Hai found a movie, a comedy about race-car driving, and as we let the flow of it get us through the next hours of that night, I thought about my mother, pouring Hieu's money—if it was true—into the Lotus Leaf Café. I had gone to college and grad school mostly on fellowships and grants. I'd never expected my mother to afford any of it, and she hadn't.

When my mother folded up her knitting and rose from her chair, she said, "Wake up early. We go at six." Though she didn't look at Sam, she was speaking to him, for the first time since he'd arrived. Ong Hai got up too and gave a little pat on the head to me and Sam—his grandfatherly good night.

Sam picked up the remote control and searched the channels. It was ten o'clock, yet somehow the whole house, the whole neighborhood, seemed closed down.

I had imagined, many times, my brother returning to our lives, but hadn't factored in how much his absence, all those months adding up, would enshroud his homecoming.

"What do you need the money for?" I asked him.

He clicked over to *The Daily Show*. "For one thing, I'm moving."

"Where?"

"California."

Of course. I didn't even need to ask why. Stereotypical sunlight and seacoast. As a kid he had often whined to our mother that we should live there—just pick a city. In high school, when one of his friends moved to the Bay Area, Sam was jealous for months.

"Why the urgency?"

He took a moment to answer. "If I don't go now, I might never go."

I understood that, more than I could admit. But instead I said, "So you're going to disappear again?"

"You went off to school. You got away. It's my turn now."

He didn't see how easy he'd had it. It wasn't personal, I told myself; this was traditional, a Confucian-influenced truth: the boy was entitled to more; the boy was subject to few verging on no obligations. Sam had always worked that system. He got our mother to buy the running shoes his friends wore and the electronics he coveted. He convinced her that he needed newer and better cell phones. He would take money from her purse and she would pretend not to notice.

Sam turned up the volume on the television, perhaps so no one else could hear us talking. "I'm not saying you owe me anything. But she sure as hell does."

"When you saw her with Hieu—why were you following her?"

"I got bored one night."

"I'm serious."

"It's her own fault. She'd go out every once in a while and refuse to say anything about it. So I followed her. They were having dinner at a Thai restaurant and he gave her something in an envelope."

"I've never known her to go anywhere other than her friends' houses."

"I told you, she's been lying to everyone." Sam stood up, turned off the TV.

21

"So that's it? That's all there is to say?"

He was already headed to the basement stairs, so certain his old space would be the way he'd left it that he hadn't even bothered to ask. Pausing for a moment, he said, "Oh, yeah, I almost forgot. Welcome back home."

In the morning Sam actually did get up early and follow me to the Lotus Leaf, driving that huge SUV. When we arrived our mother and Ong Hai were already in the kitchen, preparing the shrimp and vegetarian rolls and rinsing herbs for the pho. The morning breads, scones, and doughnuts had already been delivered, and I set to work arranging them on their trays.

Sam said he could run the cash register, no problem. He talked to customers in a friendly voice that was unrecognizable to me. If someone pronounced pho incorrectly, calling it *faux*, he didn't even correct them the way I always did.

The Lotus Leaf was supposed to be an American realization of what Ong Hai had started in Saigon: his old Café 88, a name he had chosen because the number was lucky. And look at the luck it brought, Ong Hai would say when he reminisced about it. *We had customers so loyal they wouldn't get their coffee and tea anywhere else. We met that nice American lady. We got lucky enough to make it to America.* If I attempted to point out all the bad luck—the fact of war, loss, displacement—he waved these away. *That's not good or bad luck; that's life*, he said. *Life is a temporary stop on the way home to death.* It was an old proverb he would repeat with disconcerting cheer.

The Lotus Leaf was also supposed to mean a bigger future for our family—for Sam. But that was because my mother had counted on him caring. Even after he left and she refused to speak about him, I knew she harbored hope. Ong Hai too had been patient, believing Sam could return any day, that the boy just needed some space to grow up. For me, away in grad school in Wisconsin, one month turned easily into another, and Sam's being gone didn't disrupt, really, what I'd already gotten used to. But surely for my mother every unreturned text, every phone call that wasn't his, must have felt like punishment or revenge.

Now that Sam was restored to his proper place, helming the money machine, my mother already seemed more relaxed, on her way toward glad. Maybe she imagined that we'd all head back home together, toward dinner and television again, and that slowly the summer would find a shape: our family, reunited, two kids in their twenties yet kids all over again, everyone under the same roof, working in the same place, eating the same meals. The last year could be erased or overlooked; Sam would be back in the basement room; questions wouldn't be asked and answers wouldn't be given. All very Vietnamese.

After lunch my mother went out for supplies and Sam ducked

into the kitchen, where I figured he was asking for money from Ong Hai. A few minutes later Sam returned to the front with no discernible change in expression. I was cleaning off the tables and chairs and when I looked at my brother I wondered if I had long passed the point of being able to read him. Still, I knew enough to think, *Forget it.* That dream of a family-run café was nothing but a small-time, small-town wish. Money or no money, now that Sam knew how to be gone, he was never really coming back again.

I swept up crumbs from the floor. Sam folded his apron and left it on the counter. The café was empty, and it was a good time to take a break, eat a late lunch, have a cup of tea.

"I'm heading out. Ong Hai asked me to get a few things," Sam said to me. "You gonna stay here all day?"

The question made me feel trapped. "Not necessarily."

I straightened some of the paintings on the walls—a dramatic series of wilting daffodils by a local dude who'd walked in one day and asked if he could hang his work there for sale. Before that the walls had been empty, so it was all the same to my mother. That had been many months ago now, and it didn't look like any of the paintings had sold.

"Let me know what you find out," Sam said.

I watched him drive the SUV out of the parking lot. I wondered whose car it really was. I should have guessed what he would do, should have guessed from his good-bye. I suppose I wanted to believe him in that moment, to think that he would go to the Asian market to pick up some extra rice-paper wrappers and maybe some fish sauce, and that he would be back soon, however briefly. I wanted to believe he would stay another day or two, enough to gather the rest of his things from the basement, enough to try to figure out how to get his hands on the mythical money.

Ong Hai came out from the kitchen and waved me over. He punched a couple of buttons on the cash register. The drawer popped open, revealing the empty spaces where the day's cash transactions had been. Sam had even taken the quarters.

"You saw him?" I asked.

Ong Hai shook his head. "He asked me for money. I told him no, not until he stays long enough to earn it."

He didn't have to admit that he'd all but let Sam open the register in front of him and take the cash. He had too much of a soft spot for us kids; even when he said no, he never really could deny us. Not an ice-cream cone, not a toy, and not this.

It wasn't the right time to bring up Hieu, but I did anyway, using Sam as my shield. "Sam said that Mom's been getting money from Hieu."

Ong Hai looked embarrassed, but he wasn't going to cross his own child, even for his grandchild. "That's her business, Lee."

"He said she used that money for the café."

I'd made Ong Hai uncomfortable, but he said nothing. We could hear my mother returning, the heavy back door slamming shut. There could be no hiding the cash register from her. Ong Hai and I had no words of explanation, no excuses, and my mother had no reaction. In spite of everything, just one day at the Lotus Leaf would have been enough for Sam to reclaim his spot as the favored one. He would have gotten his money if only he could just stay.

Somehow we got through the rest of that afternoon. I went home first, taking the same route, past nail salons and tanning salons, to the house on Durango Road. The basement showed no sign that Sam had ever been back. The frameless bed kept its blue plaid cover; the torchère floor lamp from the early nineties still leaned at an angle. Who knew how much damp the russet carpeting held? No doubt Sam had searched the whole place for any possible hiding spot.

I made sure to be back in my own room, door closed, by the time my mother arrived. No telling what she would do next, how her rage would vent itself.

That's when I saw what Sam had left for me.

For a long time after, I wondered at the gesture. Some days I still do. He couldn't have known what path he was pointing me toward, and yet maybe he had sensed there was something more to know. I have not asked him this; maybe one day I will.

Sitting on my worn copy of *The Age of Innocence*, the text

that had been the center of my dissertation, was a scrap of paper where Sam had written down his new phone number. Stuck to it was a little golden spear: the pin my mother had kept for some forty-five years, an accidental gift from a woman named Rose.

TWO

When my mother and Ong Hai landed here as refugees in 1975, their only plan had been to try to get somewhere warm. But then my mother met my father at the refugee camp while waiting in line for a meal, and that was that. They got married quickly so they could be resettled together, which turned out to be in a small town fifty miles west of Chicago. For the next eight years the three of them chased opportunity—a stint at chicken farming, a try at running a grocery. But mostly they worked at Chinese, or what people back then called Oriental, buffets.

My mother once said that everything was easier before Sam and I came along. Came along, as though we'd had a say in the matter. What she really meant, though, was me. Sam was the wanted child, the boy, born in Rockford, Illinois, in 1983. My arrival a year later, a surprise, no doubt, came soon after my family first moved to La Porte.

I was six years old when Hieu and my father took that fishing trip. They'd become friends in the refugee camp, and Hieu had followed us to the Midwest. To me and Sam he was Chu Hieu, Uncle Hieu, a bachelor who came over for dinner and weekends and holidays and who always brought us candy and toys. My parents had taken him in, Ong Hai said. Hieu looked up to my father, wanted to have a family like he did and learn how to run a restaurant too.

In later years, I couldn't hear the sound of his name, *hue*, *hew*, without thinking of my father, his death, what his last moments might have been. He had gotten up early to fish alone, using a pair of Hieu's waders. It may have been that he wasn't accustomed to them, or that he didn't expect the river to have such a current, calm as it must have seemed. The tow of it took him by force. When did it happen? How early had it been? How had Hieu found out? As many times as I had imagined this, couldn't stop myself from imagining, I had never dared to ask my mother or even Ong Hai. What I knew came from eavesdropping, bits of talk gleaned during the funeral and visitation, when my parents' friends, a surprising number of them, traveling from other towns where we had lived, showed up with food and money and tins of jasmine tea. I hadn't seen Hieu since then. No one talked about him, and I never knew where he'd ended up.

At the time of my father's death, he and Hieu had been making a plan to move us all to Naperville, Illinois, where a friend wanted to partner on a new venture. I didn't remember much from that year, except that my mother wanted to keep our part of that plan. Hieu had receded by then, unmentionable. I recalled how Sam and I sat in the backseat of the Mercury Marquis, surrounded by towels and bedding and pillows, the whole car rattling with cooking gear; Ong Hai was in the passenger seat, garbage bags of clothes stuffed around his feet, while my mother drove, keeping next to her the urn that held my father's ashes. I grew up keeping that urn in sight. Its place in every living room we had became a reminder, a kind of homing device, for all the ambitions he'd held. We were supposed to see them through.

We didn't last long in that Naperville business deal. Soon we were in other small suburbs, tracing a wide arc from Wisconsin to Illinois to Indiana, often near colleges, where the public schools were decent and the buffet business a sure thing. My mother picked up where my father had left off, and my brother and grandfather and I followed. Every time we drove past Chicago—the city skyline distant, cloud-covered— it seemed phantasmal to me. Fitting, I suppose, for a family on the lookout for the next thing.

So Sam and I grew up as American kids, though we might have looked to others like foreigners. That was our mother, we would have been quick to say. We learned early on to explain away her behavior—her fondness for clearance centers, her wariness of school sporting events, her absolute disbelief in compliments. She was one of those fresh-off-the-boat types, we would have said to our friends. Old-school, old-fashioned, old-generation. We called her a total immigrant, made fun of her accent—whatever got a laugh. We'd sell her out in a second if it would make anyone understand that we, Sam and I, were different. We didn't like weird food. In fact, the only way we liked Chinese food was the same way our friends did, deep-fried and covered in syrupy sauces. Once, in a bid to boost popularity, we told our classmates they could eat for free in whatever restaurant our mother was running. This backfired, of course, when she came around to demand payment from everyone. But at the very least, we made sure people knew that we were nothing like her. If they thought she was strange and scary, we agreed. We had never been to Vietnam and had no desire ever to go there. We'd much rather go somewhere like Australia or Fiji or Iceland.

It was a given that Sam, as the son, and firstborn at that, didn't have to wash dishes or get As or justify every dollar spent. I don't think I ever questioned this. The resentment I sometimes felt was directed toward our mother instead. I would have said that Sam was a good brother. He had no problem letting me play his *Legend of Zelda* and *Super Mario* games. He showed me how to roast marshmallows over the gas flame of our stove. As we got older, he would sign field trip permission slips for me, forging our mother's name.

In high school we drifted into different crowds, and there

were days, weeks, when we didn't really say anything to each other. But there wasn't, I thought, any real animosity or rivalry. We watched the same sarcasm-driven sitcoms and action blockbusters and could always fall back on shared jokes about our mother. But mostly we got absorbed into separate circles. I took AP classes; he hung out with the skateboarders who sold weed out of their cars in the school parking lot.

By the time I left for the University of Illinois, Sam was already flunking out of his first stint at community college. But at least he stayed at home. My mother liked the idea of education just fine, especially since all of her friends did, but everybody knew that Vietnamese kids were supposed to live with their parents until they got married. College and grad school were just a temporary leave of absence.

That's probably why my mother never questioned my coming back. Didn't ask what happened to my roommates or why I didn't get another apartment in Madison. She didn't know that most of my cohort already had their plans set, from tenure-track and visiting assistant professorships to postdocs secured in hand. I was one of the walking losers, stuck in the wait-and-see, having to hear people say things like, *Something will turn up. Hang in there.* I told my mother and Ong Hai that a job offer could come in anytime and all I had to do was be patient, but I needn't have bothered. For my mother, home was the only answer.

We'd lived in worse towns. Franklin had an art museum

and a farmers' market and neighborhoods of colonials butting up against McMansions. We stayed at the edge of the gentrification, though, in the grotty section overrun with strip malls and payday advance shops. And, as always, we were renters. First apartments, then duplexes, and finally a whole house: your standard middling ranch, bricked, carpeted, and vinyled, in a neighborhood where tricycles were left to rust in the winter, TV satellite dishes clung like bats to eaves, and empty houses still had *Beware of Dog* signs stuck to metal fences.

Being home was endurable only because of Ong Hai. He and I could have been retirement buddies: listening to NPR, sharing a pot of tea, playing cards, him telling stories about the eccentrics he'd known in Saigon. It was the antidote to my mother's thousand criticisms and complaints. Nothing was too minor for her to notice: from the way my ponytail sagged to the way I folded towels to the mealy state of tomatoes at the store. Hers was a lifelong habit of pointing out the loose threads on a stranger's shirt buttons, scorning the groceries in other people's carts. She would criticize a bride's makeup (but scold me for commenting on the duration of the wedding), find fault with every other restaurant—too expensive, too slow, too fast, music too loud, utensils too scratched. If I microwaved leftovers for two minutes she would say it should be two and a half. I chopped vegetables too loudly, too slowly. The lightbulbs I bought weren't the right wattage. My umbrella, drying on the back porch, stayed there too long.

In many ways my mother was a traditionalist, and that meant she had to defer to her father, the oldest in the family and therefore head of the household, even though the gesture was symbolic. This made for a tricky power balance that Sam and I had always used to whatever advantage we could. For me that meant making sure Ong Hai was on my side. He was the one who told my mother I should be allowed to go to homecoming and prom. He helped me with security deposits for apartments. And he had always given me money. Restaurant wages, was how he justified it, a supplement to whatever job or stipend or fellowship I had. A few hundred-dollar bills slipped into my book bag. Whether my mother knew about this, I never asked.

If it was true that she had been accepting—demanding?—money from Hieu all these years, then it went against her stance of self-reliance, what she called the *Ronald Reagan pull-up-your-bootstraps way*. Like a lot of Vietnamese immigrants from the older generation, she had a hatred of communism that defined all of her political views. Had my father been like that too? I didn't really remember my mother before his death, though a part of me wanted to believe that she had been sweeter then, softer, and that his dying had changed that. A part of me wanted to believe maybe she simply couldn't pull herself up and had had to turn to Hieu. And as always, the children didn't need to know about it.

Those first three weeks at home, before Sam's arrival and

rupture, I worked at the Lotus Leaf during the day and tried to avoid revising my dissertation at night. I sent my CV to a bunch of colleges in the area, some I'd never even heard of before, asking if they needed any adjunct instructors in the fall—the higher education version of substitute teaching. My adviser, Valerie, had said I should use the summer to shape my chapters into articles and submit them to journals. *Your degree won't be fresh for long*, she warned. Meaning that the more distance that came between it and a decent job, the less viable I would seem. We had often met at coffee shops and when she crossed her legs I couldn't help looking at the surprisingly high heels she wore. They made a resolute kind of sound when she walked, which I guessed was the point. She was one of the younger professors, recently tenured, and she had a collection of scarves—cashmere in the winter, chiffon in the spring—that seemed intimidating. When she talked she leaned forward, sipping her coffee, and I would think, *Yes, I want to be like her. I can do this, I can write this, I can wear heels with a purpose.* Valerie was the one who'd asked what none of my other professors had broached: Was I sure Wharton was my thing? Ethnic lit, she reminded me, was hotter right now and might make me more marketable. What she meant was: Why was an Asian girl so interested in studying such white American lit? I didn't blame her for wondering. But I couldn't explain why I'd loved Edith Wharton—the escape, the very whiteness seeming like escape, the fact that her life

35

was the opposite of mine. At least, I'd loved her until we spent so much time together. Now that she and I had crossed the finish line, I was almost as tired of her words as my own. Newland Archer and Ellen Olenska had begun to seem stilted and caricaturish, waxen figures of elegant misery and stifled longing. I would think of them sometimes while washing dishes at the café or handing change to a customer. I would see Archer sitting with his crate of imported books, dreaming of touching the wrist of his would-be lover. He would be too far away for anyone to approach, me least of all. I was becoming that sullen, dirty-haired daughter consigned to a lifetime of scrubbing out restaurant kitchens. The fact that I had no desire to leave the café early, hurry back to my desk to do what was supposed to be my real work, was an altogether new kind of despair for me.

Late at night, shut in the third bedroom with its twin bed and the ceiling light that looked like an upturned ashtray, I stared at my laptop screen. I e-mailed, read food blogs, edited the sentence structure of Wikipedia entries. I clicked the hours away, link by link, from news sites to recipes, celebrity gossip, celebrity babies, fashion bloggers who posed like flamingos in the middle of SoHo streets. I wondered if I had the guts to leave the way Sam had. My best friend from college had a two-bedroom condo in San Francisco where she worked for a pharmaceutical company, and she'd been saying I should move there too. Back in undergrad Amy and I had both applied to Stanford, she for med school, me for a literature PhD, but I hadn't gotten in. Now we could be roommates again, she said, and it sounded so simple, so *normal*. I could do that, I told myself: gather my things, sell my car, put a plane ticket on a credit card, and get the hell out of here. But then I'd feel guilty, start weighing Amy's offer against my grandfather's worries about the Lotus Leaf. He hadn't put any pressure on, but it was there: If I didn't help at the café, who would? If I didn't help, how would it last?

I had already started suggesting improvements, irritating my mother with every one. If they couldn't change the name of the café or the exterior—it was in a strip mall that had been designed to look like a village, albeit a cheap one, with forest-green awnings and false fronts—they could at least change the Lotus Leaf sign, which had calligraphic letters evoking gongs and Far East bamboo. They could replace the white-tiled floor and the plastic teal-green countertop and those black metal chairs with fan-shaped backs. One afternoon when my mother wasn't around, I threw out the artificial orchid plants and the credit union calendars. I ordered a chalkboard menu to re-place the ugly whiteboard. I told Ong Hai about my ideas: add banh mi to the offerings; negotiate a new plan with the bakery that supplied our pastries, cutting back on bagels and upping the doughnuts; set up a display of Sriracha bottles because white people loved Sriracha now. Why not have a prettier-looking menu, font, and logo, start up the social media accounts that had become, for every other business, a requirement? He didn't disagree, he said, but what about the cost? Mainly, he knew as well as I did that my mother had to call the shots.

As it happened, the day after Sam left us again was the day the chalkboard arrived at the café. I'd ordered it a week before, with a plan to install it secretly, figuring my mother would have a harder time objecting to it once it was in place. But she was standing right there when the UPS guy delivered the box and she said, "What is *that*?" like she'd just spotted some gross mold.

I tried to convince her that the chalkboard would bring some warmth to the place. "It'll be more like a cozy coffee shop."

"Says who?" She stood, thick-legged, hair kept in a continual no-fuss bob, a small but solid tyrant. "How much did this cost?"

"Hardly anything."

"Nobody said you could do this."

"I'm trying to make the place look better."

We were standing in the fluorescent-lit back room next to the kitchen, where my mother kept all the nonrefrigerated supplies. She folded her arms, ready for a fight, and said, "Oh, now you think the business is your business."

I knew better than to challenge her, especially in the wake

of Sam's fresh absence. But I couldn't stop myself from saying, "I'm just trying to help out here."

"It's such a good thing you got the PhD, then."

"Tran," my grandfather intervened, emerging from the front with a yellow canister of Café du Monde in hand. He looked at the half-opened chalkboard box and said, "Maybe it's nice-looking, eh? Maybe we keep it here."

"This is a restaurant, not a school. Have you ever had a Viet teacher? Do they make enough money? I don't think so. Vuong, Thi, Hanh," she named some of her friends. "Their kids are engineers."

"Can we just try it out for a while?" I said. "See how it goes."

"You been here a few weeks and now you think you own the place. You think you're some hotshot, big degree, big decision maker now. You don't know anything about a restaurant."

I looked at Ong Hai, who shook his head, silently advising me to back down.

"Whatever," I said. "What do I care? It's your place."

"Don't forget it," my mother said.

When she left, Ong Hai said to me, "No sense fighting mean."

"Sometimes it's hard not to."

He smiled a little but said, "That's the trouble, Lee. You and your ma both think that."

He urged me to go home early, since business had been

slow. "Jennie will be here later," he said. She was their one part-time employee, whose hours had been so reduced lately that she'd mentioned she might have to quit.

I knew Ong Hai just wanted to put some space between my mother and me, and he was right. When I looked at her now I thought about money, Hieu, and all my brother had claimed. Probably when my mother looked at me she thought of my brother too—his disappearance, my failure to fill his space. We both had reasons to stay away from each other.

I knew that Sam's leaving me his new phone number, stuck through with that gold pin, was supposed to be a message, some sibling code that we were in this together. Maybe he thought I'd round up the money, call him when it all got fig-ured out. But when I returned to the house that afternoon, twenty-four hours after Sam's second escape, his offering seemed just another mess he'd left behind. He had gotten away and I had not.

I went to put the pin back in my mother's room. It looked just as it had when Sam had searched it, what I used to think of as a widow's spare landscape. I wondered what would have happened if Sam *had* found a stash of money. Would he have taken it—would I have let him? Would he have slipped away without ever facing our mother?

I opened the bottom dresser drawer and reached for the

ballerina box. I thought I knew my brother well enough, yet I didn't figure that the rest of the jewelry—the gold necklaces, the jade and gold bracelets—would be gone. The only thing left was the pin in my hand.

I turned it over and over, hating Sam, fearing my mother. I remembered myself at eight years old, imagining the pin as something more real than it was. Mostly I had known it— Sam and I both had—as the vestige of a story that didn't really belong to us. Still, it seemed wrong, somehow, to leave it in the dresser drawer by itself. So I didn't.

When my mother and Ong Hai came home that night I was hiding out in my room. Ong Hai knocked on my door and handed me a bag of leftover summer rolls and pastry, understanding. Soon enough I could hear their two televisions murmuring. I thought about telling Ong Hai about the jewelry but worried that he'd feel obligated to tell my mother. There was a good chance it'd be a while before she uncovered it herself. Sam's renewed absence and theft at the café were bad enough; knowing this could only cause more trouble for me.

Laughter rose from Ong Hai's TV show, while a blast of commercials came from the living room. He liked sitcom reruns and competitive reality shows; she preferred legal dramas, medical mysteries. It was a collapsing sort of moment, these sounds of made-up lives overlapping in my solitary room.

I set the gold pin back down on *The Age of Innocence*, where Sam had left it, as if to point out how old-fashioned both were. In my childhood imagination the image of the house sitting in a field of tall grass had seemed so important, come to life from a *Little House on the Prairie* book. In actuality it looked like something from a garage sale, which was probably the real reason Sam hadn't taken it.

The jewelry, the stories—they all referred to a gone time, long before my mother and grandfather fled the country of their birth and landed in the country of my birth.

Opening my computer, I checked my e-mail again, still wishing for a good-news message, a *Congratulations, this job is yours!* But nothing new had arrived.

I picked up Rose's pin once more. And it was then that I considered what had never seemed significant before: Hadn't Ong Hai always said that Rose was a reporter working on an article about Vietnam? If that was true, had she written the article? And if so, couldn't it be found?

I pulled up Google, my default page, and stared at the blinking cursor. I typed, *Rose article Vietnam*. Before I hit return I thought to add the year: *1965*.

I didn't expect anything to come up, but the third result listed the Rose Wilder Lane Papers in West Branch, Iowa. Rose. Born 1886, died 1968, daughter and only child of Laura Ingalls Wilder. Author of the once-popular, now-obscure novels *Free Land* and *Let the Hurricane Roar*. Alleged ghostwriter of the *Little House on the Prairie* books. And correspondent in Vietnam for *Woman's Day* magazine, 1965.

In the closet I had a collection of books and college papers kept through our years of moving. I didn't have a lot—my mother thought owning books a waste, especially when libraries were free—so I had cherished the ones Ong Hai had bought for me, like *The Great Brain*, *Anne of Green Gables*, *Superfudge*, *Sweet Valley High*. And my favorite: the *Little House on the Prairie* box set circa 1986, the spines wrinkled and softened by countless rereadings. *Little House in the Big Woods*. *Little House on the Prairie*. *On the Banks of Plum Creek*. *By the Shores of Silver Lake*. *The Long Winter*. *Little Town on the Prairie*. *These Happy Golden Years*. And the two outliers—*Farmer Boy*, about the childhood of Laura's future husband, Almanzo, and *The First Four Years*, a posthumously published account of the early, difficult years of Laura and Almanzo's marriage.

I slid out the copy of *These Happy Golden Years*, turning to that passage where Almanzo gives Laura a gold pin as a Christmas present. *On its flat surface was etched a little house, and before it along the bar lay a tiny lake, and a spray of grasses and leaves.*

I hadn't read or thought about the description in so long. Now a shiver went through me as I wondered what *was* real. Could it actually be the pin my mother and grandfather had kept? Was it a call, or maybe a message, staring straight at me as it had all these years, though I'd never before noticed? Was this the same Rose?

I opened *The First Four Years*. It didn't belong to the

original arc of the books and didn't read like it either. Here the language is spare, the feel of something private and unedited, a space where a storyteller's voice hasn't yet tempered the rawness of remembering hard times. Maybe because of this, I hadn't liked the book when I was a kid. The heartache, the deprivation, had little redemption: Laura and Almanzo lose their wheat crops to hail and heat, get themselves into terrible debt, have a baby boy who dies soon after being born, and lose their house in a fire. The only bright spot is the child who survives it all: Rose, described by Laura as her precious flower of December.

Surely, if the gold pin were real, if it had existed, Laura would have handed it down to her daughter.

Back at my computer it was easy enough to find the *Woman's Day* article from 1965. Titled "August in Vietnam," it was Rose Wilder Lane's last publication before her death a few years later. She gives a genial tourist's view of the country, describing the "resilience" of the Vietnamese people, especially the women, whose skin seemed to her as "smooth as cream and yellow as gold." It was a little too *Miss Saigon* for comfort, but I didn't care. I was looking for Ong Hai. Yet nowhere did Rose mention meeting a family in Saigon, a man and his daughter who served her coffee and fruit at Café 88.

I stepped into the hallway with my laptop, intending to talk to Ong Hai, but my mother called my name. She was knitting in front of the living room TV.

"What are you doing?" She sounded suspicious, as if guessing the trouble I was about to court.

"Just going to talk to Ong Hai."

"He's asleep."

"Are you sure?" But I realized his door was closed, his television off.

"What are you talking to him about?" Her gaze turned back to the screen, where good-looking med students were arguing with each other as a way to build up sexual tension. She made a little *tsk*ing sound and her needles clicked as they seesawed against each other, shaping a baby blanket. I had never learned how to knit and my mother had long since given up trying to teach me. Whenever I saw her at it, no matter what argument we'd just had, I couldn't get over the magic of being able to get a spool of yarn to build and bend into something like that.

"What are you talking to him about?" my mother repeated.

She didn't sound angry but I knew that was never more than a blink away. We could never have conversations the way parents and kids did on TV, all banter and affection. What would she say if I dared to admit what Sam had stolen, had left? What if I told her about Rose? What if I brought the name Hieu out into the open?

"Hold on," she said before I could answer, nodding at her show, which was heading toward its sound-track-thundering denouement. She pulled out more yarn from a plastic grocery bag. She was always carrying things around in these plastic bags and tying the handles together too tight. Finally: "Hurry up—next show's coming on."

There was nothing to say to her. My mother, who had once referred to a PhD in literature as a fake degree for a fake doctor, was so focused on the television, expectant and almost docile, that I suddenly wondered if *she* was the one who couldn't discern the real from the fake. It was startling and new to think of her this way—compliant, complacent, given over to a lifetime of watching. Someone getting older.

"Nothing," I said, and she didn't pursue it.

I stayed up too late, rereading the *Little House* books, thinking about what was fact and what was imagined. What did it mean, anyway, to be based on a true story? How many times had Ong Hai told the story of Rose? How many times during the years of my *Little House* obsession had I pretended the pin was Laura's secret gift to me?

In a way, Rose had been part of the dream, the memory, that had pushed my mother and grandfather out of Vietnam, back when the city of Saigon was crumbling around them. They had taken only a few things. Photos, money. The jade and gold jewelry. And the gold pin. Maybe to my mother and Ong Hai it had been some kind of proof—that Rose had mattered, maybe, or that she and Ong Hai had mattered.

So much immigrant desire in this country could be summed up, quite literally, in gold: as shining as the pin Rose had left behind. A promise taken up, held on to for decades, even while Sam and I were reckless with our own history, searching for things we couldn't yet name. If this Rose was the same Rose of the *Little House* books, the daughter of Laura Ingalls Wilder, then she had defined a part of American desire that my mother understood just as well.

THREE

America is mostly made up of small towns, and no matter where you go, mountains or seaside or flatness, you will always find, just off an interstate or county road or tucked into a strip mall on a commercial pass, a worn-out-looking Chinese buffet. It might be called the Golden Panda or New China or New Golden Panda Buffet, or just plain Asia Buffet—Oriental Buffet if it's a real backwoods area—the words spelled out in Kung Fu chop suey font or, depending on the economics of the neighborhood, utilitarian block lettering, sans serif. Some of the buildings will have a pagoda look to them, with faux-clay tiles and gold trim. Others will be more to the point: cement, windowless, cheap real estate. They will have rutted lots, signs that say *More Parking in Rear.* When you open the door an electronic two-tone bell will announce your arrival.

Inside, the lighting will be dimmed, concealing the fine

layers of grease that have settled into the surfaces, settling even now into your hair, your clothes, your skin. But don't think about that. Look, instead, at all the Asian stuff! Dusty red lanterns; pictures of dragons and fishermen; paper place mats printed with the signs of the Chinese zodiac. Everywhere you look there will be plastic, vinyl, PVC: the plants in the corners, the seat of each chair, the amber-colored cups at the water dispenser, and, at the cash register, the little altruistic trays that tell you to go ahead, take a penny, leave a penny.

But remember what it is you came for. The goal, the crux, the mother lode: gleaming rows of inset chafing dishes where steam rises to meet the plastic roofs known as sneeze guards. The setup will tell you about the restaurant's ambitions. Are there two buffets, lined up like parallel stalwarts, dependable, traditional even, or do they form one line as in a middle school cafeteria? Are they perhaps angled, even perpendicular, in a nod to a newer, avant-garde style of enterprise? Are the buffets close to the kitchen, which is easier for the workers but more of a trek for some of the diners? Or do they take the center of the room, proud to claim the spotlight?

You might agree that one of the best things about a buffet is no waiting. The plates and bowls are always ready and someone will always take away the dirty ones. As experienced diners know, time can work for you at the buffet. Play it right and the span between walking in the door to biting into an egg roll is no more than two minutes. But what is your methodology? Do you move from left to right, appetizers to dessert? Do you pace yourself, dish by dish, or do you crowd as much as you can into each helping? How do you gauge your hunger to your greed? How do you figure the difference between eating and consuming?

You might choose to begin at the tureens of soup: wonton, hot and sour, yellow egg drop, thickened into goo. From there you might be distracted by mounds of fried rice, shining with oil (white rice available only upon request), sesame balls, and steamed buns—plenty of carbs for the rookies who fill up on them first. There will be piles of those cabbage-filled egg rolls, their skins turning obstinate under the heat lamps. The whole array of fried will be impressive: fried wonton strips, fried shrimp, fried chicken wings, fried crab puffs, fried dumplings, and the essential crab rangoon. All that happens even before the entrees: lo mein, spare ribs, Mongolian beef, sweet-and-sour pork, sweet-and-sour chicken, cashew chicken, almond chicken, sesame chicken, and, of course, the famous deep-fried nubs named after the mysterious General Tso. It's all gloriously American, brought in by food distributors, defrosted, reheated, refried, doused with the sweet, sweet, viscous sauces that arrive in giant plastic jars or frozen blocks almost arbitrarily labeled *Kung Pao*, *Garlic*, and *Szechuan*.

This is not to say that all buffets are alike. No, each has its own personality, its own special offerings, like fried corn on the cob or Shanghai noodle burritos. Some buffets take a pan-Asian approach, with California rolls, pad Thai, chewy parcels of bulgogi. Some rely on incentives, like all-you-can-eat king crab legs for an additional four dollars. Others go for broad ethnic variety, adding spaghetti with marinara, Swedish meatballs, quesadillas, hot dogs, chicken fingers, Tater Tots, a bin of mixed romaine with ranch, Italian, and Thousand Island dressings parked next to the dessert puddings.

Dessert, of course, is a crucial part of any buffet. You need the soft-serve ice cream with the "fixins" bar of chocolate and caramel and sprinkles. You need your grocery store cookies, cannoli, brownies, orange jelly rolls, slices of sheet cake and red-dye cherry pie. You have to have your syrup-soaked fruit cups, your red and lime Jell-O, your Jell-O mixed with Cool Whip.

All this and so much more for just $5.99 at lunch and $8.99 at dinner (not including tax and drinks).

Most customers don't leave tips, maybe a dollar or some change, though they do make as many trips as possible to the chafing dishes, hauling food like it's a sport. The same people who tell their children to eat every bite on their plates at home will heap on the sweet-and-sour, take a couple of bites, and move on to a fresh plate. When presented with a buffet, a kind of determination tends to come over people. Maybe you know what I mean. Maybe you start to feel, as I have, like the food is free, that the whole of it is yours. That you ought to claim more and more, even if you don't eat it.

You wonder if you can sneak some leftovers home—you're paying for this, after all. You find yourself getting caught up in the allure, the expanse, dizzied by the promise, the challenge of all you can eat, all you can get, all you can demand. In your haste you might spill food on the tables, grab at the serving spoons and drop them wherever you like. Doesn't matter. Eat now, forget tomorrow. Ask for more fried shrimp, more white-meat chicken. You must exercise your right for endless refills, bottomless cups of soda pop. You must do whatever it takes to get your money's worth.

When you see these restaurants, especially in the many areas of the United States referred to as fly-over country, when you're driving past them, glad to be heading somewhere else, somewhere better, no doubt, you may feel sadness and amazement and pity, and you may wonder: How did that restaurant happen? Are actual Asian people running it? How did those poor souls end up here in the middle of nowhere?

My family was one of those you might have wondered about. In 1989, if you had driven past the Golden Dragon restaurant in La Porte, Indiana, and perhaps decided to stop in and check out the place, why not, you're hungry, you might risk it, you would have seen my parents replenishing the buffet, unloading ribs and wings, wiping the tables, stacking plates. Interchangeably waiters, busboys, cooks—my parents ran the place in tandem. They weren't Chinese, and neither had any training as a cook. But it didn't matter because the customers didn't know the difference.

I was five years old then and had no idea what it meant to run a restaurant, to be one of the few Asian families within a wide radius. In a year my father would be dead and not long after that the rest of us would be in a different small town in a different midwestern state.

But the Golden Dragon was the first buffet I remembered. We had moved to La Porte because my parents had heard of a family with jobs available at their restaurant. That was how it worked in the community—relying on friends of friends who were trusted, even if unknown, simply for being Vietnamese.

The town was about twenty miles away from a nuclear power plant in Michigan City, where we had gone once to see that great lake. Sam and I were fascinated by the cooling towers, and by the fact that you could swim and lie on the beach within view of those thick hourglasses, the steam that lifted away from them in slow motion. Ever after I couldn't help associating La Porte with those towers—vaguely menacing, yet something people seemed to take for granted.

Sam and I used to go to the Golden Dragon with our grandfather for a late dinner. Late, because we could eat the dregs of the buffet for nothing, and with no customers around the restaurant felt like our own playhouse. We crawled under the tables, pretending to be on submarines, secret missions. We crammed our mouths with wonton strips and drank as much Sprite as we wanted. If any crab rangoons were left, we fought over them. Our grandfather shook his head at the very idea, sickening to him, of cream cheese flavored with fake crab, stuffed in a wonton, and deep-fried. Sam and I knew we were American because we loved those things the most. The oily crisp giving way to the salty ooze. Ong Hai would wrap up the chicken or beef dishes to take home and my mother and father would scrub down the stainless steel vats, preparing for the next day. At the time I thought we owned the place, that it was fancy, *ours*, and that by right of daughterhood I could think of myself as some kind of Golden Dragon princess.

It took me until middle school, long after we'd left La Porte, to feel the abjection of my family's livelihood, to understand what did and did not belong to me. By then I had started busing tables, and saw that buffets in other towns and states followed the same structure, the same skewed ratio of fried to nonfried.

A lot of the customers assumed we didn't speak English, and therefore we were invisible to them. If white people thought I couldn't understand them, what might they say? As it turned out, people liked making jokes about eating dogs. They said no matter how much they ate they were going to get hungry again in an hour—a line I never really got. Sometimes they took on exaggerated Asian accents right in front of me, like Mickey Rooney doing yellow-face in *Breakfast at Tiffany's*. "Five dolla, five dolla," was a common phrase. "Ah, Grasshopper!" was another. "Bonsai!" And the yodeled, cringing cry of Long Duk Dong from *Sixteen Candles*, the thing I could never forgive John Hughes for: "Oh, sexy girlfriend!" It was all a joke, of course. Can't you take a joke? It's funny! Why get offended? Why be so sensitive!

Even if I was tempted to say something, fling back some kind of retort, if I could come up with something to say, I never would. Always my reaction was to retreat, conceal the humiliation of my race. That was what Asian people were supposed to do, wasn't it? Stay nice, slip from view.

But then there were times people would want me to talk. They would ask me what I was. "What are you?" "Where are you from?" Answering "America" or "Here" was not sufficient. It didn't matter that I had been born in La Porte. They wanted to know where I was *really* from, what I *really* was. They would take guesses. They might ask if I knew such-and-such Vietnamese person in a different city—was I related to them? Once in a while someone would try out a few words in mangled Chinese or Vietnamese and I would just nod and try to smile. Occasionally people would mention that their father or uncle had fought in the Vietnam War. And a few times, people asked what right I had to be in this country. That was when I started realizing that not everyone knew the basic history of the war, that there were those who viewed all of Vietnam as the enemy, the "Charlie" of so many fucked-up movies.

In retrospect, most of the customers were forgettably normal, predictable, easy. A number of vets frequented the buffets and they were always kind, prone to leaving tips, lingering to chat with my grandfather. But of course I remembered the rough patrons most. I let their words linger, reiterate themselves in so many moments of reflection.

I often wondered how my mother, with that proud lift of her chin, had been able to stand it. But she was pragmatic: If the money was good and the money was steady, what else mattered? It didn't make any difference, she said once, if all the customers were fools, so long as they paid. My grandfather seemed to agree. He made friends with the regulars, told them to call him Ong Hai. Mr. Hai, his first name. Soon, Sam—lingering on the edges of the restaurant, watching the rest of us toil—started calling him that too. But Ong Hai even took mockery in stride. He said you couldn't blame people for still learning, even if some of them were pretty slow at it. He traded jokes with customers, talked weather and snow and lake effect, smiled no matter what. When people complimented him on his English he thanked them with sincerity. Ong Hai became the name he answered to at work and at home. This is good business, is what he said. This is our American way.

FOUR

My mother had planned to have, one day, a Golden Dragon she could call her own, but Sam changed her mind. Sometime when he and I were in high school, American eaters had started looking for authenticity. They wanted true ethnic food, whatever that was, and they'd go to a hole in the wall to get it, in fact preferred that, in order to feel like it was the real deal. Whenever Sam said that buffets were gross, full of fake food, my mother would tell him to be quiet, that he was being disrespectful. She didn't let on that she was listening when he said that Ong Hai's cooking was better than any we could find at a restaurant. But that's what had led her to the Lotus Leaf.

The day after my discovery of Rose Wilder Lane, my mother discovered the deal I'd struck with the bakery that supplied the café's pastries. I'd been so preoccupied with Rose and the gold pin, wondering what and whether to tell Ong

Hai, that I wasn't prepared when my mother came boiling out of the kitchen. *Stupid*, she spat out. *Who do you think you are?* Then she switched to Vietnamese, and though I had no great grasp of the language, I knew the basics. *Think you know everything.* She pointed a sharp finger at my nose. The silky-poly button-down she wore was trembling. *Stupid. You know nothing.*

A customer was standing there, waiting for to-go summer rolls for his lunch, but my mother ignored him. I grabbed a paper bag while my mother amped up her voice, repeating herself. Ong Hai appeared with the packet of summer rolls and handed them to me, steering my mother back to the kitchen.

"Whoaaa," the guy said. "That lady's tough. She your mother?"

I hated these kinds of chatty customers, especially when there was no one else in line.

"Enjoy the summer rolls," I said.

"Hey, how come your English is so good and hers isn't?"

Some things, buffet or not, didn't really change. And I still didn't have a good comeback.

"Who knows?"

After the guy left, Ong Hai came back out. He looked sorry for me. "Maybe you should go take a break again."

I started to say I couldn't believe she was really that mad, but of course it was my mother—she really was that mad. Sam, the chalkboard, now this. The previous night, watching TV, had been the lull in the storm. "What am I supposed to do, stay out of her sight until Sam comes back?"

"Let's just keep more trouble away from us."

"I'm just going to go home, then. Which I'm sure will make her even madder." I sounded like a petulant teenager, which was what I felt like too.

"I'll talk to her, Lee."

When I got back to the house on Durango Road, I filled a plate with grapes and set them near the photograph of my father. Growing up, I'd often taken care of the altar just to hear my grandfather tell me I was a good daughter. *Your ba would be so happy about a PhD*, Ong Hai would say whenever I called from Madison. Sometimes I thought this hypothetical affirmation was what had kept me in grad school. According to Ong Hai, my father had prized education so much that, whenever he could, he'd helped his friends pay for their classes. That was the kind of guy he was.

As I dusted the oak console of the altar, I told myself to be more like my father. Think forward, look up. That's what Ong Hai would have said too. I resolved to collect my computer and spend the day anywhere else—maybe sit in a museum or library until it closed, get some work done, try for some sort of progress toward making good on my degree.

But Rose had another plan for me. On my laptop, where my e-mail inbox showed no new messages, the website for the Rose Wilder Lane papers was still up on the screen. Index of letters and writings; chronology of her life. It was all housed in the Herbert Hoover Presidential Library and Museum. I mapped it. A twenty-minute drive from Iowa City, which was a three-hour drive from Chicago. I thought of Sam fleeing to California on the wings of his theft. For him, a breaking free. For me, a different way westward—for that's what Iowa once was, the west, not the middle—was coming into view.

The lie formed itself easily: I would tell Ong Hai that I was going to Iowa to help an old college friend move apartments.

But first, I called Alex.

In college we had gone on a few road trips with friends—to Graceland, Dollywood, even Disney World. Being undergrads in the humanities, we had an overdeveloped sense of irony and camp. We used the word *meta* too often. And we purposely avoided organized social life—the fraternities and sororities, the clubs and associations pinned to ethnicity, race, and religion that were constantly posting "call-outs" and advertising bowling nights, dance nights, movie nights. Alex and I made sure to hang out at bars and coffee shops and living room sofas with other English and arts majors. We had met during our second semester at the UI, and, whether by sheer proximity or boredom, we'd slept together a few times, late after a party or study session, when there was nothing more interesting to do.

I hadn't seen him since before his move to Iowa City a year earlier, when he'd been boyishly pleased to have gotten into the MFA program there. When I called to propose an impromptu visit, that nervousness was gone. He talked about his cohort, his workshops. He used the phrase *my collection* to refer to the short stories that would become his thesis and, he hoped, his first book. The MFA was only two years, so he was dedicating the summer to holing up in his studio apartment and writing every day, living on savings, a summer stipend, and his parents' good graces.

And when, hours later, he opened the door to his apartment, the guy with the hair that never looked washed had a new look of cleanliness. His clothes seemed ironed. He looked like the kind of guy who could put together a killer Power-Point. It didn't seem very writerlike, I thought, and said so.

"*You* don't look like someone with a PhD," Alex returned. But he spoke lightly, watching me leave my overnight bag on the floor next to his bed. The sheen of early evening, early summer, lent his face and the room around us a kind of expectancy. I knew, as no doubt he did, that we'd be sleeping together that night.

He saw me noticing his built-in shelves, well filled with books; the mod-floral rug and the striped curtains; hardwood floors that reminded me of the apartment I'd had in Madison— old, softened, scratched, in need of a refinish but still cozy-making. I wondered which girlfriend had decorated the place.

"So who are you with right now, Edith Wharton or Laura Ingalls Wilder?" Alex asked, bringing out two mugs for tea.

Over the phone I'd explained my plans to look through the Rose Wilder Lane papers. I hadn't yet said anything about the pin and the connection I thought it had to my mother, to my family.

"Both, I guess."

"My sister was obsessed with those *Little House on the Prairie* books when she was little. She always wanted to call our parents Ma and Pa."

"Apparently her daughter wrote those books, or at least cowrote. Some critics even call them ghostwritten. Did you ever read them?"

He shook his head. "Too girly."

"You'd be surprised. There's a lot of hunting and building stuff. Plus slaughtering pigs and digging wells and all that."

"I remember my sister wanted to churn butter and bake biscuits."

"There's that too. Also headcheese." I described how Laura's ma would take the head of a pig and boil it until all the little bits fell off, then mix them together with spices and potliquor and wait until it all congealed, the gelatin seeping out from the skull. Then it could be cooled into a loaf and sliced. "I bet some place around here still serves it."

"Way out in the country, maybe. Too many vegans and hippies in this town." Alex brought me a cup of tea and looked at his watch. I thought he was going to ask me to clear out for a while so he could write, but instead he said, "Want to go to this party later? I forgot about it until a couple hours ago. It's at Jonah and Silvie's."

"Jonah and Silvie are here?"

"She got her MFA in poetry last year. Jonah's at the law school now."

They had been the first of our friends from undergrad to marry, not long after graduation, and their wedding had seemed a little silly, a little young. *We* were young. Kids dressing up in formal clothes from T.J.Maxx, one step beyond prom, insisting on being adults, while parents and elders looked on with amusement.

It wasn't like I had anything better to do, so a while later we headed out. Alex's neighborhood was lined with Bradford pear trees that I remembered from Urbana-Champaign— white bunches of bloom giving off an odor of ash and old fish. I could never understand why they were so popular. Like the battered sofas that reigned on front porches, the smell brought back the sleepy, pleasant feeling of being alone in a college town in the summer.

"Did I tell you it's a baby shower?" Alex said as we walked.

"Oh, Jesus."

"There'll be alcohol, though. And obviously guys are invited. It's just a party."

"Wait a second, Jonah and Silvie are having a baby?"

"Didn't you see their news on Facebook?"

"I try to avoid Facebook."

"Well, they're popping it out at the end of August."

"But I don't have a gift. And where's yours?"

"I'll get them something later."

"You can't show up to a baby shower without a gift. That's the whole point of a shower: to shower people with gifts."

"I always wondered why they called it that."

"Did you know that an anagram of *shower* is *whores*?"

We laughed.

"Another thing," Alex said. "They're going to announce the gender. I think they officially called it a gender-reveal-slash-celebrate-baby party."

"It's not accurate to say gender. They should say sex."

"A sex-reveal party? Anyway, apparently they asked the doctor to write down the gender—or sex—on a piece of paper and seal it in an envelope, and they gave that to the baker. When they cut into the cake at the party it'll be either pink or blue."

"Next thing you know, people are going to turn the whole delivery into a party. An all-nighter with kegs, and shots for every contraction. You know, in the olden days pink signified masculinity and blue signified femininity. Somewhere along the line that got reversed. What if the baker forgot or mixed up the pink and blue? Or just decided to play a trick on them?"

Alex caught my hand and held it for a moment. "Why don't we just let them cut the cake and be happy about it?"

I didn't know anyone at the party except Alex, Jonah, and

Silvie. Her belly kind of freaked me out, the conspicuousness of it. She kept running her hands lovingly over its expanse. We were pretty much all the same age at the party but it felt like everyone else had, if not the rest of their lives figured out, then at least the next few years. And of course everyone else had brought bags and boxes of gifts, covered with bright paper and ribbons and images of teddy bears.

Alex, a natural partygoer, made the rounds while I helped myself to the deviled eggs, mini-cheesecakes, and spiked pomegranate punch. I noticed him talking to a couple of girls who were leaning toward him with that unmistakable interest of intent. I wondered if they were previous dates or dates about to happen.

At last Jonah and Silvie approached the cake—tall, piped with flourishes and rosettes—that sat in the middle of the dining table. As everyone gathered around, it was like their wedding day all over again. I well recalled that moment, Jonah's hand covering hers as she held an engraved silver knife. Here was the old-timey notion of marriage and the promise of a baby carriage done in real life. I'd read enough literary criticism to have earned a healthy suspicion of this, and yet I found I couldn't so easily dismiss their joy. I slipped to the back to pour myself more of the punch.

"I'm so nervous," Silvie said. Earlier, I'd heard people gossiping that she really wanted a girl.

"I hope it's not green," Jonah said.

People whipped out their phones to take pictures as Jonah and Silvie sliced into the cake. Those nearest them started exclaiming and everyone else craned to see: the innards saturated a deep Cookie Monster blue. Shouts rose up and in spite of myself I joined in too. Alex took a picture and showed it to Silvie. Tears came to her eyes and she said, "Oh, my god, I'm having a baby boy."

Jonah hugged her close and I couldn't help it: I felt something for them.

When Alex brought me a piece of cake he said, "Pretty good sex reveal, don't you think?"

I took a small bite—too sweet, as expected, the buttercream leaving a film on my tongue. "That's a lot of toxic-looking blue dye. Must be some boy they're having."

We decided to sneak out before the gift opening. We talked about going to a bar but ended up just walking around the empty campus. I remembered why my friends and I had spent so much time in college rotating among each other, as if seeking out ways to develop wounds. We needed some small dramas to forget the bigger ones, and to make us feel like we could be the protagonists of our own minor story lines. Being with Alex helped numb the guilt and worry about Sam and my mother and Ong Hai and the café; my unwritten future could recede with each further minute we spent together. As much as we talked, I didn't mention much about the Lotus

Leaf or my brother; I didn't tell him about Hieu. It was easier to present Alex with an edited version of myself.

I'd been ready to poke fun at the MFA world Alex had immersed himself in, but he seemed so truly glad to be there that I didn't have the heart. Besides, I didn't want the talk to turn to my own prospects. How I would have to force myself to revise my diss and turn it into articles; how I would have to try to get those articles published and do presentations at conferences. I would try to make the whole thing a book, or *monograph*, as people in academe irritatingly called it; I would hit the job market again and try, try, try to land any kind of tenure-track assistant professorship or visiting assistant professorship, no matter if it involved a heavy teaching load in some rural county in Oklahoma a hundred miles away from the nearest Target. The saga of my family, round two.

It was so much easier, and preferable, to block out such thoughts with Alex. He was the second person I'd ever slept with (the first being a guy in my dorm, freshman year, who took me to free lectures on global filmmaking), and neither of us had ever endured long relationships, with each other or anyone else. Somehow we managed not to feel jealous. We could go months without calling or e-mailing and still be able to pick up where we'd left off.

So when we got back to his apartment I kissed him first. We were on the bed soon enough, the sex faster than I remembered, his hands a little rougher as he moved on top of me.

When it was done I asked him to order a pizza and he laughed. "Mushrooms and olives, right?"

We stayed in bed and Alex checked his e-mail on his phone.

"Are you going out with anyone right now? One of those girls at the party?"

"Did you meet Allison? Blondish-reddish hair—"

"The one wearing boots on a warm spring day."

"We broke up a few weeks ago."

"Is she the one who prettied up your apartment?"

"I guess so. She's in poetry here. It was only a few months."

"I'm not involved with anyone at the moment either," I said, though he hadn't asked. "Aren't the hookups at this school supposed to be legendary and incestuous? That didn't happen so much at mine." This was true, disappointingly so. I'd kind of hoped to find some agreeably distracting escapades, but most of the guys were already married, engaged, or involved in long-term or long-distance relationships. "You know what, I can't imagine being Jonah and Silvie right now. I wonder if they planned the pregnancy."

"They did, and that's why he's in law school. He said he decided to grow up finally."

"Maybe that surprises me more than it should. Aren't we just a little too young for this?"

"And then one day very soon we'll wonder what the hell happened to us. Once upon a time, you'd be a spinster by now."

"And you'd be 'baching' it, trying to learn how to cook your own salt pork and pancakes," I said.

Our grandmothers would turn in their graves, Ma Ingalls had said at the idea of sewing sheets by machine rather than by hand. *But after all, these are modern times.*

Yet my mother still believed children should live at home until marriage. And spinsterhood might now be called single-hood but it still elicited private worry and pity. I thought of Laura's sister Mary, the pretty one, whose luxurious blond hair Laura had envied. As a young girl, Mary pieced together a quilt for her trousseau, planning ahead for her future house, husband, and children. Then illness left her blind. The *Little House on the Prairie* TV show gave Mary romance, marriage, and babies, but none of that actually happened. In real life, blind-ness ended her dreams. The Ingallses scrimped and saved in order to send Mary to the Iowa College for the Blind because they knew that her education there would be the extent of her adventures. Then she would return home to live out the rest of her days. Which she did. Mary died at age sixty-three, only a few years after Ma Ingalls. How had Mary reconciled all her lost potential, all those lost wishes? Could she even have talked about it with anyone?

When the pizza arrived Alex and I ate it straight from the box as if we were undergrads again. Afterward I showed him the *Little House* box set I'd brought in my overnight bag, explaining that it had been an eighth-year birthday gift from Ong Hai, after he and Sam and I had gotten hooked on reruns of the TV show. Gamely, Alex opened to the first page of *Little House in the Big Woods* and we started reading together, slipping down into the plot of land near Pepin, Wisconsin, where Laura Ingalls had been born in 1867.

One thing I loved about the books this time around was how they were a DIY guide to frontier living: how to make butter and cheese from the cow you milked yourself; how to make sausage from the pig you butchered in the yard; how to make a smooth pine floor and a door with hinges; how to sew a lady's dress with all the requisite flounces and bustles. I saw myself living alongside Laura as she grew up, as her family left Wisconsin for lands unknown. I could have been her invisible twin or make-believe friend, helping her trick Nellie Oleson into getting leeches stuck to her legs, rushing to bring in the woodpile under threat of a sudden blizzard. I imagined myself living in a dugout, saw myself timidly attending a fancy birthday party where oyster soup, codfish cakes, fried potatoes, white cake, and whole oranges were served. At Thanksgiving I too might have enjoyed stuffed rabbit roasted with slices of salt pork. At Christmas I too would have rejoiced over a piece of horehound candy, a cake sprinkled with white sugar, a tin cup for my very own, and a new, gleaming penny.

Yet the books were also filled with shadows of hunger,

sickness, violent storms, worries about money. And they had a baseline white entitlement: the Indian lands should, of course, be given to white settlers; the only good Indian was a dead Indian. (Pa and Laura, at least, objected to that.) The Ingallses roamed as if any parcel of land out West might be theirs for the taking. Once, the family spent a winter subsisting on little more than tea and brown bread. Laura grew up knowing the meaning of sacrifice and stillness, the same way she knew she'd always have to wear a corset and keep house for a man. All of this for "freedom," homesteading, the will and claim of land—of assumed ownership.

Sometimes the *Little House* books mentioned life "back East," that distant apparitional place that supplied workers, goods, and coal from the railroads. Also mail, newspapers, and magazines that provided glimpses of politics and fashion. Ma Ingalls had to wait for *Godey's Lady's Book*, or word from other women with connections to the East, to find out if hoop skirts had come back into style to replace petticoats. Even on an empty prairie, style mattered. There was satisfaction in owning a new dress made from poplin freshly arrived from the East, each imagined pin tuck traceable to the prominent families of New York that floated and fretted through Edith Wharton's pages. While those women dressed in satin gowns, Laura Ingalls, during that same time period, sewed her own calico aprons and helped to stack the winter's hay.

Alex and I had gotten through the first book and part of

the second when he started drifting off. I sank down next to him and closed my eyes. At some point I wasn't sure if I was dreaming yet or merely thinking images of empty houses and unfamiliar beds, struggling to know where I was in the first place.

FIVE

Long before Laura Ingalls Wilder became Laura Ingalls Wilder, she was simply Mrs. A. J. Wilder, wife of Almanzo, known to her daughter as Mama Bess. They lived on a farm named Rocky Ridge in southern Missouri. For a while she wrote a column called As a Farm Woman Thinks for the local *Ruralist* newspaper, covering observations about chickens, horses, gardening, and weather. But she had bigger, secret ambitions. After Rose left home and became a writer, Laura completed a small memoir about growing up in the 1800s. She called it *Pioneer Girl*. She wanted to sell it to the publishers, and surely Rose could help her. After all, Rose had connections and Laura needed money. Rose was the one who had encouraged her mother to write her memories down in the first place.

This was right after the Crash of 1929. Laura was sixty-two years old, Rose forty-three. By then, Rose had made a name with her articles, stories, and biographies; she had traveled in Europe, found friendships with other writers, mapped out ideas for future trips, future books. But she wanted to be a novelist. So she went home to Rocky Ridge, thinking she could have her own quiet space for work, and in her spare time help her mother with *Pioneer Girl*. For years, both women wrote the same territory of the Ingalls family's adventures westward.

Rose sent *Pioneer Girl* to her agent but he returned it soon enough, rejected by numerous publishers. An editor friend suggested that the memoir could be made into a series of books for young readers. Quickly Rose and her mother reshaped the pages into a new manuscript, *When Grandma Was a Little Girl*, what would later become *Little House in the Big Woods*. Harper & Brothers published it in 1932, the same year the *Saturday Evening Post* serialized Rose's novel *Let the Hurricane Roar*. Over the next ten years the two women would collaborate on the rest of the *Little House* books.

Laura wasn't a born writer; her personal jottings, her column for the *Missouri Ruralist*, and *The First Four Years*, which Rose never edited, show a spare, wooden style. If Laura's narration was the flatness of prairie, then Rose's was all hills and mountains, metaphor and suspense. Still, it wasn't until the early 1990s that a critic, William Holtz, brought this discrepancy to the forefront, going so far as to argue that Rose had ghostwritten the *Little House* books. But Rose never had any interest in claiming them under her own name. She had no desire, she said, to attach herself to "juveniles." She couldn't have known how the future, its legacies and obscurities, would shake out. By the time *These Happy Golden Years*, the last planned book in the series, came out in 1943, she'd achieved her own literary renown with the 1938 best-selling novel *Free Land*.

Except I'd never heard of it. Who had? Until recently, all I'd known of Rose had come from the TV show and *The First Four Years*. Her name had so fallen into obscurity that she had become a mere afterthought.

These were the baseline facts, gathered from the web and from the Holtz book I'd found at a used bookstore, that were circling through my mind when I stepped into the Herbert Hoover Presidential Library and Museum in West Branch, Iowa. Rose had been pals with Hoover back in the day and been his first biographer, which was why her papers were there. Pictures of him, looking stern but trying to smile, lined the walls, leading the way to a back room where archives were kept.

I'd always loved the stillness of academic libraries, the comfort and competition of being surrounded by people involved in slow, scholarly endeavors. The library at the Hoover wasn't exactly a Newberry or Beinecke, but the kind of place that reminded me of home: a reading room time-warped to three decades past, with rust-colored carpet and microfiche readers the size of early IBM computers. A small band of researchers squinted over Hoover's notes and newspapers, setting up cameras on tabletop tripods to record their findings. They were a standard lot—frumpy and frowning, pallid and disheveled. Only a couple of them glanced at me, disapprovingly, I thought. Suddenly I felt silly in the bright turquoise ballet flats that I'd thought were so cute, with their little gold lamé bows. Like a lot of Asian people, I probably looked younger than I was.

The librarian, a skinny guy who looked a lot like an engineering grad student I'd dated a couple years back, looked up from the journal article he was reading as I approached the desk. He asked me to sign in and list my affiliation. "I'm Ron," he said. "I'm here to help but, just so you know, we can't provide any change for the Xerox machine." He printed out an identification card and handed it to me. *The researcher, Lee Lien, has duly applied to use materials in the Herbert Hoover Library.*

When I explained that I wanted to look at the Rose Wilder Lane papers he led the way over to a shelf that held the index: a row of three-ring canvas binders, nearly two dozen in all, cataloguing Rose's diaries, letters, and mementos.

"Seems like every few weeks or so someone new wants to see these," Ron mused. "Some are fans, some are researchers."

"I'm a researcher," I said, a little too stridently. I mentioned that I'd just gotten my doctorate.

"That's cool," he said. He seemed to regard me with a new respect, I thought. "So, first, take a look at these catalogs. All the Lane papers and documents are listed. See which ones you want to take a look at, then fill out a request sheet and I'll bring them out from the back. Of course, the diaries are photocopies of the originals."

I thanked him, already reaching for the binder marked *1930s*. I sat down at the nearest table and turned the pages. As Ron had said, it was just a list, generated long ago on what was probably a manual typewriter, with brief descriptions of what the papers held.

RWL diary, 1930, Jan.-Feb. Rocky Ridge, Mo.
RWL diary, 1930, March, part I-II. Rocky Ridge, Mo.

I went back to the shelf to look at earlier years, marveling at how they tracked Rose's moves—California, Missouri, Albania, New York, Texas, Connecticut. It was so overwhelming I just sat there for a few minutes: I hadn't expected there would be so much information. Hadn't realized how large her life had been.

On the request sheet I asked for a few of Rose's journals from 1930, when she and Laura would have started working on *Little House in the Big Woods*, and the diaries from 1965, when Rose visited Vietnam. Ron disappeared into the back and after a while wheeled out a cart with several boxes, like the kind used to store file folders.

"Here you go," he said. I must have looked surprised, because he said, "I know, it's a lot. She was prolific. Take your time."

He left the cart next to the table I'd claimed. It was ten in the morning and as I stared at the boxes, my resolve started to slip. What was I doing here, anyway? Was this all I knew how to do—research and read? The idea of Rose at her desk, piecing together the origins of her parents' lives, then wandering the earth to the end of her days, brought back an old anxiety: my mother and grandfather, also searching, landing, restive in the Midwest. I had to banish this—them—from the room. I remembered Alex, instead, tapping away at his laptop. I remembered Iowa City and the evening drinks, dinner, and bed that were waiting for me. Alex would want to know if I'd found anything here.

I opened the box that held photocopies of Rose's 1965 journals and saw that it included a pile of Vietnam souvenirs as well. Blank postcards, with faded, dreamy drawings of the old opera house in Saigon and the Hotel Caravelle. Boarding passes from Pan Am and United. Hotel bills. Her passport and visa, which displayed a photo of Rose wearing a turban and looking like the famous portraits of Laura in old age. Most of the journal entries from the trip were scattered notes about the history of the country. Her handwriting took time getting used to—sprawling, loop-filled, an old style people had stopped learning more than half a century ago. I couldn't see where she'd written about anyone in particular in Saigon. No young man and his daughter, no Café 88.

Instead, she mostly wrote scraps of grand abstraction—about colonization, about civilian dignity in spite of war—and travelogue remarks about weather and rice fields.

Ao dai is the V dress.
8 acres. Rice crop garden palms bananas. Village destroyed by V.C.
All admire adaptability, flexibility, the bamboo reed.
Foreigners are disliked, admired, & respected.

Nothing so far corroborated my theory that Rose Wilder Lane was the American woman who had visited my grandfather's café every day for two weeks. Ong Hai had said he'd helped her cross the street, navigating the traffic that flowed without signals or stops. He was worried about her being by herself in Saigon. He told her his home would be hers as long as she ever wanted it. And she had thanked him, pressed his hand. This American woman was both old and young, Ong Hai tried to explain once. She'd possessed joie de vivre, and a mind completely intact. But the Rose of the archives, Rose Wilder, had died in her sleep three years later, at the age of eighty-two, at her home in Connecticut.

Nowhere in these journals was there mention of a gold pin. If Almanzo's gift to Laura in *These Happy Golden Years* had been real, it would have been an heirloom, no small thing for Rose to lose or give.

I had nearly emptied the contents of the box onto the table and now, disappointed, I started to put everything back. The items had been out of order in the first place—just light penciled numbers on them to correspond to the index—so I didn't worry about keeping everything neat. There were a few black-and-white photos in the mix, small snapshots encased in plastic. Most were scenes of Saigon life—people on bicycles and cycles, French colonial buildings—the standard images one would find even now in *Lonely Planet* guides. There were pictures of Rose too, standing amid all of this. Only one of them wasn't of her. It was a faded, blurred portrait of a man standing on a sidewalk. The photo had been taken at an angle, as if Rose had impulsively turned to get the shot. The man looked out at the street traffic. My grandfather had no pictures of himself from his younger days. But I thought it could have been him. Like the man in the picture, Ong Hai often wore light short-sleeved shirts and flip-flops. Café 88 could have been on that street.

In the index the image was simply listed as *Photo No. 12, Saigon, Vietnam, 1965.*

I looked up to where Ron was manning the front desk. He was staring at a computer screen, clicking a mouse. I wondered if he was playing some online game. Around me the other scholars and researchers kept on with their own work, making no noise except with the shutters of their cameras.

For the second time in a week, I turned into a thief. I didn't even think before the photograph was in my notebook, closed between blank pages where I had yet to write anything down about Rose Wilder Lane, or Laura Ingalls Wilder, or why I was there at the Hoover Library, looking them up, searching for, maybe hoping for, my own claim on America's favorite pioneer family.

That night Alex and I ordered Thai food in. While we waited for it to arrive, I showed him the photograph and the gold pin.

"Who knew you'd turned into such a sly little klepto?" he said, holding the picture up to the floor lamp near the dinette table where he kept a stack of *New Yorkers*. "If I turn it just a little to the right and close one eye, I can see how you maybe do kind of look like him."

"Yeah, yeah, his face is hardly visible, I know. But there's something of my grandfather in the guy's deportment. It's like the signature Ong Hai stance."

"Did you just use the word *deportment*?"

Alex's buzzer rang, and he tossed the photo back to me on his way to the door. "You're going to stay and find out what's next, right?"

The ease of his generosity, right after my theft, which couldn't help but remind me of Sam's thefts, shamed me. Perhaps my brother and I were more similar than I cared to admit.

"Rose Wilder must have been rolling in royalties," Alex said as he spread out containers of larb gai and noodles and tom yum soup.

"Only late in life."

There were no other direct descendants of Laura Ingalls Wilder, I explained, and none of Laura's siblings had had children. Rose did have a child but he died shortly after birth. "Rose, Laura, and Laura's mother all at one point gave birth to baby boys who ended up dying in infancy."

"You know, so many people can't bear the thought of not going on, of not continuing somehow in the world. But there are her books. That's Rose Wilder's legacy."

"Sort of. If anyone remembers her books. Anyway, everything ended up with Rose's lawyer. She thought of him as an adopted son."

"So all of the lawyer's descendants are the beneficiaries of the estate? Think of all the merchandising. The TV show, movies, the millions of reprinted books. When were they published, again?"

"In the thirties, and continually in print since then."

"Jackpot." Alex helped himself to more noodles. He offered the rest to me but I declined. Thai food had been the wrong thing to get, though I didn't say so. It reminded me too much of Franklin, of the way so many Asian restaurants in suburbs and small towns had to take on a pan-ethnic identity so that patrons walking into a Vietnamese or Chinese restaurant could also find the comfort of a tamed-down pad Thai.

"No one knows who Rose is, though," I reminded him. "Laura is the one people know; she's the hero of the books."

It was something I kept thinking about, later, as we returned to Alex's bed, and on into the night long after he had fallen asleep. Aside from the known truths of Rose's life, seeing her in those Saigon photos at the Hoover Library made me consider how alone she might have felt in the world. If she resented her mother for becoming the star, if she believed herself forgotten, if her travels to my family's homeland had been an escape from the fame she'd delivered to the name of Laura Ingalls Wilder. Alex would say it was wanderlust pure and simple. Who didn't want to be free of their family's choices?

As a kid I had loved the chronology of the *Little House* books. Now I saw the narrative arcs, the threads, the foreshadowing. Of course *These Happy Golden Years*, the book I kept returning to for its passage about the gold pin, had to be the payoff to the hardship in the previous books. Here, the Ingallses' farm and garden are thriving and Laura is raking in twenty-five bucks a month as a schoolteacher. She's eighteen, she has beautiful hair, she has a new pink summer dress and a feathered hat, and she has the dashing Almanzo Wilder as her beau. He drives the prettiest, fastest team of horses in town and lets her drive them too. They get engaged, they get married. The book takes us right up to the wedding night: the new couple, sitting outside their new house, under the stars, with what seems like all the world before them.

Yet there's a deep restlessness threading the *Little House* books together. Pa Ingalls is anxious to keep looking for a better homestead, to keep seeking out the treasured West, and Laura too has that "itchy wandering foot." Perhaps her daughter Rose was able to translate and convey these feelings so well because she had grown up caged in her own desires, if not for westward exploration, then for worldliness, fame, glory, a life beyond the farm and small-town Missouri.

In our own way, Sam and I had felt that restlessness too. That desire to be free of *our* family's choices, even though at the same time we knew how much we owed—our very existence—to them. The fact was, we had grown up Asian American in a mostly white landscape. There were consequences for that: a sense of imbalance, a subconscious avoidance of mirrors. Who wouldn't want to be rid of that, untethered from such fixed identity?

For the first time since Sam had left his number stabbed through with Rose's pin, I felt compelled to make use of it. Sliding out of Alex's bed, I tiptoed over to my bag and took out my phone. *Where are you?* I texted. *I'm in Iowa.*

Back under the covers, I waited for a reply. But there was

none, of course, and soon I was falling asleep, phone idle beneath my pillow.

took up Alex's offer. By day three, Ron and I were exchanging small talk about the drive from Iowa City. He saved my table and the papers I requested, told me which sandwich he thought was best at the deli down the road.

I was reading the letters that Rose and Laura had written each other during the years the *Little House* books came to be. I was looking for clues, figuring that if it was true that Rose had cowritten these books, then the gold pin must have been inspired by something real—if not her father's gift to her mother, then perhaps someone else's gift to Rose.

She was eight years old when her parents chose to settle in Mansfield, Missouri. They had done some wandering already, with failed farms and crops in South Dakota, Minnesota, and Florida to show for it. Mansfield, near Ozark country, promised good land and temperate weather. They stuck it out through years of near-poverty, slowly building Rocky Ridge Farm. Though Rose learned how to manage this kind of life, how to sew and save, she longed for the pleasures a city girl might have. She wanted new dresses and shoes, lavish hats, and restaurant food. With her sharp wit and book smarts, she stood out in Mansfield as a loner, a snob, a dreamer, so much so that her parents let her spend her last year of high school in the larger city of Crowley, Louisiana, where Almanzo's sister Eliza lived, in order for Rose to gain a more advanced education. As soon as she could, Rose got away. She was college-girl material but had no money for it, so she went to the nearest metropolis, Kansas City, and learned how to become a telegrapher. There she finally felt free and, even more importantly, financially independent. She could go out to lunches without guilt, have beaus, and keep hours as late as she wished. She started traveling for her job, going where telegraphing skills were needed. Eventually she landed in San Francisco, where she met and married Gillette Lane.

In photographs, young Rose looks more cautious than girlish. She has that early 1900s look of gaiety and verve, with her broad, flower-trimmed hats and rounded cheeks and soft, glimmering eyes. She looks ready to see what the world has to offer. But there's a canniness in her steady focus, the set of her mouth. Part determined, part amused.

Gillette was supposed to be a land developer but turned out not to be skilled at much of anything but charming and socializing. Their precarious finances kept them on the road, searching for work. They were in Missouri in 1910 when their son was born; he died within days. Rose threw herself into real estate work, telegraphy, whatever could be found. The more she did, the less Gillette did. He was constantly thinking up schemes and losing out by them. She was constantly saving his ass. More than once Rose had to sell whatever she had—clothes, housewares—in order to buy groceries for dinner.

By the time they returned to California, their marriage was pretty much over, though I loved how she pretended otherwise in her letters to her mother. Rose was a master of the double life. She humored Gillette too, making another go at real estate ventures with him but really heading out on her own in the farmlands of what are now San Jose and Silicon Valley. She made her own friends too, artists and writers who encouraged her to write and whose connections got her a job at the *San Francisco Bulletin*. Under the guidance of editor Fremont Older, Rose quickly learned to churn out the kind of articles and opinion pieces the public wanted to read.

Back in Mansfield, Laura worried about her daughter's newly glamorous life as a reporter girl and wondered about the state of her daughter's marriage. She resolved to visit during the summer of 1915, just in time for the World's Fair. Laura also had mercenary reasons: Rose and Gillette owed her $250 and she had promised Almanzo that she would get the money back. It was astonishing to read Laura's letters to him from her trip, gathered as they were with Rose's correspondence like some schizophrenic epistolary novel. Laura's effortful descriptions of San Francisco and the fair, her anxious reminders about the chickens and gardens and chores at the farm—these were far from the prose style of the *Little House* books that would make her famous. Her assurances that she had not lost sight of why she was in San Francisco—to collect that debt—dominated her letters with a vigor that reminded me of my own mother, whose whole day could be made by catching a price error at the grocery store checkout.

In truth, most of Rose and Laura's correspondence revolved around the getting, saving, and making of money. For Rose and Laura both, it was the main reason for writing anything at all.

I do not think you will make a great deal of money out of this book, Rose wrote during the drafting of *Little House in the Big Woods, but it should go on for years and years, paying a little all the time.*

If you find it easier to write in the first person, write that way. I will change it into the third person, later.

At times, Rose did more than suggest how to shape the stories. It wasn't enough to mention a party Laura had attended in De Smet. Rose instructed her mother to describe how nervous she had been, how she'd braided her hair and wound it around her head—hadn't she?—and brushed and pressed her dress and looked in the mirror. The dress was brown poplin—wasn't it?—with shimmering plaid trim.

If such details really had come from Laura's account of her childhood, how much prodding had Rose done to draw them out?

I couldn't fathom the lengths I would have had to go to in

order to get anything more than a yes or a no out of my own mother. Even Ong Hai, who loved telling stories, always stuck to anecdotes, like old Rose in Saigon with her largesse and Americanness, or the customers who had to have their coffees just exactly so, or his pet mice that had such a good sense of direction he could release them half a mile away and they'd return. If I asked him about anything tied to the war he would always manage to veer away from it. He didn't want to talk about his wife—my grandmother—or the relatives he had lost, and I couldn't blame him, couldn't force him. The same went for the nitty-gritty about my father. Sam and I had grown up learning almost nothing about our parents' marriage, much less what our father's life had been like in Vietnam. All we knew about him came from the scraps of our own memories, the few photos we had, and from the stories Ong Hai told about our father's spirit for adventure, his high hopes for the restaurant business. My mother always met my questions with frowning silence, a suspicious counterquestioning: *Why do you want to know?* Eventually I stopped asking.

Maybe if there'd been money in the telling I'd have had better luck.

Instead, this silence became a subject itself, formidable. Sam and I rarely broached it with one another, though once in a great while, in one of those mysterious, unpredictable moments of sibling bonding that could happen out of nowhere and vanish just as quickly, impossible to make or re-create, we would agree on some unifying truth about our family. Like how hopeful our father had been—by now, as Ong Hai often intimated, he might have built an empire. Or like the way our mother would never get free of her first-generation immigrant mentality. Once in flight she was always in flight, glancing uneasily around before pushing on to another vista that promised better prospects. Maybe it kept her feeling safe. She couldn't have known that it would leave Sam and me feeling the opposite—permanently unsettled, unable to know what could be called home.

Look how massively she's controlled our reality, Sam said once, when we were in high school and discovered what *Forrest Gump* was really about. We had seen the movie as a rental when we were kids and our mother had fast-forwarded through so many parts that we didn't fully realize what had happened in it. Watching it on TV a few years later, Sam and I shared the same reactions: *Jenny was a stripper? Forrest and Jenny had sex scenes?* Our mother had cared for only one of the movie's threads: Forrest striking gold in business over and over again.

Of course, Rose never had a sibling to collude with, to speculate with about her mother's withdrawn nature, or the horizons the Wilders had chased for a better plot of land. Rose, above all, had believed in self-sufficiency.

And now I didn't have much of a sibling either. In the library I pulled out my phone; no text, but the clock display read four o'clock, meaning I had only an hour before the Hoover closed. I'd made it through several years' worth of correspondence, with no sign of a gold pin or a Christmas gift from Almanzo. At the rate I was going, it'd be another Christmas before I was done.

Because the more I delved into the collaboration on the *Little House* books, the more slow-going the search became. So many researchers, or fans, had been here before me, and it was clear that the documents hadn't been reorganized in years. Notes, addresses, and scribbles, some of them not even numbered or indexed in the catalogs, lay out of order within the packets of longhand letters and postcards. I kept getting distracted by the receipts—more evidence of the money fixation Rose shared with her mother. If she was manic-depressive, as critics claimed, her finances were too, jumping between debt and savings. Rose kept track of every cent of commission that went to her agent, and every cent that went to her, and when, and how. Yet she was also a spendthrift, unable to stop herself from purchasing a bit of land here or there, or some new furniture to spruce up a new apartment. On the backs of some of the receipts were more notes: details about architecture, books she wanted to get, ideas for novels. A list of possible titles: *Trundle-bed Tales. Long Ago Yesterday. Little Girl in the Big Woods.*

One slip of paper caught my eye because, unlike the rest, it was dated 1918, and because it was enjambed like a poem.

She wasn't supposed to know. They told her

not to know. A boy, again,

a gain, would always be wanted on a farm.

Rose's looping cursive seemed almost illegible, as if a larger force were bearing down on the letters.

The note wasn't numbered, didn't correspond to anything in the catalog.

I read the words over and over again, until they took on another meaning. Another light. The third-person perspective.

I looked back through my own notes. Rose's child had been born and buried in 1910. Eight years of discord and separation later, she and Gillette divorced. In her journal Rose noted that she had finally "got rid" of him.

So what happened in 1918? *A boy, again.* Was I misreading, overreading? Was it possible that Rose was writing about herself? Or was it possible this note was written by someone else entirely?

There was nothing else I'd found to sustain the thought, but it persisted: what if Rose had had another child?

Finding everything you need?"

I jumped at Ron's voice right next to me. He was leaning over a rolling cart filled with spiral-bound Hoover papers, idly glancing at my notebook. The room had nearly emptied out, and it was just me, Ron, and one other guy at the copy machine.

"So," he continued, "where are you on the road to Saint Laura?"

I closed my notebook. "What, you think I'm some sort of hobbyist?"

"Quite the contrary. Only the die-hard scholars follow the trail to the Lane papers. She's the one who kept track of everything, after all. I'd say the serious fans make it as far as the various libraries holding original manuscripts. The amateurs stick to the houses and museums, although it's an industry secret that the museums are the best source of pay dirt."

I knew that the Ingallses' house in De Smet, South Dakota, where the family had finally settled in 1880, had been turned into a museum. But the main stop was Rocky Ridge Farm, where one could pay homage to Pa's fiddle and Ma's hair combs. Only now, hearing Ron, did it occur to me that if the gold pin in *These Happy Golden Years* was preserved among Laura's effects—if it had nothing to do with that pin now pocketed in my tote bag—then Rocky Ridge would be the place to find out.

"You have industry secrets?" I asked.

He picked up a couple of the Hoover documents and started to reshelve them. "To be honest, it's not really my thing. But I hear that Rocky Ridge has some material. Most of it on display, but apparently some is still boxed up."

"Papers?"

"Mostly clothes and trinkets and stuff like that, but supposedly a few papers and letters too. There isn't much money to keep up the place, and it's more or less run by volunteers."

"Their website looks pretty good."

"That's fairly new. I think the heirs of the *Little House* enterprise are providing a little more support these days. They used to keep their money pretty tight. I think technically it's the Laura Ingalls Wilder–Rose Wilder Lane Museum but you know how no one calls it that."

I didn't, but kept that to myself. "So how do you know there are more papers there?"

"I don't—it's just what I've heard from a few other people who've been through here. Just a rumor."

"Aren't you guys interested in bringing whatever it is here?"

Ron glanced at a booklet he was holding, frowned, and set it back on the cart. "This doesn't belong in this section," he muttered. "You scholars are never as neat and tidy as I think you're going to be. You know, we've tried to see about getting some more of Rose's things here but there's not much urgency about it in Missouri. Actually, no one's even confirmed that there are any real documents left. Bit of a biddy brigade over there."

I glanced at the clock. Nearly five. "I guess I should get going," I said.

"If you're coming back tomorrow, I'll save everything for you again right here," Ron offered.

"Thanks," I said.

"No problem." He kept on with the Hoover items and I gathered up my notes. Conscious of Ron's presence, I tried to straighten the letters I hadn't yet read, keeping them in chronological order.

As I left the library, Rose's words—*a boy, again*—swam in my head. Maybe it had to do with the missing people in my own life—my father, and now Sam. Maybe it was simply the scholar's thrill of excavation that had eluded me throughout my grad school career. Somehow it had popped up here, in this relic of a presidential library in the middle of a literal cornfield. Either way, I knew I had to keep looking. And then I had to find a way to get to Rocky Ridge.

SIX

Don't was my mother's favorite way to begin a sentence. Don't forget to wash all the vegetables. Don't forget to scrub the sinks, mop the floor. Don't leave the kitchen without disinfecting the countertops. And don't forget there are a thousand ways to do these things wrong.

Those ways—the mistakes in waiting—seemed to come at me as I parked in front of my mother's house in Franklin, Illinois. Iowa seemed so much farther than hours away; it didn't seem possible that it was evening there, too. Already, my reflection in the car window seemed smaller.

I was born small, my mother liked to say, on a Saturday night, the contractions deepening right before the dinner rush at the Golden Dragon in La Porte, where my parents had started working a few months earlier. We had only one car, so Ong Hai drove my mother to the hospital, where he and Sam dozed off in the waiting room; at the restaurant, another waiter had agreed to drop my father off after his shift. But by the time he showed up, at ten-thirty, I had already arrived. My father recognized me in the nursery right away—the only Asian baby, with a shock of black, black hair. The nurse let him bring me into the room where my mother was sleeping. She woke up, she said, at the smell of oyster sauce and grease emanating from his clothes.

My mother would tell this story sometimes as proof of my early and innate sense of bad timing. Sam, after all, had been born on a sleepy Sunday morning in a town where everyone went to church. No disruption in schedule, no disruption in pay. He'd been an easy baby too, with little fussing or crying, content to spend hours playing with toy cars or watching television, while I apparently threw up a lot, screamed for no reason, and refused to sleep through the night.

Ong Hai neither verified nor disputed these reports. He tended to take the line of neutrality where things concerned my mother and me. And it was hard to make him mad or even frustrated. "Your ma," he would say, shaking his head, his only way of criticizing her. "You kids." His gentle nature had a way of making Sam and me listen; we wanted to gain his quiet favor and approval. I remembered long days, just the three of us, hanging out in a patch of backyard, walking to a playground, counting the tiger lilies we passed. My mother would be gone from breakfast to late at night, sometimes working two different restaurant jobs. She smelled too of frying oil and soy sauce.

Even though she showered as soon as she got home, the odor lingered in the sofa cushions she'd sat in, the fibers of all her clothes. In later years, when Sam and I could fend for ourselves after school, that smell would become Ong Hai's as well. Whatever place we lived would retain the scent of their restaurant hours.

After La Porte, the towns blurred together—Elgin, Waukesha, Aurora, Kankakee. I didn't realize until I was in high school that the one midwestern state we avoided was Michigan, where my father had died.

Sometimes I thought I didn't remember his death at all. Sometimes I thought I didn't remember him. In my mind he was a still-life figure: smiling at my brother and me as we clutched matching balloons; holding us, one in each arm, while on a carnival ride called the Scrambler. The active memories were hazed over, influenced by too many images of old-reel home movies from television shows. Slow-motion details appeared in dreams, in unexpected moments when I was TAing a class or opening the cupboard to search out something for dinner. Then I would see my father again, standing in one of the buffets he and my mother managed; offering me a chopstick bite of shrimp; already starting to clap while Sam leaned forward to blow out the candles on his fifth birthday cake.

Ong Hai said my father was the kind of guy who made friends wherever he went. He had a big laugh—I thought I remembered that too—and he was always up for trying something new: foods, shows, cities. One of his dreams was to visit every state in America. He had plans to build a restaurant franchise, eventually importing Asian goods to American grocery stores under his own label. He could have done it, Ong Hai said. He was a natural in business. His only weakness was his kindness; he would help anyone out, even to his own detriment. Sometimes he lost money on ventures simply because he'd been too nice, too trusting. In La Porte, he loaned money to friends but never got repaid; he gave other people his business ideas.

When we offered our respects to the urn with my father's ashes, we lit red candles and incense, we bowed to his photograph, and we set out plates of fruit. But none of these helped me keep a true image of him. I don't remember my mother getting the news of his death, or seeing her or Ong Hai crying, or me or Sam crying, though we must have. I don't remember the words *death* or *died* being uttered in either Vietnamese or English. I just remember always knowing he was gone.

Somehow, my father's being an immigrant made his death seem that much more tragic. To have escaped a war, to have fled his own country, to have started over, to have come such a distance, only to have his life cut short, drowned in a strange river far from home—it seemed unbearably unfair.

All the same, Sam and I grew up being careful to say little, if anything, about him. It wasn't that we were afraid of hurting our mother—she was no delicate flower. We were afraid, or at least I was, of enraging her. My father was a topic that required so much respect that almost no one, at any time, would be worthy of it. And I more than anyone else knew the depth and capacity of her anger. Before the fight that had led to Sam walking out that first time, she seldom turned on him or Ong Hai, though there was one time when Sam bounced a ball that knocked over one of the candles on our father's shrine, almost toppling the urn. My mother very nearly raised her hand to smack his face. I had never seen her do that to him, though I'd been the recipient of a few such slaps myself.

We could go weeks in peace, she and I, then suddenly break down over the way I said I needed to do homework. "Don't you talk that way to me!" she'd yell, and we'd be off. Then the next day all would be calm again, my mother offering to teach me how to cable-knit with a new ball of acrylic yarn, me pretending to learn.

"You are alike," Ong Hai sometimes remarked, and I didn't know whom that irritated more.

I could never deny, however, that I had inherited some of my mother's neuroses. In the same way that she would never stop looking for a better job opportunity, and would never think to miss a day of work just because she was sick, I wouldn't go to sleep until I had memorized every date in a history book's chapter on the Depression, preparing for an exam. School became my domain of control: story problems were solvable, grades were attainable, and results and right answers were on every page. Literature became my favorite because of all the symbols and metaphors, easy to manipulate into the thesis statements my teachers so desired. In math, you could have a right answer or a wrong answer. In literature, you could have the best answer. Whenever I developed a formula for interpretation, coerced a few images into defining an entire story, or text, as my teachers said, it was a little bit like winning a game show.

Whenever Ong Hai says my mother and I are alike he means it as a compliment. He means tenacity, determination. And perhaps he means to remind me that I am beholden to her. That, I've always known. I could only vaguely ever imagine what she and my father and Ong Hai had gone through to come to the United States, though sometimes I thought I recognized it in her saving face.

I'd always looked to Ong Hai as the benevolent contrast, the one who would sympathize when I pouted after a punishment, the one who would sneak me a piece of fruit if, after refusing a dinner of leftovers, I was sent to bed hungry. My mother must have known these things too, but it was in her power to let them go. Her silence always made me hold my breath—for its rarity, its way of preceding fury, its promise of more scolding to come. She was, like a lot of Asian people, disconcertingly blunt. Anyone she saw, including me and Sam, might be deemed too thin or too fat, too ugly, too tired-looking, too slutty, or simply stupid-looking. By the time I got to middle school I was in the habit of checking my appearance in the mirror not out of vanity but out of worry, paranoid about what my mother might target next. *She can't help it*, was what I told my friends when they expressed their shock at some of my stories. *That's how those old-school Asian people are.* I never admitted how her watchful assessments seeped into my own consciousness, and how much effort it took simply not to listen.

And I never wanted to end up like her, working that hard, moving so much, finding solace only in a few hours of television and sewing each night. Every fellowship, stipend, or loan, every research gig, even Ong Hai's secret help—each windfall was a form of deliverance from that fate.

What I hadn't expected was that I would be so unremarkable in grad school. Forget being a star—I wasn't even close to a gleam. When a few classmates dropped out after the first year, I both envied and pitied them. I didn't dare think about doing the same, as it would have been an admission of failure to my mother. Instead, I chose Edith Wharton as my dissertation subject because I'd read *The Age of Innocence* so many times and hadn't yet grown to hate it. I told myself that maybe everyone took their vocational cues this way. Maybe everyone felt like an imposter and this was why my classmates drank so much. Me, I wasn't so good at that, not since my first semester in Madison, when after two glasses of wine at a reception I bit into a cherry tomato and the juice shot out onto a professor's sweater. He didn't notice, just kept on talking about Cixous, but another student stared at me in horror. I never drank that much again.

By the time I turned in the prospectus for my dissertation, grad school had become one big ruse that I had backed myself into and couldn't get out of. So I kept on with it, forced my way through the diss as fast as possible, and decided that this was how all academics felt, that everyone slogged through the semesters and lived for summers and sabbaticals.

It had taken being away from all that, hiding out in the Herbert Hoover Library, in a place that felt as far from civilization as the Ingallses' house on the prairie had been from a city, to understand what so many of my peers must have already known. At one point, I looked up at the library's old schoolhouse clock and realized I'd been reading Rose's journals for five solid hours. I had fallen headlong into her world. Was that what research was supposed to feel like? Was it supposed to render a person spellbound, the archival stuff so vivid that one's own life faded in comparison?

I hadn't wanted to go back to Franklin, to that shadow of a life.

In the kitchen Ong Hai was making two different kinds of banh mi. The counters were crowded with plates of pickled carrots, daikon, leeks, grilled pork and shrimp. He would layer these together, fleck them with jalapeños, coriander, mint, and Thai basil, then dash a split baguette with Sriracha-fish-sauce mayonnaise.

"Are you trying these out for the café?" I asked.

"Now you're back, you can be the taste tester. How's your friend?"

I'd almost forgotten the lie I'd told. I wanted to confess, tell him about Rose, show him the photograph I'd stolen from the Hoover Library, but my mother was within earshot in the living room, the television casting its ghostly light onto the walls. So all I said was that I'd spent some time doing research at a library near Iowa City.

Ong Hai pointed at the plates. "Try," he said.

I popped a slice of daikon in my mouth. Its vinegary crunch even tasted translucent. "This banh mi could change the whole business."

"Hope so, or your ma is going to start talking about going back to the buffets," Ong Hai said.

"It hasn't even been a year and a half yet." I'd read somewhere that more than 60 percent of restaurants didn't make it past that mark, but had figured my mother's pride alone would make her hold on longer.

"Well, at least things look a little prettier now, thanks to you."

"Did *she* say that?"

"Doesn't say it, maybe, but I think she thinks it. And there's more to do."

He was pulling me in, pulling me back. *But what about my own work?* I wanted to say. How had my mother managed to disparage my contributions to the café and then enlist me for more without uttering a single word?

"It's all for Sam anyway, right?"

"What does it matter? He's your brother." As usual, I was proving way too petty to be the Buddhist Ong Hai was. Changing the subject, he said, "You know who loved banh mi? Your ba. I bet he would have talked about making a franchise. What do you think? Like a Viet Chipotle place except with banh mi."

"Works for me," I said.

"Here, try the pork and shrimp."

We turned our focus back to food, our favorite subject, talking about how to layer the ingredients toward a better balance. I took pictures, jotted down some notes. Ong Hai sliced the baguette on the diagonal. I'd buy this every day, I said, after the first bite. He chewed slowly and decided it wasn't bad at all, then told me to eat the rest and decide for sure.

This habit, of being incapable of eating without sharing, was so ingrained that it had become mine as well. I had irritated every roommate I'd ever had by asking and reasking if they were sure, really sure, they didn't want some ice cream or toast or pancakes or croissants. They called me a food pusher.

When Ong Hai brought half a sandwich to my mother I took the moment to slide past them, down the hall toward the bedroom that I still refused to think of as anything other than temporary, borrowed space. Opening my overnight bag, I pulled out the Laura Ingalls and Rose Wilder biographies I'd found at Defunct Books in Iowa City. It was comforting to return to them, get lost even in these scholarized accounts of the pioneer life, especially when it came to Rose's involvement—as collaborator, editor, writer—in shaping Laura's descriptions of crops and holidays, fried potatoes and chicken pie.

But of course, my mother wasn't about to let me get away so easily. After her shows she walked into my room without knocking and said, "You going to the restaurant tomorrow?"

I sat up from the bed, feeling like I'd been caught at something far worse than wondering if maybe the *Little House* books had so much food in them because they'd been written during the Great Depression. She made a face, of course. She thought it was a lazy thing to do, reading. Like who did I think I was, some leisurely empress dowager?

"Yeah." I closed the biography partway, keeping my place with the edge of my pillow.

My mother was dressed in what Sam and I referred to as classic Old Asian Lady garb: loose, comfortable pants with an elastic waist, button-down tunic blouse, velvet-trimmed house slippers. Hers was a wardrobe of clearance items and clothes kept so long they'd become vintage. Sometimes her look crossed over into accidentally hip, like when she rolled up the sleeves of a nineties plaid shirt and paired it with Bermuda shorts and a sun visor.

Surveying the room, the clothes I'd thrown over the back of the chair, the books I'd piled on the floor, she made a little *hmmph* sound, the one I knew too well, had memorized from my earliest days, earliest memories. That sound managed to express disapproval, disbelief, and disdain all at once. She was good at that, and she was punishing me for going to Iowa.

"You get a job for the fall?"

"Not yet."

"Why can't you get a job at the college here?" she asked for about the thirtieth time, referring to the community college where Sam had halfheartedly taken classes.

"Because that's not how it works. I already told you that."

"It's a job. You go in, you apply. It's just a job." *Don't think you're so special*, her tone conveyed.

Both Sam and I had learned, early on, that it was usually easier to lie or play dumb or both. This shirt? I got it on sale, five dollars! That iPod? Great deal from the university—practically free! I had always lied about where I was going. Lied about the roommates I lived with. Everything was a bargain; everyone was always nice, quiet, and studious.

"What were you doing in Iowa?"

"Helping out a friend and doing research."

"They must have very special libraries there," she remarked. "Well, now you're back. You can have Jennie's job now."

"You let her go? Why'd you do that?"

"You should be happy to have a job."

And with that—midargument for me, the finale for her—she turned and left, not even closing the door. I heard her own door shutting and I pictured her peeling back the old bedspread that I had smoothed out less than a week earlier, worried she would suspect that Sam had searched her room. I pictured her opening the bottom dresser drawer and realizing all the jewelry was gone.

I understood that my fleeing to Iowa had wounded my mother more than it had angered her. Which was worse, because instead of triumph there was just that strange sensation that I could only call immigrant guilt. If my mother had ever felt this way, she never let on. She was one of those stoic Asians that my other Asian American friends and I would sometimes joke about. No nonsense, all business, and a little scary.

Once, on a holiday visit home back when I was an undergrad, I had asked my grandfather if she'd been different years ago, before my father.

"No," Ong Hai said. He laughed as he said it. "Your ma is always serious. Even when she was very young. Little serious girl. That's your ma."

It's what made her a hard worker, he said. She had apprenticed her way into running her own business. She knew how to balance books, keep track of cash flow, maintain supplies, and do the taxes. She did as much as she could herself, because she was cheap and because she liked to be in charge. But it seemed that whenever I began to respect her for this she would pick another fight and I wouldn't back down. By this point, we had spent more years unhappy with each other than anything else.

The days resumed in pointed silence. We woke up early, worked at the Lotus Leaf, watched TV. But Rose had made me restless. With every swipe of a customer's credit card and every fold of a spring roll I was planning my next departure.

Sam sent me a text on the day of the week when my mother and Ong Hai liked to watch a dance competition show involving D-list celebrities. Ong Hai asked me to join them, so I sat on the sidelines, in a creaky wicker chair my mother had picked up a decade ago at a garage sale. Like most of our furnishings, it was a temporary solution that had become permanent. Any effort I'd made over the years—a throw pillow or decorative vase—only looked pitiful. My mother called such things a waste of money, and she went out of her way not to use them, making a point to serve food on the Fiestaware she'd had for decades instead of the Crate & Barrel outlet dishes I'd brought with me from Madison.

In Calif, Sam wrote. *What did you find out?*

I thought about taking my time answering—wait a few days, as he had. On the TV screen a couple was gyrating around, some kind of dirty dancing hip-hop mix.

Nothing, I texted back. Which was true. I wasn't going to be Sam's personal assistant. And what was there to find, anyway? I didn't remember Hieu's last name, so I couldn't look him up. Ong Hai had made it clear he wouldn't be talking about the subject. And my mother was the unapproachable fortress she'd always been.

Sam persisted. *Did you find out about the $*

Where are you in CA? I wrote.

SF.

I didn't answer his question about the money. Instead, I looked up at my mother and grandfather.

Ong Hai was nodding off on the sofa, having had a rare third beer. The TV show hadn't even gotten to the judging yet but he stood up and said good night. I got up too, went to the kitchen to get something to eat. The refrigerator was packed with leftovers but I put a pot of water on for pasta. I waited there, flipping through clothing catalogs.

My mother appeared as I was about to drop a handful of spaghetti into the water.

"What are you doing?" she asked, in her voice that meant,

What's wrong with you? "Don't use so much spaghetti. You waste it."

"I'll eat it."

"You better," she said. She got herself a few saltines, letting the cupboard slam shut.

Don't engage, I told myself, but I couldn't help it. "You don't even like pasta."

"You think I need to eat it to know it? I know you waste it. Next day you make it all new again and waste it some more. You never know how much to make."

I didn't reply, hoping she'd go back to the living room.

But then she said, "Lee," in that universal mother voice of command.

Whatever she was going to say I didn't want to know—didn't want to hear it. So I said, "Sam's in San Francisco."

She kept her focus on the saltines, crunching them. She said, "Tell him we buy a house. He always wanted one. Maybe one of those condos. What they call a town house."

So she was going to pretend I hadn't thrown her off at all.

"I like a brand-new house," she said, like one of her customers considering a menu.

Of course she remembered that Sam had always envied his friends' homes and never brought anyone over to wherever we lived. Neither had I. Nothing could ever be ours, Sam had complained, until we owned. We couldn't even paint the walls. My mother had, in the past, made vague promises of buying—*Soon, soon*, she would say—but we knew better than to believe her. How could we cement ourselves to a home and mortgage when there was, at any time, a chance of moving somewhere else?

Here was my doorway to the Hieu question. "How could you even afford it?"

"That's not your business."

"Hieu?"

Whether I'd finally uttered the word for Sam's sake or my own, I couldn't have said, but I felt myself backing away a little, preparing for my mother's wrath.

Again she surprised me. "Not your business," she repeated simply.

Sam had figured out how to make it his business, by leaving. I pushed: "I don't think your plan is going to bring him back. He's not a kid. He's twenty-seven years old."

"*You're* here."

"Temporarily."

She waved a handful of crackers. "Same stupid talk. You'll learn one day. You just make sure Sam is back." She returned to the living room, stepping out of her pink Dearfoam slippers and leaving them next to the sofa.

I'd done so well resisting her, but I couldn't resist following her. I would have muted the television but my mother had the remote in her grip.

"I'm not going to do that, even if I could."

"You do what I say." It wasn't a threat; it was a forecast. She was counting on me to follow her directions.

Without another word she aimed the remote, increasing the volume of an insurance commercial. She wasn't going to look at me again.

She had won. I went back to the kitchen. Even before I drained the spaghetti I knew my mother was right again: I had made too much. I always did. I was the kind of person who always had to add a little bit more, just in case. Just one of my many deficiencies. And as my mother knew, behind every deficiency lurked a greater danger and menace.

Once, when I was in eleventh grade, she'd announced, "Your friend Erin might have leukemia. She's always sick, always sneezing."

"She has allergies," I'd explained. "She has to get shots for them."

My mother shook her head and said, "You just wait and see." I worried about Erin for years.

If Sam or I showed a hint of a cough or stuffy nose our mother would make us eat enormous bowls of a flavorless rice soup called chao, and apply the noxious-smelling Tiger Balm to our chests. She had a way of making us believe that we would perish if we didn't heed her directions. I didn't recall ever going to a doctor for anything but vaccinations, because my mother suspected that Western medicine was one big scam. She was convincing—so able to mix her conviction with our fears—and if I didn't exactly trust her, I couldn't help believing her.

At the time, I'd chalked it up to the stereotypes I'd absorbed at school: *That's how old-school Asian people are*. But what if it was something else? What had my mother suffered that made her so fearful of others' secret intentions and maladies?

The previous week, at the café, my mother had glared so intently at a customer using an hour of WiFi over one cup of coffee that he finally left, probably never to return. Later I joked to Ong Hai that only she could manage to turn free WiFi into a detriment to business. But of course my mother would be suspicious of the Internet. She had wanted no part of it in the first place. It was the apotheosis of a wild wood, with too many ways to get in trouble.

Sam's abandonment must have felt to her like a confirmation of all her worst suspicions about us and the world we'd grown up in—and into, despite her attempts to cloister us. Yet she had spoiled Sam, was what I'd always insisted to Ong Hai, whether he agreed or not. I blamed her for not making Sam grit his way through school like everyone else. I blamed her for relenting. If she got upset when the school called again about his cutting classes, Sam would tell her she was too controlling. He'd go off with his friends, sometimes returning drunk, hung over, or smelling of weed, and the next day my mother would glower, but that was it. She didn't ground him, or even, as far as I could tell, stop giving him money. And eventually the argument would recede and the flow of our household would go on. We all got along fine, I would have said to anyone. But I also wondered how we had ever managed. Did we have laughs? How had we spent all those years?

On the morning that Sam left for the first time, my mother was just two weeks away from opening the Lotus Leaf. It was a couple days after Christmas and my plan had been to sleep in, have lunch with Ong Hai, then drive back to Madison. But I awoke to the sound of arguing: my mother's voice rising, reaching every part of the house. She was yelling about Sam's car.

I got out of bed and lifted a slat of the window blinds. Outside, the gray Honda Civic my mother had bought for him was smashed in along the front and one side. One of the headlights looked like it had been cleanly carved away.

In the living room, Sam was slumped on the cracked leather sofa, somehow managing to yawn and roll his eyes at the same time, while my mother stood over him. He'd gone out the night before and it looked like he'd slept in his clothes, a uniform of dark jeans and hooded sweaters. Now he was chumbing through one of the cookware catalogs my mother kept on the coffee table. Our artificial Christmas tree, prelit and predecorated, stood near the altar to our father and Buddha, looking sorrowful in the morning light. Ong Hai had left the fleece-lined slippers and winter boots we'd given him under the tree. *It's a foot-themed Christmas*, he had said, and I thought of that later. An ominous thing that Sam and I had accidentally done.

My mother grabbed the pages from Sam's hands. "Drunk driving," she told no one in particular. "So much money to fix the car! Maybe it can't even get fixed!"

She was mixing her English with Vietnamese, her hands balled into fists. Ong Hai popped in from the kitchen, holding a carrot and a peeler. "Hey, Lee," he called out, as if a fight weren't erupting before us. "Come over and help."

As I went to the kitchen Sam said, "It's not like I got a DUI. It was just an accident."

Ong Hai pointed me toward a bowl of mung bean noodles, freshly rinsed and ready to be chopped into smaller pieces. It would be mixed with shrimp, pork, carrots, fish sauce, sugar, garlic, and seasonings, spread carefully into cha gio egg rolls. I took scissors and, as he had taught me years ago, started cutting within the bowl of noodles, lifting up handfuls of the fine, translucent threads and snipping whichever ones seemed too long. The noodles gave off their peculiar sweetish, musty scent that always reminded me of browsing through the narrow aisles of Asian grocery stores.

Ong Hai whispered, "He said he ran into a fence. A guardrail. You need some tea?" He filled the kettle with water.

"Was anyone hurt?"

"Said he was by himself."

It was impossible to know what was true.

Ong Hai added, "This is more about their fighting from the other day. Before you got here."

I'd figured as much, since the holiday had been tenser than usual, marked by their sullen faces. "What was that about?"

"Oh, she was mad and he wouldn't apologize."

"What is this, the apocalypse? She asked him to apologize for something? What was it?"

Ong Hai shook his head.

In the living room my mother was saying, "No more of this. No more car."

"What's the big deal? I'll get it fixed," Sam said.

"How? How are you going to pay?"

Sam had always had jobs, mostly at retail shops and restaurants, though he refused to work at any place our family ran. He never kept a job for long but he never seemed to lack money either. Partly this was due to our mother, but by the time I finished high school I assumed that he'd found other, less legal ways to get cash. By high school, his friends were the ones who sold weed right out of their cars at lunchtime.

"I can pay," Sam insisted.

"Where you get the money?"

"I have some saved up."

My mother made her little *hah* noise. Then: "No. The car is gone. I say *no more*."

I looked at Ong Hai, who raised his eyebrows. I knew he was thinking what I was, that she had never spoken that harshly to Sam.

"I have to have a car."

"Then buy one with all that money you saved. Because I say no more car. No more of this."

"Whatever."

I could hear Sam getting up from the sofa and stalking away to the basement. Probably he didn't think my mother meant what she'd said.

She huffed off to her room. Ong Hai and I prepared the egg rolls and drank tea, believing the argument would dissipate, never imagining it could end any other way.

"You should see how fast I could make these in Saigon," Ong Hai said as his pile of rolls grew larger. He had far outpaced me. He started talking about his old Café 88 and the morning became just the two of us. That was always the best part of being back home. He never asked questions about school, and his voice never took on a tone of puzzled disapproval over what I could possibly do with a graduate degree in literature.

As we were setting out bowls of nuoc mam and plates of herbs and lettuce leaves, a tow truck pulled up to the house.

My mother emerged, went out to the front stoop, and waved. Two guys, Vietnamese, got out of the truck.

Sam came bounding up from the basement.

"The fuck!" he shouted.

We all watched as the guys hitched up the Honda. Sam ran outside, yelling. He started pulling things from the trunk and backseat—old CDs, clothes, a sleeping bag, shoes. He had no way to stop the guys from taking the car. It was in my mother's name, and she paid the insurance.

When he came back into the house he didn't say anything, didn't even look in our direction. I wondered if maybe I was more shaken than he was; I couldn't help feeling like a little kid again, scared of getting into trouble. And I couldn't believe that my mother had gone through with it. Why was she making a show now?

Ong Hai turned on the television. Football. Something mindless and background enough to diffuse the tension in the air. Quietly the three of us ate the egg rolls along with the braised short ribs and tofu tomato soup he had prepared the night before. When Sam finally reappeared the game was almost over, yet another beer-sex-car commercial was on, and Ong Hai had just brought out a pile of orange and pineapple slices.

Sam carried a backpack and an enormous duffel bag—the kind that made me think of kids in movies going to sleepaway camp, something we'd never done—out to the front stoop. My mother narrowed her eyes but didn't move. On the television, a bunch of players were on the field, slapping each other's asses. Then an old red Pontiac, the kind that looked perpetually dirty, unironically nineties, turned onto the street. Behind the wheel was Gabe, Sam's best friend from high school. The three of us—my mother, grandfather, and me—watched Sam carry his belongings to the car, heave them into the trunk, and climb into the passenger seat. He made sure not to look back at the house as Gabe drove off.

Since high school Sam had been increasingly remote, cultivating an air of self-possession and his own group of part punk, part slacker, part skater, part pseudo-artist-philosopher types. Still, I didn't believe that he was doing anything more than what my mother was doing: putting on a display, parading a point.

Ong Hai flipped the channel to another game and my mother returned the dishes to the kitchen. Then my grandfather looked at me, and he shook his head just the smallest bit, conveying, finally, the weight of what had happened. Sam hadn't just left; he was gone.

The crazy thing was that he stayed within reach: our mother still paid his cell phone bill every month. We could see the numbers he had called and texted; we could see the times of day. But whenever I called or texted him there was no response. I wondered how long my mother tried it, letting the phone ring into voice mail a dozen, two dozen, a hundred times a day. Sam didn't cave. It was a brilliant bluff, I had to give him that: he knew that if our mother canceled his phone he would be lost to us. Secretly I called some of the numbers that appeared on the bill. Sam's friends from high school, who claimed not to know where he was staying. Maybe my mother called them too. In any case, the Honda was sold and the basement where Sam had stayed became off-limits for all of us—a new addition to her litany of unspoken rules. These measures didn't make a difference, though, because now my mother was locked in the position of having to wait to see what would happen.

A year and a half later, she still was—with both me and Sam. It must have driven her crazy, not being able to corral us with the same power she'd exerted when he and I were kids. Ong Hai's benevolence now seemed a way of placating her. It hadn't occurred to me before that his patience was a gift she was aware of, might even be grateful for. It hadn't occurred to me that her commands—*Don't do this, don't do that, just do what I say*—might actually be entreaties.

The next morning I hid out in my bed, waiting for my mother and Ong Hai to leave for the Lotus Leaf. I could hear them hurrying cups of tea, opening a package of the cereal bars Ong Hai had discovered a few years back. He had a taste for sugary breakfasts, especially things like Pop-Tarts that could be held in one hand and eaten while driving.

After I saw my mother's Toyota pull away I went into the kitchen. Ong Hai was at the door, about to put his shoes on.

"Water is still hot for tea," he said. "Here." He reached into his shirt pocket and held out a cereal bar.

I shook my head. He placed the cereal bar in my hand anyway, along with an envelope he'd been holding. "Where you going now?" It wasn't the first time he'd guessed my intentions.

"I just need to get away from her, just for a little while." And then, "Sam's in California, by the way. San Francisco."

Ong Hai nodded. "He always wanted that."

I had a feeling he didn't believe it was for real. I wondered if, in his own way, he assumed as my mother did that the family would, must, stay whole. I could see the narrative: Sam was just continuing his rebellion, boys will be boys and all that, but one day he'd figure things out, shape up, and come back home. How else could we get past Sam's stealing? The prodigal son was worldwide, historical, cross-cultural.

Ong Hai gave me a quick, awkward hug; in our family hugs weren't normal, weren't natural. Too American. "See you soon," he said. And then he left, offering up a small smile before closing the door. I listened for the sound of his car as it started and rolled down the street. I didn't know if I had his approval. I didn't know what he would tell my mother.

I opened the envelope he had given me. Five hundred dollars. When I was a kid, it was thrilling to get twenty bucks on my birthday or on Tet and I would spend hours thinking of hiding places. Now all that money made me ashamed, made me want to get away even more.

My mother had left a stack of junk mail on the table, including the Restoration Hardware catalog that Sam had torn to write down his phone number. It was a longtime hobby of hers, to glance through catalogs and turn corners of pages she liked. The people who had rented the house before us had diverse tastes, spanning L.L.Bean, Brookstone, Victoria's Secret, and Burpee Seeds. I didn't think my mother ever ordered anything, but she seemed to savor the possibilities the way some people like to get lost in a good book. Out of habit I picked up a Chadwicks of Boston mailer and peeked at pages she'd marked, thinking, as I often did, that it might be a way to see into her mind a little, but as always it was impossible to know which item on the page was the one she liked. That boiled-wool sweater? That sterling silver necklace? So far, I'd never gotten it right; her standard response to holiday and birthday gifts never deviated from benign dismissal.

I tossed the catalog back in the pile and fixed a cup of tea. The hours alone in the house spread ahead of me. Guilt about the café and not helping out there—these I could feel filling me up as the hot water filled the teacup. Maybe I should have gone to the café after all, letting the day and every one that followed subsume me with their monotony. Sam would stay in California. My mother would continue to brood. The café would continue to struggle. Then my mother would find another restaurant to run. Ong Hai would trail along, both of us doing what we were told. It could all happen just like that.

And then there was the alternate history that my mother and Ong Hai preferred, believing in the beauty of time, its passage a cleansing. In this version, Sam would come back, maybe not right away, but one day soon. My mother's business was her business and the money was her money. We would all go on, staying home and saying little, each day turning into the past that repairs its own self.

In the stillness of the house I felt like I could see our future bodies, spun through the days into older impressions. Every movement I made was a choice between becoming visible and remaining unseen.

I picked up my phone and found Alex's number.

On my way back to you, I typed. It sounded more suggestive than I'd intended, but I pressed SEND anyway.

SEVEN

1869. The Ingalls family leaves their log cabin in Wisconsin and heads out in a covered wagon for the yet-unseen "Indian Territory" of southeastern Kansas because Pa yearns to see the country and find fresh land. Their patch of Wisconsin had become too settled, he said—too many neighbors, too little hunting. He wants to explore. So they set off near the end of winter in order to cross the Mississippi while it's still frozen, waving to all of their family who've gathered to bid a predawn good-bye.

It isn't a good decision.

In Kansas, Pa is so certain that the government will seize the Indian Territory and hand it to white settlers that he begins a farm there, about seven miles from the town of Independence. Their nearest neighbor is Mr. Edwards, an aw-shucks, heart-of-gold "wildcat from Tennessee" who can dance a fine jig and spit tobacco farther than Laura has ever seen. He helps

Pa build a log house, a well, a stone fireplace, and furniture carved from tree trunks. Ma plants gardens, Pa plants crops, and they all look ahead to harvest days.

But *Little House on the Prairie* is really about failure, Manifest Destiny, and the tension between whites and the Osage Indians whose lands are being threatened. Ma repeatedly says she hates Indians, while Pa is all about negative capability: he has respect for the leaders, makes a point to learn some of their customs, yet he also believes that their land should be his by right of whiteness.

As it turns out, Pa makes a lot of mistakes, like building their house too close to a trail. The family narrowly avoids a violent clash with the Osage, saved only by Chief Soldat du Chene. In the end, two years after arriving in Kansas, the Ingallses are kicked off the land by federal troops. Pa's surprise is surpassed only by his outrage, but there's nothing he can do. So he and Ma load up the wagon again. The books do not cover the defeat of returning to Wisconsin with nothing gained. The books never admit that Pa made any errors at all.

After Indian Territory, the Ingallses try out Minnesota, where the only housing they can afford is a dugout near Plum Creek, not far from the town of Walnut Grove. When Laura and Mary go to school they're mocked for their too-short dresses, especially by the wealthy and well-dressed Nellie Oleson, who becomes Laura's enemy. At home, Pa's questionable judgment leads him to borrow against future crops so that he can buy lumber for a new house. He predicts a splendid wheat harvest, never imagining that firestorms, bad weather, and literal plagues of locusts will destroy it all. Pa has to walk back East to look for farming work in order for the family to get by.

Then come the two missing years, the years that Laura and Rose avoided, beginning with the birth and then death, at nine months, of Laura's brother Frederick. The sole boy. The Ingallses, unable to afford seed wheat for crops, move to Burr Oak, Iowa, and run a hotel. Laura is nine years old at that point. For the family, hotel work is rock-bottom, far worse than a dugout. It means serving customers and cleaning up after them; living by someone else's clock; being denied the autonomy of farm life. It means exposure to the rough language of townspeople and to the sights and sounds that come from the proximity to saloons. And always, of course, there's the haunting memory of baby Frederick's death. Eventually they get themselves back to Walnut Grove and another piece of farmland—and then Mary falls ill with a fever that renders her blind.

The Minnesota and Iowa years are the worst in the Ingalls family. Even though Grace, the last child, is born during that time, she is yet another girl, guaranteeing that there will be no boys handing down their name. No wonder that Laura and Rose, writing, skip ahead to *By the Shores of Silver Lake*, with young Laura realizing she is no longer a little girl, that she must, as her father tells her, be the "eyes" for Mary. When a long-lost aunt unexpectedly shows up and helps Pa secure a job with a railroad company, he takes the chance to push westward, settling the family at last near the brand-new town of De Smet, South Dakota.

After their first miserable *Long Winter* of near-starvation, the Ingallses get on track: everything—the crops, gardens, chickens, and cows—grows as surely as Laura herself, who stays at the head of her class in school, popular and sur-rounded by friends, and who gains the notice of Almanzo. (Their real-life age gap had to be shrunk down so as not to have a twenty-five-year-old man courting a fifteen-year-old girl.) Finally Laura is able to enjoy social hours, parties, little luxuries like embossed name cards and an ostrich-feather hat from Chicago—the kinds of things her daughter would one day gather in abundance. Laura earns it all by being a seam-stress and schoolteacher, and by being a good girl with a bit of a temper, a cleverness, that makes a guy like Almanzo fall for her.

Rose Wilder, who had mapped the arc of the *Little House* series, knew that it had to conclude in the happiest of ways: with a wedding. She'd made sure to set up Almanzo's charac-ter early on, and to portray him as someone who could equal Pa: savvy, kind, wiser than his peers, and excellent at all things homesteading. That depiction begins with *Farmer Boy*, the one-off volume describing Almanzo's boyhood in upstate New York. The Wilders had a lot more money than the In-gallses, and it shows in their fine-spun clothes, their horses and buggies, their house with a wallpapered parlor and horse-hair sofas just for company. And especially in their meals. While salt pork, potatoes, and cornmeal mush make a rich breakfast for the Ingallses, a typical Sunday breakfast for the Wilders calls for stacks of pancakes, sausages, oatmeal with cream, and apple pies topped with cheese. The Wilders, especially Almanzo, eat constantly, which is evidence of their wealth. Even after an enormous dinner of ham and potatoes and bread and stuffing and fried apples and onions, they nibble on popcorn and apples and milk during their evenings of sewing and whittling. *Farmer Boy* makes sure that readers know Almanzo is a smart, sensible boy from good stock, who can thresh wheat, shear sheep, train horses, and grow pumpkins with equal adeptness. Which is to say, an ideal farmer and the ideal future mate for Laura Ingalls. He becomes a hero too: in *The Long Winter* he and Cap Garland risk their lives to find wheat so the townspeople can survive until spring. Later, Almanzo woos Laura by driving her around in his new buggy, pulled by the quickest team of horses in the county.

In the books, Almanzo and Pa Ingalls are parallel characters. Both smart, judicious community leaders, with a sense of humor too. Pa could build houses, farm like mad, and play a mean fiddle. Almanzo could build houses, farm like mad, and fry a mean buckwheat pancake. And in real life both men made the wrong calls time and time again.

That comes through not in *These Happy Golden Years*, the

finale that Rose worked on, but in *The First Four Years*. Rose found Laura's handwritten manuscript after her mother's death but opted not to pursue its publication. After her own death, her lawyer and heir, Roger Lea MacBride, released the book and added it to the *Little House* box set. So Rose's wedding conclusion gets contradicted by doubt. Where the Ingallses in *These Happy Golden Years* enjoy a flourishing farm, in *The First Four Years* they're struggling, days marked by dust and worn calico. Laura confesses to Almanzo that she doesn't want to marry a farmer. He asks her to try it out for three years, and if it's not a success, then he'll do something else. The three years quickly turn into four, each more disastrous than the last. Still, they end up sticking it out for the rest of their lives.

Like Pa Ingalls, Almanzo Wilder is no stranger to borrowing against unplanted crops, and he conceals the debts from Laura. He fashions for her a pretty little house with a custom kitchen but when the note comes due there's no way to pay it after his crops are dashed by windstorms and hail. Their daughter, Rose, thrives but their second child, a boy, dies a few days after his birth. Almanzo suffers a bout of diphtheria so severe that he would walk with a limp the rest of his life. The last chapter of *The First Four Years* provides no break from misery: their house burns down in a fire that was accidentally started by Rose. Throughout the book Laura repeats a bitter refrain: *The rich man gets his ice in the summer; the poor man gets his ice in the winter.* She and Almanzo would not have their summer ice for many years. The worry of that, the all-consuming daily relentlessness of it, shapes the core of the book, and shaped much of their daughter's life.

It was a near-seven-hour drive from Iowa City to Rocky Ridge Farm, with a stop in St. Louis. Plotting the route, I warned Alex not to expect much more than grassy plains linking little towns named for faraway places. Lebanon. Peru. Siena. Cairo, pronounced Cay-ro. This was fly-over territory, all right, the midwestern landscape that was so easy to dismiss.

We had spent the last few days in Iowa City together, he revising short stories while I returned to the Hoover Library, where Ron greeted me by name. I kept searching the stacks of papers, but unearthed no further evidence of my grandfather's Café 88 or the subject of that mysterious 1918 note about a boy and a farm. Alex and I spent our evenings in bed, sometimes with books, sometimes without.

As soon as he knew that I wanted to visit Rocky Ridge, he suggested the road trip. He'd actually bought the complete box set of the *Little House* books from Prairie Lights while I was back in Franklin. "Huh," he said when I told him I was impressed. "Hadn't realized this is a good way to get girls." His favorite volume, he said, was *The Long Winter*.

"Of course it is," I said. "It's the most stark and depressing one."

Like Alex, I was fascinated by how those blizzards of 1879 get reflected in the narrative of isolation and howling winds. As the months go on, the snow piles higher over the train tracks, preventing coal and grocery trains from reaching De Smet. By spring Pa's cheeks are dark hollows and he's too weak to lift a bag of grain on his own. "Laura and Rose had wanted to title it *The Hard Winter*," I said, "but their publisher thought that was too severe for children."

We were in Alex's bed, looking at maps on our phones. Nearly four hundred miles lay between us and the house where Rose had spent her childhood.

"But so much of what goes on in all those books is messed up," Alex said. "Like when Laura says she doesn't want to have the right to vote? Or the casual descriptions of all those people who freeze to death in winter storms. Or the depiction of Indians."

"The TV show was worse," I told him.

Alex didn't seem to believe me, so I found some clips on YouTube. The show didn't futz around with all the traveling the Ingallses had done; it set them down in Walnut Grove, perhaps because it sounded sweeter than De Smet, conjuring the idea of old-fashioned Minnesotans, plain-faced and hard-working. Growing up, I had watched reruns of the reruns with Sam and Ong Hai, the three of us believing that that was how America used to be. I believed it even though I knew how far the show veered from the books, and how crazily. Like the episode when the TV Laura's adopted brother, who didn't exist in real life, becomes addicted to morphine, or when his girlfriend is raped and impregnated by a man dressed as a clown. Still, as a girl I couldn't help feeling persuaded by the show's opening scenes of dusty walks and distant water mills, men in dingy suspenders and women in faded floral bonnets. I liked Doc Baker and Mr. Edwards and Mr. Oleson, poor soul, who owned the general store with that shrill and snooty wife of his. I liked the folksy theme song, little Laura running through a field while her parents smiled from their covered wagon. Everything in the town went back to the Ingallses' log cabin and the laddered loft that Laura and her sisters shared. The Ingalls family was the moral compass of that town, and not much passed without their input. That was true of the books as well. Ma and Pa were supposed to be the ideal parents. As a kid I decided that, had my father lived, he would have been a lot like Pa. Always there, helping out anyone in trouble, good-hearted and filled with optimism.

Alex and I were well into watching the clown attack episode—an homage to seventies slasher flicks, according to viewer comments—before I realized I wasn't helping my case. Though he liked the idea of the road trip, Alex was skeptical that we would find anything more than kitsch and souvenirs at Rocky Ridge Farm. He doubted that the scribble I'd found in Rose's archives—her almost-poem, I called it—meant anything more than a few dashed lines of regret—possibly about the death of her child, or possibly about something entirely fictional.

Don't forget she was a writer, he said.

The night before our trip, Alex mentioned that we'd be driving right past all the casinos, shows, and rides that Branson, Missouri, had to offer. When I said no way he said, "Come on. It'll be fun." It could be a campy little holiday, he said, a nostalgic throwback to our undergrad days. "Good old-fashioned fun."

"It'll be research," I said.

"Don't get your hopes up."

"I won't," but of course, I already had.

EIGHT

Driving south on U.S. 54 in Missouri, I tried to envision what could have seemed so magical about the place to Laura and Almanzo back in 1894. The handbills had promised bountiful apple and cherry orchards, and Laura wrote in her travel diaries that their journey, by covered wagon, had taken them through immense expanses of wheat and corn fields. I tried to picture rows of apple trees, groves of peaches, lush leaves everywhere. And a well-worn path where horses and carriages passed each other, coming and going from the Ozarks, once known as the Land of the Great Red Apple. Laura was twenty-seven then, Almanzo thirty-seven, and Rose eight years old. They were rebounding from a disastrous stint in the Florida Everglades. Drawn by advertisements touting the farming possibilities in Missouri, they'd set out once again, weary, hopeful, determined to make a permanent home.

It was taking a lot of imagination—a kind of movie light, with matching sound track—to transform the highway and median strip and dismal expanses of rural neglect into something golden and beckoning.

"Are we in the Ozarks now? Aren't they supposed to be hilly?" Alex asked.

Neither of us could tell where they started or what they were supposed to look like. The terrain looked as flat as ever, though according to the map we were very close to Ozark country.

I slowed to turn onto a county road and Alex pointed at the Tastee-Freez sitting at the corner. He started singing "Jack and Diane." *Two American kids doing the best they can.*

"That's probably where we're having dinner," I said.

We had hardly seen a gas station in the past thirty miles, but we had passed plenty of anti-abortion signs and stern religious placards. *Hell Is Real. Jesus Is Real. Jesus Saves. Be Saved Today. Will You Be Left Behind?*

Then, not far from the turnoff to Mansfield, I saw it in the distance: the unmistakable red and yellow of a "Chinese" restaurant. A windowless cinder-block frame, bulging-eyed Chinese dragons painted on either side of the door. *Golden China Inn* read the sign, and a plastic banner: *Buffet 11 AM–9 PM Everyday.* I remembered reading somewhere that the birthplace of American deep-fried cashew chicken was Springfield, Missouri, an hour west of Mansfield.

A little shiver went through me, as it usually did when I saw these kinds of restaurants. It felt like a secret, some sort of private knowledge or shame. In grad school, no one I knew would have dreamed of eating at such a place; everyone wanted *authentic* food, street food, real food, none of this boneless almond chicken bullshit. It still felt embarrassing to admit that, for me, these kinds of buffets *had* been an authentic American experience.

Whenever I did tell people that my family used to manage buffets—with a great show of irony, of course—they were always intrigued. Everyone asked the same questions: did we eat the food ourselves (sometimes, but mostly as leftovers); did the busboys scrape half-eaten plates back into the chafing dishes (it maybe happened in some places, but not that I'd seen); did the workers make fun of the customers (yes, if they were obnoxious or rude). Sometimes that was all the levity my mother seemed to get—complaining about the cook, going over the tedium of each day, recounting stories about customers, especially the ones who were messy, dirty, overweight, or loud. She had grown immune to the piles of fried chicken parts, the cornstarchy sauces that ranged in color from fuchsia-pink "sweet and sour" to dark brown "Chinese gravy." Ong Hai, who worked alongside her after Sam started fourth grade and I started third, which was when we were judged old enough to look after ourselves, took his usual stance of observance and amusement. You wouldn't even know he was paying attention to everything, but later in the evening he would chuckle about the man who'd been caught filling up a Tupperware with General Tso's.

Once, in college, I made a list of all the places we'd lived before Franklin and how I knew them.

Rockford, Illinois: Sam's birth.

La Porte, Indiana: My birth.

Battle Creek, Michigan: Air smelled like sweet puffed-rice cereal.

La Porte, Indiana: Golden Dragon. Dad dies.

Naperville, Illinois: Great Wall. Brief stay. Endless divided highways and car dealerships.

Joliet, Illinois: Asia Garden (or was it Jade Palace?). First apartment too close to the prison; second apartment too close to the casino.

Waukesha, Wisconsin: Jade Palace (or was it Asia Garden?). Annie, Asian best friend in fourth grade, who introduced me to *Laverne & Shirley*; we decided when we got older we'd go to Milwaukee to see where they worked.

Valparaiso, Indiana: Grand Asian Buffet. More strip malls than anywhere else. Frozen custard shops.

The last buffet my mother and Ong Hai ran was the New City China in Franklin. This was after my mother agreed to stay in the area so that Sam and I could go to the same high school through graduation. The New City China was no different, really, than all the other buffets. Same foods, same steaming chafing dishes, same dark carpeting, same mottled plastic cups the color of amber. But somehow the place made my mother and Ong Hai different. Maybe that was where they finally reached the saturation point, for he grew quieter and she grew even moodier. The customers were no worse than any others in any other town, but somehow this particular restaurant, squatting on the edge of a strip mall of tanning salons, with its vinyl sign that flapped in the wind, seemed to take all the energy out of us. And maybe it coincided with my becoming even more aware, or more self-conscious, of that inexorable deep-fry smell. Even when I didn't go anywhere near the restaurant, I could smell it in our apartment. For years after, and still, I couldn't stand the odor of fried food. When the owners of the New City China shut the place down, my mother and Ong Hai managed a Viet-Thai-Chinese restaurant. A couple years later, the Lotus Leaf Café came along.

In my anxiety dreams I often find myself back in one of those buffets, unable to find entrance or exit. I wake up with the sound of the interstate in my head—cars muffling past, the rush of them, in darkness, going right past us, the drivers missing us entirely with blinks of the eye.

That's what I wanted to do, what I wanted to be: the

person in the car. The driver driving past. I had come all this way so as not to think about my family, the Lotus Leaf, the way they paired and weighted me with obligation.

And yet Mansfield, Missouri, reminded me of how the past will not be banished. So many small, dying, basically dead towns in the Midwest looked like this. Where once-graceful, ornate courthouses and libraries—back when libraries meant something important, something civic—had been, if not torn down or boarded up, converted dozens of times over into shops and offices and apartments and barely surviving histor-ical societies. There might even be the remains of an ambitious opera house. The nicest building in town was likely to be a funeral home.

Main Street had been built broad, to accommodate horses, buggies, and hitching posts. And surely local efforts tried to preserve the "historic downtown" area. Surely there were sad little parades on Memorial Day or the Fourth of July. In Mans-field a few local "shoppes" offered "olde-fashioned ice cream" and "sewing notions," but it looked like most of the money was flowing in and out of the paycheck advance and pawn shops.

It was all claustrophobically familiar, but because I didn't know how to explain this to Alex, didn't know if our relationship—whatever it was—could sustain that kind of talk, I kept it to myself. Alex had grown up in the suburbs of Northern Virginia, where his point of reference was D.C. and the bustle of power it represented; he'd gone to Urbana-

Champaign because his father had. He had no expectation of staying in the middle of the country forever. For the time being, Iowa City, with its multitude of coffee shops, vegetarian restaurants, and boutiques, with its writerly quotes embedded into the sidewalks, was a novelty. The Midwest itself was quaint and charming—two words that, to me, had come to signify a deception that went both ways: while the outsider might deign to peek in, the midwesterner knew the darker isolation that waited behind Victorian facades and re-created soda fountains. As we drove through Mansfield, Alex was startled, then fascinated, by signs that read *Communities Against Meth* and stores with names like Farm King and Smokes for Less. He had never really lived, and never would, in this kind of waning small town.

There wasn't much more to Mansfield except the markers directing us to the Laura Ingalls Wilder Historic Home & Museum. We followed them to another rural road, at last glimpsing the farmhouse ahead at the bend of a curve. A gravel parking lot had been set up across the street and I pulled into it. There must have been at least thirty other cars already there.

"Stuff of dreams," Alex said as he stretched, getting out of the car. It seemed to be the phrase he'd chosen for the trip. Crossing the Mississippi in St. Louis: "Stuff of dreams." Seeing billboards for Branson slots and comedy acts, a life-sized replica of half of the *Titanic*, $9.99 all-you-can-eat steak dinners: "Stuff of dreams."

We could hear singing as we walked toward Rocky Ridge. The house was all white clapboard, with a wide front porch and dark shutters, sheltered by a canopy of trees. It was what Alex termed "respectable," meaning large enough to command some authority but not so overly large as to appear to be trying to impress. Though it sat close to the curve of the street, perhaps a victim of years of widening roads, it still felt remote, set apart from any discernible neighborhood. This was what Laura and Almanzo had finally deemed home. Where Rose had come of age. Where she had returned again and again, loving and hating her mother, writing her books, writing her mother's books.

The singing turned out to be an a cappella group—a dozen kids, ranging from about ten to eighteen, holding sheet music and standing in a circle in the backyard of Rocky Ridge. A few mothers stood off to the side, watching, and Alex asked one of them what was going on.

"Rehearsals," she explained. She smiled at Alex's confusion and I regretted that her hair was done in a typical suburban mom-bob. "For Wilder Days. It's not till September, but we have to start early because of camps." For the festival, the kids would be dressed in the long flowered dresses, bonnets, and hat-and-suspenders that signaled pioneer garb. For now, they were in halter tops and cargo shorts, practicing a musical about Laura and Almanzo.

You drove a team of horses that caught my eye; it's there
I'll be sitting by and by.
By and by you'll be taking my hand; by and by we'll settle
our own land.
Oh, Manly, Manly, what a wonderful life we're living.
Oh, Laura, Laura, what a wonderful life we've been given.

"It's probably the big event of the year," the woman said. "There's lots of music and games, there's apple-bobbing and all kinds of fun things from the books. People come from all over. They dress up and have picnics and there's a trivia contest and a Laura look-alike contest. Where are you two from?"

"Iowa," I answered.

"Oh, I love Iowa," she said.

I could see Alex about to engage in an earnest conversation with her, so I grabbed his arm. "Let's go."

I pointed ahead to the museum, a flat-topped building that looked like a public rest area, sitting right next to the farmhouse. The cost of admission included access to the house as well as the second home, Rock House, which Rose had built on the property in 1928. Alex and I paid for our tickets. The strains of the singing rehearsal started up again as we stepped into the world of Laura memorabilia.

Ron had mentioned that the place lacked funds, and it showed. While most of the trinkets and photos were shelved behind glass, some were simply exposed to the summer humidity. If there was air-conditioning, it was either broken or running on the lowest possible setting, supplemented by a giant whirring fan stationed near the open doorway. The place was what it was: a low-budget, overly specific museum, musty, cramped, and vaguely organized, the labels and signs handmade and hand-typed, with a scent of mold, mildew, and sleepy Sundays in the air. Yet it was thrilling too to see bits of the *Little House* stories coming to actual life. Here was Pa Ingalls's famous fiddle. Here was Almanzo's last buggy. Here was a display of Laura's hair combs, lamp mats, knitting needles, serving spoons. Here was Laura's writing desk, stocked with her favored pencils and tablets. Mannequins were dressed in some of her outfits and hats. The lace fichu that Ida Brown had given Laura on her wedding day lay folded on a shelf. The glass platter, etched with the words *Give us this day our daily bread*, one of the few things Laura had been able to save from the fire, sat on a dining table.

Laura's jewelry was also scattered throughout the glass cases. Her engagement ring, a pearl-and-garnet set, was granted prominent display. As told in *These Happy Golden Years*, noted the label. No sign of Laura's gold pin, however. Its absence gave me a moment of validation when I considered that its likeness—my mother's pin—was tucked in a pocket of my handbag.

One corner of the museum was devoted to Rose. Though some of her books and newspaper articles were laid out, mostly her role seemed to be that of daughter of a proud mother. See Rose all dressed up, ready to board a train out West. See Laura and Rose and Almanzo all living together with their horses at Rocky Ridge, 1930. See Rose and Laura posing in front of a World's Fair exhibit, San Francisco, 1915.

San Francisco. The name of the city brought Sam back into my mind, and with him my mother, my grandfather, our dwindled family. I shook my head, refusing to allow them entrance.

"Hey," Alex said, coming over from a cabinet of keepsake items he'd been checking out. "Did you see Laura's jewel box with the tiny porcelain teacup? Remember that? It's really real."

I could have stayed for hours, trying to keep track of all that was real, but I knew we had to make our way over to the main house. The first thing I noticed as I stepped into the book-lined living room was a cordoned-off door near the hallway. A tour was in progress and Alex and I tagged along for a few minutes. The guide explained that the door led to a second stairway, now too delicate for use, that led up to Rose's old room. The guide, an aging, no-nonsense woman who could have played a schoolteacher in the television version of *Little House on the Prairie*, was one of the volunteer biddies Ron had mentioned. They all seemed territorial. Possessive.

They knew more about Laura and her legacy, had memorized more of the books, than anyone.

She talked about how Laura and Almanzo had lovingly built each room, with some later modernizing financed by Rose. But I was struck by how the parlor seemed the only warm place in the house, with its varnished wood and stone fireplace. Nearby, Laura's library bookshelves were crowded with titles she and Rose had selected. The kitchen was dim, a place to get work done rather than a place to gather. Standing there, gazing at the few cupboards, enamel cookstove, and narrow counter area, I felt like I needed to drape a shawl over my shoulders. In the two small bedrooms on the first floor, the iron bedsteads were twin-sized and I told Alex that I bet the mattresses were as hard as bone. Here was where Laura and Almanzo had slept, their beds nearly toe to toe.

Though Rose's room upstairs was tiny, it seemed at least a little more welcoming. I could picture a child dreaming away the seasons there, staring out the window with her books. Plotting her future, determining her escape. The rest of the second floor was closed to the public, and yellow strings were taped over two closed doors. When I saw that, I knew I was done just imagining what might happen next. I knew I would have to see what was in those rooms.

As the rest of the tour started back downstairs, Alex and I dropped back to the end of the line. There were no other guides around and I doubted the house had any security cameras in use. Alex stood guard while I tried the doors. It was almost too easy: they weren't even locked.

The first room looked like a meeting space: folding table, metal chairs, filing cabinets. Stacks of brochures sat on the floor, along with diamond-patterned curtains that had probably hung at the window. The paneled walls had been painted a dull gray, and someone had laid a cheap mauve rug over the oak floor. I poked through the cabinets—museum papers. I decided to move on to the second closed-off room. This one had had the allure of clutter: half-open storage boxes pushed against the walls. It was here I shut myself in, feeling the heat of stilled objects rising all around me. It felt like a chamber, filled with things to be dealt with in the vague future. I wondered if it was Laura or Rose who had chosen the wallpaper of tiny bud-sprouting vines that covered even the steep slant of the ceiling. Who had hemmed the green-striped fabric for the tiny square window? Like any proper attic, the room smelled of forgotten things.

Glancing into the collections of clothes, books, newspapers, magazines, I couldn't tell what was Laura's and what was Rose's, or if perhaps the items belonged to someone else entirely. Who had wanted to keep what? One box contained purple mimeographs of Laura's As a Farm Woman Thinks column. Another held cross-stitch hoops and yarns.

Dust spun in the air when I pulled out a small crate that had been shoved under a faux-Chippendale-style chair that no longer had a seat. On top of the crate lay a few yards of pink floral jacquard, maybe meant for pillow shams. Inside: an old apron, a collection of plain, unused stationery, three copies of Rose's novel *Free Land*, and two slim soft-bound journals. They were, disappointingly, empty—not a single line of writing in the yellowed pages.

I paused at the *Free Land* books. They were first editions, perhaps saved from the copies that Rose had received upon publication. The cover appeared to echo the gold pin: a wooden shanty sat near a pond, bordered by sheaves of golden wheat and grasses. I had never held such old original editions before. Maybe that's why I felt compelled to open each copy, to touch the brittling pages and imagine how it must have been for Rose to see her work come to such tangible fruition, to hope it would launch her to the literary success and acclaim she had so desired.

It was the middle copy of *Free Land* that held the letter, though it wasn't so much held as it was captive, pressed as thin as the pages of the book, and easily missed. It didn't fall out; the book didn't open to it. I just happened to flip past that particular page.

The paper was carbon-copy type, like the old onionskin I remembered from Ong Hai's earliest ESL classes at a community center. The ink had blurred, and I had to bring the letter to the small window at the far end of the room to read the words.

October 14, 1918

To Whom It May Concern at San Francisco General Hospital:

Two days ago, I was made a mother by a woman at your hospital. I wish her to know, if it is acceptable, that I am profoundly grateful. If it is irregular to write this letter, I apologize. May she know that the boy's name is Albert? He will be well taken care of all his life.

Yours,
Mrs. Louis Stellenson

The handwriting was scratchy, calligraphic. All at once I imagined a woman sitting down at her husband's desk, her hand traveling over the thin cream-colored paper edged in blue. A burst of feeling, an impulse sent off in the mail. And what about the recipient? Was she still in the hospital when the letter arrived? Had a nurse handed it to her silently, apprehensively? How had the letter found its way to this book?

I forgot I was in the dim heat and dust of Rocky Ridge Farm, that even now another tour group was right outside the door, surveying the little room where Rose had slept and grown up. I forgot about Alex playing watchman. I forgot everything but the two women poised on either side of this letter, bound forever by a child. Rose's child?

I was startled by two soft knocks on the door. Alex opened it and whispered, "Better hurry up."

I had to take the letter. I refilled the crate with its contents, but I must have arranged them wrong, because the lid wouldn't fit. Alex tapped on the door again, so I added the copy of *Free Land* to my bag too, secured the crate, and slid it back where I'd found it. Then Alex and I were down the stairs and out on the front lawn, walking away from Rocky Ridge. The choral group was still at it, now singing about Charles and Caroline Ingalls. More children and families were streaming in from the parking lot, eager to visit Laura's life, while Alex and I hurried to his car like a pair of bandits.

NINE

Whatever it was that befell Rose in San Francisco in 1918, she left it behind two years later, when the Red Cross Publicity Bureau offered her a writing job in Europe. She spent much of the next eight years traveling—Paris, London, Vienna, Albania, Armenia—before returning to Rocky Ridge for what she thought would be a respite. Always big on resolutions and always obsessed with money, she'd set a goal of storing up at least $100,000 in savings. At the same time, the extravagant part of her couldn't resist another plan: to add modern electricity and plumbing to the farmhouse and to build her parents a new stone cottage, English-style, accented with Mediterranean tiles and tall, diamond-paned windows— a generous overture but also, perhaps, an attempt to absolve herself of the devastating fire she had accidentally caused as a child, decades earlier in De Smet.

Either way, the new construction would be a gain for Rose

too. By moving her parents a half mile away to Rock House, as she named it, she could have the old farmhouse for herself and some quiet from her mother. Then she could finally concentrate on her writing and, in her spare time, be on hand to help her mother's.

Mama Bess had other ideas. Happy to have her daughter back at home, she agreed to the move but showed little regard for solitude and privacy. In her diaries Rose complained about her mother's incessant visits, knocks on her door, repetitive questions, and efforts to draw her into the ladies' social groups Mama Bess had formed in Mansfield. Rose had no patience for these perceived wastes of time, not to mention the provinciality of her mother's friends. *Days on the farm do not fill diaries*, she wrote. No doubt too she felt disapproval from her parents' friends for being a divorcée, and she didn't bother to dispel the reputation she'd always had for being snooty. Over the years of distance, Rose and Laura's correspondence had been filled with proclamations of love and of how deeply they missed each other. Now, in person, there was strain. A lot of it.

The Mama Bess Rose describes in her journals and letters doesn't much resemble the Laura Ingalls of the *Little House* books. Where bravado and spark defined the heroine I'd often thought I knew better than my own sibling, a sense of distance, a withholding, characterized the Laura of Rose's journals. Rose, one of her friends once remarked, had never gotten over the despair of a childhood marked by literal and emotional deprivation. Her impulses and mood swings touched everything from real estate to furniture shopping to friendships. Most of all, her relationship with her mother, whose ardor and acrimony Rose recorded. *No tongue can tell how I want to get away from here!*

Then came the Crash of 1929, which wiped out most of Rose's funds and left her trapped at Rocky Ridge, with debts coming due. On Rock House alone she had ended up spending more than twice the $4,000 amount originally estimated. The next few years were a blur of anxiety as she tried to make money through freelancing and ghostwriting, all the while working on *Let the Hurricane Roar* and helping Mama Bess turn *Pioneer Girl* into children's books.

Rose may have dismissed any interest in sharing the credit for *Little House*, calling her role as that of barely an editor, but there was no question she believed that her mother ought to defer to her on matters of craft. She was often frustrated by Laura's stubbornness during the writing process. Rose was the "real" writer, after all, with hundreds of publications under her belt. She had tons of friends in the business in New York, had socialized and sparred with the likes of Sherwood Anderson and Sinclair Lewis. And she would brook no resistance when it came to laying out the span of the books, making sure their narrative arcs revolved around the seasons, from planting to harvest.

On some level Laura must have known what her daughter

felt about her small-town circle in Mansfield. And perhaps Laura privately thought her daughter too big for her britches. She must have known she could not keep her. By 1935, following the success of *Let the Hurricane Roar*, Rose was spending more and more time away from Rocky Ridge. Laura was helper and helped, caught between wanting to mother and wanting to be mothered. By 1937 Rose had left Rocky Ridge for good and her parents had moved back to the main farmhouse. Rose would never again visit them for longer than a couple of weeks. Soon mother and daughter would be collaborating on the rest of the *Little House* books through letters. Laura would send pages; Rose would edit, correct, fix, rewrite, and send them back. Sometimes, out of exasperation or exhaustion, Laura sent anecdotes, telling Rose to use them or not as she saw fit.

When they argued about the writing of *By the Shores of Silver Lake*, Rose insisted her vision was correct, ending a back-and-forth by saying: *You will just have to take my word for it.*

Change the beginning of the story if you want, Laura conceded. *Do anything you please with the damn stuff if you will fix it up.*

At the Tastee-Freez, Alex and I argued.

We had a name—Albert Stellenson—but I refused to let Alex search it on his phone. I wanted to go back to

Rocky Ridge, to see if there was anything more to discover at Rock House.

"It's a sign," I said. "First the pin and then Rose's poem and now this letter."

"Or the pin is a chance likeness, and the poem is something you're reading too much into, and this letter is just a bookmark. They don't necessarily add up to anything at all."

"What about that photo of my grandfather?"

"Lee, you said yourself that the guy's face is barely visible." He knew that I hadn't shown the photo to Ong Hai on my brief return to Franklin, and I wondered if he'd guessed at my fear that Ong Hai would say it wasn't him at all. "Besides, you're not supposed to return to the scene of the crime. Have you even considered what you're going to do with all this contraband?"

He jabbed a soggy french fry into the puddle of ketchup he'd poured onto his cheeseburger wrapper. We had a corner booth, with a view of people tromping through the restaurant, their flip-flops slapping the floor. Skanky teenagers in cutoff shorts; old people in long pants and sweaters; no shortage of weary parents, each step signifying a sigh. All of them and their kids, sloppy and hopping around or whining, tilting their heads back to read the lit-up menu of burgers, fries, onion rings, and sundaes. I had always liked the look of swirled soft-serve cones, the tall elegance of creamy, airy spirals folding in on each other. How long had the Tastee-Freez been here? What had Mansfield looked like in 1968, when Rose died? When was the last time she had seen Rocky Ridge? Could she or Laura ever have imagined what their town would become?

"You mean," I said, trying to answer Alex, "how am I going to give this stuff back? I don't know."

"No, I mean—not that I'm saying you were planning on doing this, but if you were ever to publish an article about Rose Wilder's alleged double life, wouldn't you have to admit that you'd stolen some things?"

"I guess so." I hadn't thought that far ahead.

"If the end justifies the means, then what's to stop every scholar from breaking into archives and old houses?"

"Yeah, every academic is just waiting for her *National Treasure* moment."

Alex smiled at that. We had watched more bad movies together than good ones, preferring anything with multiple chase scenes. We'd agreed that, should villain or alien come after us, we would stick together.

Being with him had always made me feel like real life— whatever had to be faced or endured—could be postponed for a while. Even with all of his questions and doubts about what I was doing with Rose Wilder, I still felt like that, tucked away at this Tastee-Freez in a remote patch of Missouri. No one in my family knew where I was.

"I think I just need to get to the end," I said. "See where it ends. If Rose did have a child and gave him up for adoption, what happened to him?"

"I'm just not convinced. It seems too out there. Whoever had that baby could have easily been a friend of Rose's. You said yourself she had a big social circle and that she had a soft spot for helping out anyone in need."

"She did. But—" I didn't know how to justify my growing certainty that the presence of the letter and the poem among her belongings had to signify *her.* "She didn't have to keep those things. She was pretty meticulous about making copies of her letters and keeping her diaries organized. She wanted to be famous. Probably her private writing was done with the hope of future biographers reading it. She could have destroyed the evidence, but she didn't."

"Because it wasn't about her."

I shrugged.

"Anyway, we can't go back there, Lee."

"We've already come all this way."

"And it's far enough. Really. What more do you need?"

So we drove the three and a half hours back to St. Louis. I got Alex to agree not to search any variation of Albert Stellenson until we got to the hotel. His true identity would be, I said, my own personal blue-dye cake moment.

So it was at the Holiday Inn Express downtown, a rundown

stretch off the highway, that we sat on the bed and I opened my laptop. I typed the name. Stellenson, it turned out, was unusual enough to yield only three in California. One of them, Gregory, lived in San Francisco. A phone number was right there on the screen, along with a list of current, previous, and known addresses, all in the Bay Area. Gregory Stellenson, born 1979. Counting back the generations, he was the only Stellenson who matched.

"That could be Rose's great-grandchild," I said.

"Or not," Alex said. Then, "Only one thing left to do." Reaching for the laptop, he clicked on Facebook. In a matter of moments, Gregory Stellenson's profile, apparently not at all private, showed us what he looked like. "What do you think?" Alex asked, but I couldn't tell. Gregory Stellenson looked like what he said he was: thirty-two years old, blondish-brownish hair, educated, liberal, eco-conscious, with a fondness for Wilco, bicycling, Alexander Payne movies, and Bi-Rite ice cream. He had only a handful of photos, and all seemed to be group pictures with friends. He didn't mention family anywhere, didn't mention his relationship status. He had 328 friends and under his name was the tag *San Francisco*.

Google told us that Gregory had studied at Berkeley and had received a humanities award there. He had been an intern in the San Francisco Library system and he had participated in bicycle races to benefit cancer research.

"Looks like your average Berkeley do-gooder," Alex re-marked.

But all I was thinking was: *San Francisco.* California, the sun and the West. Pioneers. Rose. The Promised Land of so many migrants and immigrants, all those travelers seeking a resolution nearer to the sea. I thought: *Sam.*

Alex got up and went to the bathroom. I could hear him getting ready for bed, brushing his teeth. When he came back into the room he seemed irritated to see Gregory Stellenson's profile still on the computer screen. He grabbed a book of William Trevor stories and settled into the bed, leaning back on the chenille, gold-tasseled pillows.

I said, "They never wash those, you know."

"Did you bring one of those UV lights or something?"

"So you're done with this whole Rose thing now? Don't you wonder what this guy knows, or if he does know?"

"Assuming there is something to know. I'm sure you're thinking about going to San Francisco no matter what."

"Road trip?" I asked jokingly.

"Just keep in mind that you might be chasing a false story." Alex turned toward me. "If Rose Wilder had had a baby, why wouldn't she keep it? Especially after her first child died."

"There could be a lot of reasons. She was going through a divorce. That was scandalous enough, but to have a baby out of wedlock?"

"You said she wasn't conventional."

"Maybe the baby was Gillette's and he didn't want it. Or maybe it wasn't Gillette's. Maybe Rose had already decided she didn't want a domestic life. I could see that. She always wanted to be free and unencumbered."

"Or maybe you're overanalyzing. That baby, and that Gregory guy, could very well be related to someone else entirely."

"What about the pin?" I countered.

"Okay, say that pin really did belong to Rose Wilder. It doesn't legitimize the rest of the story."

We fell into silence, side by side on the same bed. I pulled a book from my bag—another Wilder biography—and Alex returned to his. I didn't remember falling asleep, but when I woke up he was curled up next to me, our books on the floor.

In the morning we picked up lattes and cinnamon doughnuts at a bakery and Alex drove the four hours back to Iowa. The highways alternated between steamy rain and hazy sunlight. We didn't talk much about Rose, drifting instead to our undergrad days. We kept using the word *remember*. Professors, classes, dates, the campus in winter. Then I fell asleep again, waking up to NPR just as we were crossing the river into Iowa City.

As soon as we got back to his apartment Alex returned to work, sitting down to his computer. He seemed to want some space so I headed out to a coffee shop and called my pharmaceutical sellout friend Amy. She had been a *Little House* fan since elementary school and, true to form, she encouraged me to come to San Francisco right away. *This is momentum,* she said. *What else do you have to do anyway?* As we talked, she e-mailed me a last-minute deal that left O'Hare in two days. She said I could arrive on Tuesday and by the next day be looking, maybe even finding, Rose's possible great-grandson.

Everything was directing me to California. All the signs were there, I would say to Alex. Stop using that word, he would say, and I would answer that I couldn't help it. The pioneers had looked for signs, hadn't they—checking the sky, the weather, listening for the call of a certain bird—whatever it took to keep justifying the journey. If Sam was in San Francisco, then I could find him too, talk to him for real, far from the tensions of our mother's house.

Over dinner, I asked Alex if I could stay with him a couple more days, until my flight. I couldn't see myself driving back to Franklin, aproning myself to the Lotus Leaf again, then having to lie about where I was going next. Being away from that, even for just a few days, felt like new freedom.

"You know I'd never turn you away," Alex said. "I don't know about this whole San Francisco Rose Wilder thing you're doing. But it's your business, right? So stay as long as you want." He made the decision so simple, and I wondered if he would have let me stay on and on, for weeks, months, the whole year.

He said it again later, in bed, after sex, which we had skipped the night before in St. Louis. We knew each other

161

well enough as friends, but this pattern was starting to veer toward something too risky to define, with neither of us sure, or at least I wasn't sure, who was doing the steering. Suddenly I felt a little shy about meeting his gaze, as if afraid to break a tacit, though unclear, agreement.

"You know you don't really have to go," he murmured again into my shoulder.

"I already bought the ticket."

"You could call or e-mail the guy instead."

"It's not the same. You know that. Besides, I haven't seen Amy in two years. I mean, I might move there. And Sam is there."

"Yeah, and what if he won't see you?"

The words delivered an unexpected sting, but all I said was, "You have to get back to your writing anyway. I don't want to distract you too much."

"Don't you have a book to write too? What are you going to do if your diss turns into nothing?"

"Thanks a lot."

"Well, I worry about you."

"Why?"

"You know I do."

It was too close to intimate, far more than lying there in bed together.

"I'm not a hundred percent sure what I mean by that," Alex added quickly.

"Okay." It was a dumb response, but I had no other to give. I knew then that I could have just stayed there and kept staying—it would have been an easy inertia. But there was a bigger restlessness. I was looking at the time, looking for the door.

"I'll come see you after I get back."

"You will," he said. It sounded vaguely like insistence rather than a question.

TEN

Laura Ingalls was fifteen when her grown-up life began: she became a schoolteacher, even though sixteen was the legal age to be one, and she started dating Almanzo Wilder. Not that they really *dated*. Such a word implied neutrality, even equality. In the 1880s a girl didn't date. She was courted. She was the recipient, waiting for a man to tip his hat, offer a buggy ride, walk her home from church. By fifteen, Laura and her friends—Minnie Johnson and Mary Power and Ida Brown— had to think about their future husbands and houses.

Toward the end of *These Happy Golden Years* the girls gather at a recess—they still attend De Smet's one-room school—to admire Laura's and Ida's new engagement rings. When Laura says she wants to teach another round of primary school before getting married, Ida declares, *Not I*—indeed, that's why she got a ring. All the girls laugh. Later, Almanzo tells Laura that her last stint teaching *will* be her last, and that soon she'll be frying his breakfast pancakes instead. Laura had never really wanted to become a teacher; she had done it because her mother had, and because it was one of the only ways a respectable woman could earn money. Her mother had stopped as soon as she got married, and even before Laura taught her first class she longed for the same deliverance.

A generation later, in Mansfield, Missouri, the options for girls weren't much different. But Rose Wilder had never been like her classmates, and most of her classmates had never liked her. She made it clear that her ambitions were well beyond their town. When she left she traveled across the country and then the globe, wanting to see the places she'd read about in books, and to discard the rural mores that had felt so suffocating. Independence, money, and fame: these would lift her out of the depressive plunges that often threatened to sink her.

Growing up, Sam and I had always agreed that we couldn't wait to get out of "here," by which we meant whatever little city or suburb we happened to be in at the time. We would flee to Chicago or perhaps even farther. We wouldn't be tethered to buffet bins and pop dispensers. Like Rose, we thought ourselves suited to bigger lives. Yet I saw how things ended up: Rose, despondent over her perceived failures as a writer, her inability to make or save enough money. Sam was in a limbo of his own making and I had moved back to Franklin, with little to call my own.

Just how little became even clearer to me when I stepped inside Amy's two-bedroom, very grown-up-looking condo in San Francisco, in an acronym neighborhood, SoMa, which kept resounding in my mind like a shout.

Amy and I had been friends since freshman year in college, when we lived two dorm doors away from each other and commiserated over our roommates—mine with a habit of bringing guys back to the room and locking me out; hers who kept borrowing clothes without asking. Amy had grown up in a North Shore suburb of Chicago and, like me, had dreamed of a more romantic life on one of the coasts. But now I was still in graduate student mode while Amy owned a substantial place of her own, with furniture that definitely did not come from IKEA. Whenever I admired people's houses I got fixated on the details, the cost of lamp shades and drawer pulls and crown molding. How much consideration had been given to the placement of picture frames, of candlesticks on a fireplace mantel? How much could a person, if unhampered by time and money constraints, devote to such refinement, to the pleasure of pure decoration?

The walls in Amy's condo were the creamy yellow of lemon chiffon cake, trimmed in white, and set off by drapes and throw pillows done in floral swirls of pink, tangerine, and teal. On her living room coffee table a mammoth glass vase was jammed with peonies. A matching vase sat in the kitchen, which gleamed expectantly in steel and white marble.

Gorgeous, I said, kept saying. Beautiful. What I really meant was, *Unimaginable.*

"Well," Amy said. "What else have I got to do?"

Whenever she talked about her work, which wasn't often because, as she put it, it was less a career than a job, she said she pimped for Big Pharma. I knew she sometimes felt like she'd sold out, going this route after med school—but she'd already paid off all her loans and didn't have to worry about parceling out her paychecks to make them last; she didn't have to think about money at all. I wondered if I'd ever know what that was like.

Setting out two wineglasses on the countertop—a pain in the ass, she said, pointing to stains from olive oil and tomato sauce—she wanted to talk about Laura Ingalls Wilder. Amy, with her lake-blue eyes and ale-brown hair, could have competed in a Laura look-alike contest. She had no doubts about the connection between Rose Wilder and Gregory Stellenson. "Who doesn't love a good literary mystery?" she said. And she needed the distraction. She'd broken up with a guy a few weeks earlier, or maybe it was that he had broken up with her; she still wasn't quite sure about it. They'd been dating for four months and he simply stopped contact. No calls, texts, e-mails. At some point, Amy said, it felt too pathetic to keep waiting for a return call. "Did stuff like that happen in the pioneer days?" she said. Sure, I said. Except the guy would just hitch up his horses and ride out of town, never to be seen again.

Amy had always been a planner—probably the only time she had surprised anyone was when she didn't go into residency—and she'd prepared for my visit by doing her own background reading on Rose. She'd reread all of the *Little House* books, which she practically knew by heart anyway, all those images of salt pork nestled in baked beans, shanties covered in tar paper, and polonaise dresses poufed out with hoop skirts, and had reconciled herself to the news that the books had been essentially cowritten.

"It was a bit of a balloon being punctured," Amy said, bringing a bottle of wine from the refrigerator. She opened it with some contraption I'd seen at a professor's house—one clean pull. "But then I decided, so what? If both women were happy with the arrangement, what difference does it make?"

I said I felt bad for Rose. "All she wanted was to be famous and rich but her name fell into obscurity."

"Rose was the wind beneath Laura's wings."

I felt bad about laughing. How Rose would have hated that idea!

Amy wanted to see the gold pin, so I brought out my tote bag, where I'd kept the pin wrapped up in a paper towel.

"This has to be real, right?" Amy touched the faint etching of the house. "Remember when Almanzo gives her this, how he says, *Can't you thank a fellow better than that?* and they kiss? That's got to be the only sexy moment in all of the books. Then soon enough they're married with a baby."

"And remember," I said, "In *The First Four Years*, after Rose is born, they visit the Boasts, and the Boasts ask if they can have her?"

"Oh, yeah. Mr. Boast is like, if you give us the baby then you can go into the stable and take my best horse, because you can have another baby and we can't ever have one at all. They want to trade the baby for a horse!"

"It's especially sad since, from the other books, we know the Boasts as this sweet and perfect couple."

"How could they ever have faced each other again after that?" Amy took a drink from her glass, regarded it. "Ma wouldn't approve of this drinking. Do you know what became of the Boasts in real life?"

I shook my head. I said that I did know that the Olesons moved to Oregon, where Nellie married and had children. Jaunty Mr. Edwards had gone out to Oregon too, though he hadn't been heard from after that. Laura's friends from school, Mary, Minnie, and Ida, all married and moved West as well. Cap Garland had been killed in his early twenties, in a threshing accident.

"See, everyone goes West," Amy said. "You should too."

"But I always think, once they reach Oregon or California, what next? Did they want to keep going somewhere else?"

"Not at all. This is it. The land of gold and honey and citrus, like the oranges in the Christmas stockings."

Amy brought out parcels of cheese from some expensive

169

shop—or perhaps there was no other kind there—and pastries from Tartine that were so perfect they made me want to cry. She offered me a city map, spreading it on the counter so I could see the distance between her neighborhood and the Mission District, where Google said that Gregory Stellenson lived. Google had also told us that he worked at the San Francisco Public Library, in the History Center (*History Center!* we both exclaimed), though he wasn't listed on the website.

The library was about a fifteen-minute walk from Amy's place. All we had to do, she said, was show up. She was taking the next day off for just this purpose. "We'll be like Almanzo and Cap Garland, going after the winter wheat that will save the town."

"Except we're going to say what? *Hey, Gregory Stellenson, did you know that you might be the only living descendent of Laura Ingalls Wilder?* He'll think we're crazy."

"I know. I've thought about this." Amy handed me a flatbread cracker and pointed to the melty-looking robiola. "That's why we have to be careful in our approach. Get to know him through chitchat first. You'll need to bring all of your academic credentials to bear, plus the evidence. We will have to sound stunningly lucid, is all."

Amy had always had this ability to inspire confidence in people. She was a talker, a natural saleswoman. She could make Gregory Stellenson believe whatever we were going to say, and that made me feel safe, somehow. Corroborated. It was easy, sitting there with Amy, to agree to her plan.

That night I looked all around her guest bedroom before going to sleep. Like the rest of her place, it seemed to be ready for visitors at any moment. The windows were topped with linen Roman shades. The hardwood floors were glossy, reminding me of the gleam of chestnut-haired models in hair dye commercials which always seemed to me extremely convincing. How did Amy manage to get her duvet and pillow shams looking so hotel-room-placed? Where had she learned these life skills?

I thought of Sam and the way he'd said *California* with a kind of reverence. It had embarrassed me. Had he looked at me the way I looked at Amy? Had he thought I had my shit together while he was just floundering and wandering around? What did he have to fall back on, to turn toward, to keep him going? What, I wondered, kept so many people going, every day, beyond devotion to habit? Was Sam even now in the same city I was? Was he in the same neighborhood, on the same street? From Amy's guest room I could glimpse the traffic below and the lights that were still on in the office buildings across the way. So many rows of lights, but few people. Every time I was in Chicago, or any city, I wanted to know how everyone managed to coordinate themselves in tandem, exiting buildings, entering trains, each person taking up so much space, having so many needs and desires. All scurrying toward shelter and food and safety and sleep.

It was impossible to regard San Francisco without thinking about its long history of immigration, the way it still symbolized a place of reinvention, transformation. No wonder Rose had been drawn here. No wonder my brother had. Countless immigrants had rebuilt their identities and families in this town, in spite of and sometimes because of earthquakes and fire. I had spent my entire life so far in the Midwest. I had never mentioned to my family that the postdocs I'd applied for had been at universities all over the country. I might have gone anywhere; I had hoped to land somewhere. The scarier part was thinking I wouldn't, that I would remain in the same life I'd grown up with.

But not Sam. Was he really here? Would I now, forever on, link the city to him? Not even Ong Hai knew the whereabouts of either of us. I had called home before driving to O'Hare, lied again, said I was going to spend a few more days with college friends, catching up on research at the University of Iowa. Ong Hai said he understood and didn't mention the Lotus Leaf at all, perhaps trying to spare me the guilt I already felt.

I found my phone and sent Sam a text: *I'm in San Francisco.*

In the morning Amy and I walked to the library, hoping we might be there when Gregory arrived for work. A dozen people were already hanging out in front, waiting for it to open.

Though the building was a modern beauty, with squared stones and tall, imperious windows, I felt a twinge of disappointment that the old library Rose had visited—all those arches and pillars echoing the World's Fair pavilion—was now a museum.

"The problem with this library is that it should have steps," I said to Amy. "Lots of broad, long steps for people to sit on."

She laughed. "What difference does it make?"

"Cultural atmosphere. You know, the vaunting of place through architecture."

"What was your dissertation called? 'Edith Wharton and the Reabsorption of Place'?"

"'Reifying the Aesthetics of Place.' Not much better, I know. Possibly worse."

"You could have called me for title advice. I can make contraindications sound positively symphonic."

It was fifty degrees in June and I pulled Amy's borrowed jacket tighter around me. I was glad for the easy silence she and I could fall into as I took in the bustle of people getting to work, especially the Asian women, some in sneakers and flats, some in heels, all loaded down with bags. One had a purse that seemed to be made of a hundred squares of canvas stitched together in fraying, flapping tiers. I couldn't take my eyes off them, wondering how that woman came to be in this very place, how she had selected that particular hideous purse. I'd been in San Francisco only once before, visiting when Amy was at Stanford, and had then too been unreasonably surprised by the number of Asian people populating the streets. Though I already knew that would be so, it was still startling to see them moving around in a way that seemed oblivious, like they never had to worry about being stared at.

All at once the other people around us headed to the opened doors of the library. Amy and I started to move too, and soon found ourselves standing in the middle of the lobby, a marble bath of light that revealed all the floors of the building, the stairs leading up to stacks of stacks. The ceiling, a glass rotunda, showed the sky's mass of clouds.

That's when I thought I saw him. A guy carrying a chartreuse bike helmet, evidently having arrived through a different door, pausing for a second to check his phone. Amy noticed too—she had studied Gregory's Facebook profile—and said, "It's showtime."

We got into the same elevator with him, along with an old woman with a brown shopping bag of books and a guy who could have been homeless or could have been an academic. Gregory—I was pretty sure it was him—had a book bag slung over his shoulder, stainless-steel water bottle stuck in a side pocket. His light tan and delicate freckles were a match to his photos, as were the faded collar points of his button-down. They transmitted the kind of outdoorsy, active masculinity I'd always associated with this part of the country. Probably he was a vegetarian. I could find nothing in his face that hinted at Rose or Laura except that his features seemed as unremarkable as theirs in the photographs I'd seen, and yet I decided this had to be the Gregory Stellenson I had come to San Francisco to find. It was a perverse moment that I savored, and would savor for a long time afterward: being that close, knowing something of a person who did not know me. When the elevator reached the sixth floor we all made a move to step out. It was then that Gregory glanced over at me. Just a glance. A register of another body, another person occupying a nearby space. He had no particular expression on his face, nothing to indicate a lifetime of anything but normalcy.

I had almost forgotten Amy until she brushed my shoulder.

Gregory disappeared into the back of the History Center while the old woman and the homeless academic settled themselves in the reading room. Amy and I peeked in.

From our prep work online, I knew that the San Francisco History Center housed everything from old building permits and census files to manuscripts, original newspapers, and photographs, all documenting the rise, devastation by fire, and rebirth of the city. Undoubtedly there were materials in here that pertained to Rose herself, or were written by her, like her articles and features in the *San Francisco Bulletin*. In this way she'd been in the library all this time, with Gregory circling around her. Perhaps he'd even read her work.

"Ready?" Amy said.

"Right now?"

"When else?"

She started walking toward the main desk but I stopped her. "Are we sure about this? We can't just disrupt his whole life while he's at work, can we? Seems kind of, I don't know, rude."

Amy looked at me like I was crazy.

"This could change his life," I said, all at once nervous, thinking for the first time about the irreversible nature of that. "It's a big thing to be responsible for."

"Okay," Amy said. But she looked like she was having to hold herself back from rushing into the room and blurting everything out. "What do you want to do, then?"

"Maybe we should wait. Make a clearer plan."

"It's your call," she said finally, concealing just a bit of a sigh.

For a while we lingered outside the reading room, trying not to stare too hard when Gregory came into view. He seemed to have a separate office space but emerged frequently to talk to the woman at the reception area.

"We look like loiterers," Amy pointed out.

She was right. We either had to leave the area or sit down and pretend to do research. We tried not to watch as Gregory walked into the reading room and took a volume down from a shelf.

"I need another breakfast," I said.

Over lattes and scones at a nearby café Amy tried to

convince me to get the thing over with. The sooner we talked to him, she said, the sooner everything would sink in. But now that I knew he truly did exist, the anxiety I'd felt on the plane, flying in from Chicago, shifted. Finding Gregory Stellenson had been too easy.

"I think I'm afraid of a letdown," I admitted. "Or maybe of a dismissal. It's almost more exciting this way, like being next in line for the roller-coaster ride. Because it's possible he might not care at all."

Amy's voice was resolute again as she said, "Listen. Here's what we should do. We're not going to have a crisis about this. We'll go do something else for a while, then come back. We've got time. We have hours before the end of the workday. By then you'll feel better about all this." She had the right mind for an academic life—curious, interested in the most minor and pedantic details, and not afraid to follow a tangent even while keeping her eye on the prize. She was better at the task than I was and I was glad for the direction.

We went to the Ferry Building and ate our way through it, peaches to oysters to macarons, and talked through the Laura and Rose timelines. This was why we were such good friends: we could get lost in the joy of the shared obsession, spending hours dissecting our favorite details from the *Little House* books as if the memories were our own. Like living in a dugout—a freaking dugout. Like the imagined feel of Laura's beloved velvet hat that she made herself. The bangs she cut herself, that Ma called a "lunatic fringe." The vanity cakes Ma made, all puffed and golden and melting on the tongue. How about blackbirds, fried in their own fat? Oyster soup stippled with butter and black pepper. Maple syrup poured over snow and hardening into candy. Remember the barrels of lemonade at the Fourth of July celebration in De Smet, how all the towns-people drank from the same dipper? What about the communal "roll towel" at that hotel train stop on the way to Silver Lake—one skein of fabric that everyone used, looking for a dry spot? There was a shared Christmas tree too, kept at the church and decorated with popcorn balls and peppermint candy for all. We imagined we were both Laura, going from homestead to homestead, scrabbling for the next garden, the next set of meals, and finding joy and luxury in the smallest things: a bit of codfish gravy; a handmade rag doll; a fresh ribbon for our braids.

By the time we returned to the library it was almost three in the afternoon. We'd agreed that we would approach Gregory if he was alone, introduce ourselves, and hope he didn't take us for psychotic stalkers. If he was busy, we would wait until he was heading home.

Back in the reading room, we sat for nearly half an hour until Gregory finally appeared with a cart, a shinier version of Ron's back at the Hoover. He wheeled it over to a corner set of shelves. The old lady and the homeless academic were gone but in their place were a dozen others like them. Most were reading intently; two were dozing off in their chairs.

Amy and I went over to where Gregory seemed to be organizing indexes.

She spoke first. "Can I ask you a question?"

He looked up. "Sure."

"We have a few questions about historical research," Amy said, her tone so bright that Gregory seemed a little taken aback.

"What do you want to know?" he asked.

"I'm Amy," Amy said. "This is Lee. We're investigating a bit of a literary mystery."

"Gregory," he said, and I felt the weight of his name in my chest, not daring to look at Amy just then. "What sort of mystery?" On his face, caution seemed to be turning into curiosity.

"It's about Laura Ingalls Wilder," I said. I rushed the words, wanting to gauge any spontaneous reaction, but there wasn't one. "And her daughter, Rose Wilder Lane," I continued.

Gregory nodded again, with no particular investment.

I glanced at Amy, who asked, "Do you know who they are?"

"The *Little House on the Prairie* books? The TV show? Sure."

"The show was totally different from the books," I said.

"Lee just got her PhD in English lit," Amy said. "She's spent years researching."

"Your work is on Laura Ingalls Wilder?"

"Well, nineteenth-century American."

"You probably deal with academics and researchers all the time," Amy said, smiling.

I realized then that she was starting to *flirt* with him. It sent a flare of annoyance through me, as if she were violating an ethical code. *We aren't here for that*, I wanted to say.

"I deal with people from the general public too, but it's not clear who's nuttier." Gregory looked from Amy to me and back at Amy. "You don't seem that nutty."

Was he flirting back? I wasn't even sure if he was including me in that *you*.

"Rose Wilder lived in San Francisco for a number of years," I broke in. "She was a reporter at the *San Francisco Bulletin*. Laura Ingalls Wilder visited her here in 1915, during the World's Fair."

"Oh, do you want to see the *Bulletin* archives?"

"Rose also had a child here," Amy said. She paused, waiting for me to pick up the rest.

"That is, she might have," I said. And I couldn't go further than that. Even after Amy's pep talk at the Ferry Building, I couldn't muster the nerve to come out with this history that might have been his or might have been fiction. I remembered how Alex said nothing proved a connection, that I was reading what I wanted into Rose's words, into Mrs. Stellenson's letter. And who was I to do this anyway? Gregory might not care, or he might care more than could be anticipated. What right did I have to challenge his family story like this?

I shook my head at Amy, but Gregory caught me.

"Something wrong?" he asked.

"Everything's fine," I said. "But you know what, I think we're going to have to come back another time to see the archives."

"Are you sure?" Amy asked. "After all, we're here right now."

"Yeah, I'm sure. Sorry," I said, turning back to Gregory. "I just have a few more logistics to figure out first."

"That's fine." He started to roll the cart forward. "If you end up needing help, I'm usually around."

"Thanks."

I led the way toward the elevators, Amy reluctantly following. When I glanced back at Gregory he was looking at us, but turned back to his work.

"What's wrong with you?" Amy said. "Now he probably thinks we're a couple of freaks. Or like we're trying to pick him up or something."

I pushed the down button. "I don't think we've thought this thing through."

"What are you talking about? It's all we've done today. That and eat."

"I can't get over the fact that we're potentially going to change his whole life with this information. Is that even fair? Do we have the right?"

"You need to stop thinking of it like that. Maybe he wants to know. Maybe he'll be thrilled. *I* would be. I'd be over the moon if someone told me I was related to Laura Ingalls Wilder. I'd be, like, *Where're my royalties?*"

"But that's the thing—we could end up setting off a whole chain of events that have nothing to do with us."

"Look where he works," she pointed out. "He'll probably be fascinated by this."

I couldn't disagree with that, but when the elevator arrived I got on it. Amy was quiet.

Outside, we stood in the sunshine for a moment before she spoke. "This is your deal. Whatever you want to do is yours. But if I know you, there's no way you're going to be able to leave San Francisco without finding out more. And Gregory Stellenson is the only person who can in any way confirm all these theories you have."

We started walking back to her apartment. Tomorrow, I suggested, rather than promised, but Amy said she had to work all day. Would I wait until Friday?

"Of course," I said. It was a relief. My flight back to O'Hare wasn't until Sunday. Plenty of time.

As we crossed Market Street Amy said, "He's pretty cute, don't you think?"

"So what?"

She just laughed.

ELEVEN

The next morning I was studying the map of San Francisco Amy had given me when my phone buzzed with a long-awaited text from Sam. After this cross-country chase I'd set myself on, I half expected him to say that he wasn't in California at all.

Instead the text bubble read: *Why are you here?*

I started to type back but realized: Was this how it was going to be, brief bursts of words that either of us could walk away from at any time? So I called him.

To my surprise, Sam's voice. "What's going on?"

"Hey. What's going on with you?" I asked if he had time for coffee. After a little hesitation he named a café in Pacific Heights—from the map, it didn't look to be far from Rose's old house on Russian Hill—and we settled on meeting in an hour.

I took my time walking there, figuring that Sam would

keep me waiting. Not that I minded in a place like this. I hadn't realized how hungry I'd been for hills and color and depth—the clouds hovering, chains of houses shoulder to shoulder, their various shades of mint and frost and lavender backgrounded by crisscrossing power lines.

The coffee shop Sam had named was minimalist-modern with copper counters and reclaimed wood tables, but sold homey-looking cream pies, doughnuts, and layer cakes. I was finishing my second latte and a slice of blueberry buckle when Sam finally appeared, more than half an hour after our agreed-upon time. He went to the counter first, not even bothering with a wave or nod, then ambled over with a coffee and cruller.

"So what are you doing here?" he said as he sat down, starting in on the cruller. Up close, he didn't look as drawn as he had the last time I'd seen him, but he didn't look happy either. He looked trendy—skinny pants and short-sleeved plaid shirt. He'd always been vaguely hipster-looking without much effort, but maybe being in San Francisco had put him over the edge.

"Research."

"Really."

"I've been over at the History Center in the main library." I spoke too fast, already on the defensive.

"For what?"

Instead of answering, I asked, "Why did you come here and not Southern California?"

"I know people here."

That was news to me. Neither of us spoke for a moment.

Sam gave me a mock-expectant look that reminded me of our mother—her favorite edition of the withering gaze. "Well? Any other questions?"

"Why did you take Mom's jewelry and leave the gold pin?"

He gave a heavy sigh. "Did you come all the way out here to yell at me about that?"

"They don't even know," I said. "But come on, Sam. Jesus Christ. The cash register? The jewelry? That's beyond low."

"I don't have time to listen to this."

"How is it that you're the victim here? You know all Mom wants is for you to go back home. You know she would overlook just about anything."

He drank his coffee, trying his best, I thought, to look like he didn't care at all. He took out his phone and checked it. Near us, a couple was sharing a table with their matching laptops. They spoke quietly to each other over their screens and laughed the irritating laugh of two people in complete agreement.

"What are *you* doing out here?" I asked. "Where are you staying?"

"Who's asking these questions? You or Mom?"

"I'm not her assistant."

"Sure about that?"

"Are you kidding me? You're the favorite."

"And you're the Goody Two-shoes. Always have been."

All of a sudden we were glaring at each other. At another time, last year, before the news about Hieu, I would have been afraid that Sam would get up and leave. But now I knew how much he wanted Hieu's money; I knew that he still thought I might be able to find it. "You get to do whatever you want, take whatever you want, and not have a moment's worry about it. You're free."

"I'm a constant disappointment," Sam said flatly. "You think I don't know everyone thinks that?"

"You're the favorite. And that's all that matters. You should see Mom—"

"I don't like all the expectation. I can't fulfill some role. It's ridiculous."

"It's not about fulfilling a role," I said, though I didn't quite believe that myself.

"Do you remember," he said, "how I went to the prom with Kirsten Lonski?"

Surprised, I nodded. I remembered Sam's rental tux and how he'd asked me if I knew how to fasten cuff links. I didn't, and it took us twenty minutes to figure it out. Earlier that day he'd brought home a rose corsage, bigger than a fist, and kept it in its plastic case in the refrigerator. He had been so nervous about picking up Kirsten, meeting her parents, and posing for pictures. At the time I'd been impressed that he'd asked her and that she'd said yes. She was, if not a total A-lister, enough on the fringes of it to be included in their parties. She was the kind of girl I had wanted to be, many times, growing up: conventionally pretty, blond, normal.

I didn't recall much else about Sam's senior prom, or whether or not they'd had a good time. I said so to Sam, who replied, "It was a fairly shitty event."

As it turned out, he said, Kirsten had agreed to go with him because she and her boyfriend Jim had just broken up and he'd asked another girl to the prom. Kirsten wore a strapless, sequined, powder-blue dress that was so tight her mom made her bring along a shawl, but it was all for Jim. Sam spent most of the evening hanging out with his friends and their dates while Kirsten and Jim slow-danced toward reconciliation in the local Marriott's crystal ballroom.

I was almost holding my breath as Sam talked, wondering if he was going to deliver us into one of those rare moments of sibling confidence, the two of us aligned in knowing something that no one else could.

Then he said, "Do you know why I'm telling you all this? Because you don't get it. You never will."

I sat back. The disappointment was stunning. "What don't I get?"

"Being an Asian guy is totally different from being an Asian girl."

"Every Asian or Asian American person knows what it means to feel like a freak."

"It's different for guys. Worse for guys. Especially where we grew up."

"Because media images tend to desexualize Asian guys and hypersexualize the women. I know."

"You know because you've read about it or studied it in some class, but you don't *know*. Does any guy want to be Jackie Chan, or Mr. Miyagi, or that guy from *Sixteen Candles*?"

"I get what you're saying."

"No, you don't. I'm saying I should have come here a long time ago. Look around. There are probably more Asians here than white people."

"I never knew you felt this way."

"Don't start thinking this is some psychological crisis. There's a reason I was no good in that scene back home. I needed to be somewhere else. Here."

His rant was so persuasive, I had to wonder if I'd somehow collaborated, contributed to his shame. But I said, "If you're not going back home, then at least you have to tell them."

"You're the messenger, Lee. You're going to go straight back to Franklin and tell them everything."

I was stuck and he knew it. So I said, "You must think the messaging goes the other way too. About Hieu."

At this Sam looked up. "You talked to Mom about that?"

I nodded, lying.

"And? What about the money?"

"You have to come home," I said. The words seemed to

emerge without my control, that's how natural it felt to tell that lie.

"What kind of number are we talking about here?" he asked.

I said I didn't know.

"That's fucking stupid. It's not like she can force me to stay there forever."

He tipped his empty coffee cup back and forth. "What else did you ask her? Did she tell you how long they've been together?" He looked at me—I'd never had a poker face and never would—and gave a short laugh. "I thought you were supposed to be the smart one. You didn't figure that one out, did you?"

In truth, the thought had never occurred to me. Our mother was asexual, someone who had no time for the frivolities of romance. "How do you know this?"

"It was obvious. I could tell by the way they were talking."

"That's hard to believe," I said, though as I spoke the words I remembered Hieu's laughter, his presence in those early days, all the gifts he'd brought and we'd accepted as if they were owed to us.

"Then why don't you ask her about it? Ask Ong Hai."

"You said yourself he wouldn't say anything."

"Because he knows."

"When you followed her that time, what exactly did you see?"

"Look, they were talking about money. I heard them. He

was saying something about a check. I couldn't understand all of it, but it was definitely about money. And then she said something about years. It was obvious."

In a strange way it made sense to me. I had often wondered how my mother had been able to go from one restaurant to the next, one apartment to the next, when each venture involved fresh costs and security deposits. I had always assumed that she and Ong Hai were dedicated savers who lived by bargains and deals. But maybe all that time she—we—had been cushioned by Hieu. Chu Hieu. The invisible benefactor uncle. And maybe all that time—how long after my father's death? or was it even before?—my mother had been comforted by him too.

Ong Hai had always said that my father had taken care of Hieu, had helped him out, taught him business sense. Maybe that had added to Hieu's guilt and what Sam called his blood money.

Sam checked his phone again, put it back in his pocket. "I gotta go," he said.

"We're in the middle of a conversation."

He pushed back his chair and stood.

"What are you going to do?" I asked.

He shrugged.

We were back to the beginning, then. "You don't have to go home forever. But I think it's fair to say a decent good-bye, especially if you want that money."

190

"So that's her bargain, then."

He stood there for a moment longer and I thought I could keep him there, keep him talking, if I just asked more questions, held out the imaginary promise of money. But I didn't, and he wasn't going to give me anything. Having made the move to leave, he was going to see it through.

We didn't even say good-bye.

I brought our empty plates and cups to a tub near the counter and went outside. When I faced the direction Sam had turned I could see him ahead on the sidewalk, his lean figure knowable even in the wake of the other Asians and tourists.

It was easy enough to follow him. He was talking on his phone, not looking back. Did he know me enough to guess that I might be there?

He led me into a neighborhood of homes where all the front yards had that glint of modern money. You could see it in the crisp trim, the wrought-iron fences, the just-so pattern of freshly bricked paths leading to front steps—these were crucial details, the result of countless hours considering words like *heritage, preservation.*

It was just the two of us on the street now. Sam turned at a three-story Victorian that was sandwiched into a hill among other Victorians, and painted the color of cantaloupe flesh, bay windows accented by stripes of cream and honeydew. The shrubbery and plants that made up the patch of landscaping in front looked downright molded, almost unreal. I watched Sam go up the steps and inside without a key.

I stood there for a few minutes, memorizing the street, the house number, what the neighborhood looked like.

And then I went up the stone steps too, and, as Sam had done, opened the unlocked door and walked in.

The house had that hushed feel of cleaned surfaces and cleaning services that reminded me of the rich kids in high school. They weren't my group—everyone seemed to find their own level, self-segregating by socioeconomic status—but I had been over to a couple of their houses to work on group assignments and attend graduation parties. These were the homes that had awed me with their dedication to design. It seemed that even their building materials were inherently purer than any that made up the rentals my family occupied. The purity extended down to the baseboards, to the shine of the wood floors, to the concealed spaces beneath every piece of furniture. They exuded the assumption of grace. At the very least, you had to respect all the money and care that built them.

As I stood in the front hall of the cantaloupe Victorian, I wondered what trouble I was getting myself into. Because the house was so quiet, I tiptoed toward the back. The space was open, revealing one of those kitchens where the centerpiece was a giant range, a stainless-steel hood hovering almost menacingly over it. A bar surrounded the cooking area and more living space stretched out beyond it—a cushiony twill sofa and chaise facing a stone fireplace with a huge flat-screen mounted above it like a painting. There was a second stairway to the upstairs and French doors leading to the back patio. I opened them and stepped out. Like some kind of 3-D garden catalog, the patio bore an enormous gas grill, umbrellaed tables, and lounge chairs I would have worried about getting ruined in the rain. I sat down on one of them. From this little hideaway the city felt entirely removed. That was the difference so much money could make. In a suburban rental, hiding out was the same as being forgotten; here, it was a deliberate choice and the rest of the world would just have to wait.

When Sam said my name, I started as if I had fallen asleep, and maybe I had, because he was sitting in the pillowed armchair across from me, holding a bottle of beer.

"You live here?" I said.

"Yeah, it belongs to a friend of mine."

"Are you staying here or are you living here?"

He shrugged. He looked, indeed, like he was in no hurry to leave. "Judson doesn't care."

"How did Judson get all of this money, and how do you know him?"

"He's an entrepreneur. I'm doing some work for him. I met him when he was out in Chicago. Seriously, what is with you and your inquisitions?"

"What the hell else am I supposed to do? All of a sudden you're living in San Francisco with some strange dude."

"It's not a gay situation, if that's what you're thinking."

"Well, I don't know that much about your life," I said. "No one really does."

Sam finished his beer and stood up. "Want one?"

"No." I followed him to the kitchen, pausing at the polished concrete counter. The backsplash was made of a mirrored glass tile that shimmered when Sam opened the gigantic refrigerator. It was filled with booze, Vitaminwaters, and take-out boxes.

"This neighborhood is Pacific Heights, right? Isn't it fancy?"

"Lower Pacific. I'd live in the Mission if I could, but Judson's parents own this place. They moved to Massachusetts so I stay here for free, basically. It's part of my work."

"So what kind of business is this?" I asked.

"Judson calls himself a societal entrepreneur."

"What, is he a gigolo?"

Sam smiled at that. He opened another beer and tossed the cap on the counter.

"Contraband?" I said. "Immigrant smuggling?"

"Why do you always think the worst?"

For a moment we just looked at each other, and for reasons I didn't think I'd ever understand, he relented. "All right," he said. "Let me show you."

He walked me upstairs to an office space. A row of desks lining the walls; laptops and printers.

"This is it," he said.

"What do you do?"

"Mostly number-crunching. You know, accounting. Some phone calls." At my annoyed look Sam finally said, "Judson supplies medical marijuana." I must have looked incredulous, because he went on, "It's legal in California. It goes by a doctor's prescription. Certain clinics offer it, and obviously they need suppliers."

"And that makes him a societal entrepreneur?"

"Why not?"

"Do his parents know about this?"

Sam burst out laughing. "God, you sound like a school principal. *Do his parents know?*"

"Hey, look, this doesn't exactly seem like a drug-running kind of neighborhood. I can't imagine the neighbors are pleased."

"Why would they know? Maybe you don't realize it, Lee, but this is a start-up operation. Full legalization is coming soon, and when it does, we'll be ready. We're on the verge of a boom here. IPOs and everything. You wait and see."

I held back from saying that he was just as money-obsessed as our mother.

I peeked into the room next door, which was nearly empty save for a mattress on the floor and a particleboard bookshelf in one corner. Sam's duffel lay open, clothes still inside it. "Is this your room? You didn't say how long you're planning on staying here."

"I haven't gotten around to getting furniture yet."

"So it's just you and Judson, this marijuana operation? Are you, like, employee number two at Google?"

"Look, you asked me all these questions and, as predicted, you don't really want to know any of the answers."

"I just don't want you to end up in prison."

"Oh, for fuck's sake."

"Where is this Judson anyway? I hate his name."

"You think he grows the stuff in the backyard? He's got a whole farm about an hour and a half from here."

"This is all great for you, Sam, but what about Mom and Ong Hai? What are you going to tell them?"

He made this exasperated sound, like I was too tiresome to be believed. "If you want to rule your life with obligations to other people, that's you."

"I'm trying to remember when you've ever considered anyone else."

"I think you're lying, Lee. I don't think there's any money at all. Or if there is, you don't know about it. You never even asked her, right?"

What could I say? He was my brother, in spite of everything—we knew each other well.

"You can tell her I'm fine here. I'm fine on my own."

He was making me the messenger, just as he'd said. And I knew, as well as I knew anything, as well as I knew that I would go see Gregory Stellenson later that day, that it was true, what Sam said. He would be fine without us.

So I took my leave, as the old-fashioned characters in novels I loved would have said. There was no great drama in it. I didn't know when I would see Sam again, or talk to him, and I didn't ask. He was already far away. The way we'd talked to each other as siblings, growing up in the same apartments, eating the same sugary cereals, hoping we wouldn't smell of buffet grease as we rode the bus to school, could not hold.

We walked down the main staircase. Because it was perhaps my last chance, I said, "At least tell me why you had to take the jewelry." Sam looked away. "You know she has almost nothing from Vietnam."

"I told you I needed money. You should be glad I left that ugly pin for you."

"Because you thought it wasn't worth anything."

Standing there in the foyer of his borrowed house, time zones away from our family, I realized I'd wanted to believe that Sam still had the jewelry, that he hadn't sold it all.

"It's not like she ever wore any of it. All that gold and jade looks the same anyway. She owed me."

"That's bullshit, and you know it. If anything, you owe *her.*"

"Now you're on her side? Look at how she guilted Hieu. She's been using him all this time, lying, keeping secrets."

"Even if that's true, think about how much of that money

went directly to you. You have no right to be so entitled. Why shouldn't she get some help, anyway? Why shouldn't she have someone looking out for her?"

"Wow." Sam folded his arms. "So much for loyalty to Dad."

"This isn't about Dad." But I struggled to keep sudden tears at bay.

Sam leaned against the staircase, resting his arm where the staircase railing ended, curling into itself in a shape that I remembered was called a volute.

"Maybe I shouldn't have taken all that stuff, but it's not like I'm a real thief. I was just trying to get out of there. Look around. This is where I should have been a long time ago. Anyone in their right mind would rather be here."

It was an argument I'd heard all my life, an argument I'd had with myself. Why would anyone in the Midwest, especially a nonwhite person, want to stay there? How could life not be better out West, in California? I had stayed close to home because in-state tuition was what I could afford and because I'd felt the tug of obligation to family. But I had tried to get into Stanford for grad school. My postdoc applications spanned the country. I had sent in my materials without ever mentioning to my mother or grandfather that I hoped one day to move far away. And as for the other part, well, I was a thief too. Sam had no idea how much.

I put my hand on the front door handle. It was heavy, solid, a match for the varnished wood of the door that held a single pane of etched glass. Once, we had lived in an apartment in northern Illinois where the front door knob kept falling off. The landlord didn't fix it for months, so my mother carried the knob around in her purse, for whenever we needed to get in or out. I wondered if Sam remembered that. At the moment he seemed younger than ever, as though we had switched places and I had become the older sibling. The switch had happened years back, really, for I was used to looking out for him, checking on him. I was looking for excuses.

"You're living in a beautiful house," I said, because it was so, and there was Sam, looking like he no more belonged there than I did. But perhaps he would. Soon he would. He would learn the language of this new place and his room would begin to fit with the rest. He would find friends, people like him who had no desire to go home for holidays. They would deep-fry Thanksgiving turkeys and exchange white elephant gifts at Christmas. They would eat at exquisite restaurants and dives and form very specific opinions about dumpling wrappers. They would have cheesy-movie marathons and themed parties and brew their own beer. And then Sam too would become one of the Asian Americans who made up more than a quarter of this city, whose thinness and quick walk and cool clothes would inspire a visitor like me to marvel at how many driven, successful, capable Asians lived here, and how happy and easy their lives must be.

I left Sam the way he had left the coffee shop that morning, not looking back. I wondered when I would hear from him next, or if he would ever take the initiative. He was more than capable of holding out. If I felt anger then, it had more to do with the stolen jewelry and the lost years of my own than with Sam himself.

Down at the sidewalk, I couldn't help thinking of Newland Archer—that old companion of mine, suddenly reappearing— turning away from the life he wanted but didn't dare to choose. *In reality they all lived in a kind of hieroglyphic world, where the real thing was never said or done or even thought, but only represented by a set of arbitrary signs.* Somehow, Sam and I had both found ourselves at the western coast. Did we even know what real thing we were trying to find?

On Fillmore I started north toward Vallejo Street, toward the house where Rose had lived in Russian Hill almost a hundred years before. She too had created her own community in this city. Her own free life, far from the confines of Mansfield. It was no mistake that she had found a house on top of a hill, with a view of the Golden Gate waterway, not yet bridged, opening out to the Pacific. She had loved even the chill of the fog, even the despondency that came from being surrounded by other people's wealth while she herself had to keep struggling and striving. Maybe Sam would keep striving too. It was impossible to tell what story he would make for himself.

And impossible to know what story I would bring to my mother and Ong Hai. They would be folding chilled noodles and shrimp into summer rolls, stocking bottles of water and juice, setting up cups for coffee and tea. They would be coming home, making yet more food or microwaving leftovers, eating while the familiar television shows laughed and clapped around them. I had always hated the image of TV lights flickering in someone's living room as I walked by. Probably because they always reminded me of my family and how I pictured them: sitting in near-invisibility, taking in whatever news or information that was presented.

I really did want to see Rose's house. I got as far as locating the exact route on my phone. But the absurdity of Sam's plans—that mattress on the floor, his dreams of weed—had left me with the lost feeling I had long associated with moving, packing, deciding which belongings had turned out, after all, to be discardable. The house on Vallejo was just another temporary home for Rose. As much as she'd prized the view and the height, she'd left soon enough for Sausalito, for Europe, even for Rocky Ridge Farm. I didn't want, right then, to see another temporary home. I wanted an answer.

So I returned to the San Francisco Library, even though I knew I wasn't supposed to until the next day, with Amy. In a way, I almost hoped Gregory wouldn't be there. In another way, I desperately hoped he would.

He was in plain sight, sitting behind the reception desk this time. As I approached, he said, "Hey, you're back."

"I'm back."

"Where's your friend?"

"She had to work."

"What about you?"

"This is my work. Sort of."

He nodded. No doubt he'd seen thousands of people dragging themselves through research and notes day after day. "You wanted to take a look at the *Bulletin* archives, right?"

"Not exactly. Or maybe. It's related to that. It's kind of strange."

"A lot of strange things are housed here."

"Well, stumbled across some pieces of information while I was researching Rose Wilder Lane. You know, the daughter of Laura Ingalls Wilder?"

"This is the literary mystery your friend mentioned."

"Right. Amy mentioned that."

Once again, with Gregory right in front of me, I hesitated. I could have backtracked as I had the day before and nobody else would have to know. I could have waited until Friday, as promised to Amy, whose help I was betraying by standing there.

But when Gregory glanced at his computer, already starting to focus on some other idea, some other piece of news, I decided to keep going. Here, now, just me and him.

"It has to do with a child," I said. Gregory looked back at me. "I think there was a child, is what I mean. That Rose Wilder might have given up for adoption. This was in 1918, here in San Francisco. As far as I can tell, no one in her family knew about it. But the thing is, that child was her only descendant, and therefore Laura Ingalls Wilder's only descendant, because Rose was her only surviving child."

When I paused, Gregory said, "Interesting. And then what?"

"So I tried to see if I could figure out what happened to that child. And I found the answer, or at least what might be the answer. It led—well, I guess it led to you."

I was almost afraid to see Gregory's reaction. He sat back, as if trying to put distance between us. "What do you mean, me?"

"I mean you, Gregory Stellenson. Or that is, your grandfather Albert, who was, or might have been, Rose's child."

After a few moments, Gregory said, "This is kind of creepy."

"I'm sorry," I said quickly. "I really debated saying anything at all. But I just wanted to find out if it was true. I wanted to know the rest, whatever it is."

"Wait, who are you again?"

"I'm Lee. I'm a researcher. An academic, I guess."

From my tote bag I pulled out the pilfered copy of *Free Land* and the letter that Mrs. Stellenson had sent to San Francisco General Hospital. I explained how it had been tucked into the pages of Rose's novel, stored away in an unused room at Rocky Ridge.

"You stole this."

"I needed proof."

Gregory read the letter several times, turning it over. I

could tell that he believed it. Of course, he would know what a letter from 1918 would look like, feel like, smell like.

This part of the library, the reading area and research area, and the hallway leading back to the archives kept under lock and key—all felt so empty that a humming noise rose in the place of voices.

"My grandfather was Albert Stellenson," Gregory admitted, and I felt that weight in my chest again, becoming something larger, a thrill. "And he *was* adopted. I only found that out a few years ago."

"Do you know anything about his birth parents?"

"No. But there are boxes I've never looked through, sitting in my mother's house."

"You've never looked through them? Why?"

"My mother meant to go over them with me. But she was sick with cancer—she died two years ago."

"I'm sorry."

He nodded. "I just never got around to those boxes on my own."

"Even though you work as a historian."

"Information science, actually." Gregory handed the letter back to me. "How did you get on this trail in the first place?"

I told him about my grandfather and mother, about a woman named Rose who went to Vietnam in 1965. About the gold pin that she had, whether by accident or design, left for my grandfather, who had in turn given it to my mother, who had brought it with her when they fled for America in 1975. I told him about the oblique lines of scrawled poetry I'd found in the archives of the Hoover Library, and how they had led me to Rocky Ridge, and the room where I'd trespassed and found the letter from his great-grandmother.

"There appears to be a lot of theft going on in your life," Gregory remarked.

"It's not the norm."

He seemed to consider this, then said, "Wait here for a minute." He left the reception area and headed toward the employees-only office. I had the fleeting thought that he was calling the authorities or something, but he returned with his book bag and stainless water bottle.

"Let's go," he said.

I went to Russian Hill after all, with Gregory, to 1019 Vallejo Street.

We got to the house from Taylor Street, where we had to climb a steep stone staircase to reach Vallejo. Rose's former house was tucked away among overgrowths of greenery. It was a mansion, really, a rich person's summerhouse, Tudor-ish, with dark brown shingles and many-mullioned windows. More than a century ago it had been a single-family home, then a series of apartments during Rose's era, and now it was one person's house again. A high-rise obstructed part of the view to the water. The great bridge hadn't existed when Rose was here.

At the top of the stone stairs we landed on a sidewalk that curved around a cul-de-sac of parked cars.

"Funny thing is," Gregory said, "my father's last name was, or is, Wilson, and so was mine. But he left when I was five, and hasn't been a part of my life since. When I went to college I changed my name to Stellenson. If I hadn't done that you might not have found me so easily."

The high sun glared off the windows of Rose's old house, making it impossible to glimpse anything inside. *But I would have found you*, I wanted to say.

"I feel like I've been past this place before," Gregory said.

I told him how Laura had visited Rose here during the 1915 World's Fair. While Rose worked at the *Bulletin*, her mother took in the sights. They were years away from writing the *Little House* books.

Was she still living here three years later? Gregory wanted to know, but I wasn't sure. I knew that Rose and Gillette finally divorced in 1918, and sometime that year she left the *Bulletin*, moved to Sausalito, and turned her focus to full-time freelance writing. Two years after that she left California altogether. If she had lived at 1019 Vallejo during a pregnancy it could have served as a hideout. A safe place high in the hills. Rose could have kept writing from home, quitting the newspaper when her belly grew too large.

"What about the father?" Gregory asked, but he knew as well as I did that the question was unanswerable. Even if we found a birth certificate it probably wouldn't have listed either parent's name.

Gazing up at the house again, I wondered if someone inside was looking right back at us. What would *we* look like?

My phone made a little chiming sound in my bag and I checked it, remembering, abashedly, Amy. But it was Alex. *Did you find Mr. Long-Lost?* I texted back: *Not yet.*

Gregory shaded his eyes. "Around 1918, did she have any male friends she wrote about?"

"Well, there was Fremont Older," I said. I had thought of him already. As longtime editor of the *Bulletin*, he had hired and mentored Rose, and she had become close with him and his wife, Cora. Sometime in 1918 Older left the *Bulletin* as well, taking a job at the competing *San Francisco Call*. He and Cora had had no children.

Gregory was intrigued. "I know who Fremont Older is. Have you seen his house in Cupertino? It's an architectural explosion, mostly designed by him and his wife. It makes sense that he and Rose would have had a relationship from the *Bulletin*."

"I don't know if it means that."

"But think of it. If he was her mentor. They worked together. Socialized together. Maybe Rose was afraid that he and his wife would want the baby, to raise as their own. Or maybe he didn't even know."

I thought of Alex and his skepticism: *maybe it wasn't Rose at all.* "Or maybe the baby was Gillette's. Years later, after he remarried, his wife said that Rose had always been the love of his life. Or then again, maybe it was just a nameless affair. She wasn't a prude. She even wrote somewhere that part of the reason she married at all was for sex."

"Not unusual for her time period," Gregory said.

In high school, Rose and her friends had wondered if they could get pregnant from kissing. But a couple of years after that, while she was working as a telegrapher in St. Louis, Rose made sure to lose her virginity before marriage—driven, apparently, by curiosity.

"She never remarried either. She had some relationships, but they didn't last. Or she took care not to say much about them in her journals."

"She knew people would read them. You know what?" I thought Gregory was going to suggest another possibility, but instead he said, "We should go before someone thinks we're casing the place." He led the way back down the stone steps, which smelled of moss and ruined leaves, to where 1019 Vallejo became invisible once again.

We walked on, to what purpose I didn't know, and I couldn't help glancing back; a casual passerby would never be able to tell that Rose's old apartment, full of history and mystery, existed there.

Gregory said, "You only looked through some of her

papers, right? Maybe she wrote about the guy somewhere and it hasn't turned up yet."

"What about those boxes you have? Maybe someone in your family knew something."

"I had a feeling you were going to say that." He looked at his watch. It was early afternoon, and though I was hungry for lunch I was more anxious about what else we could find.

"They're in my mom's house in Corte Madera," Gregory said. "My house now, I guess. I haven't been there in a while."

"Is that far from here?"

We stopped at the corner. Up ahead, a classic touristy cable car slid heavily down a hill, stuffed with people.

Turning to face me, Gregory said, "I can't do this right now."

"Why not? Because of work?"

"It's not because of work."

"But the thing is, I'm only here three more days."

"I understand this is important to you." He pushed his hands into his pockets. "I'm sorry."

"Will you take my number, then?" I practically forced him to add my number into his phone and hit dial so that his number would show up on mine.

"Think about it?" I pleaded.

Gregory nodded okay. He slid his phone into his book bag, shifting the strap over his shoulder, and walked away from me down Taylor Street.

TWELVE

I had intended to give Amy every awful detail from the day. Together, I figured, we could convince Gregory to change his mind. Amy could make anything seem logical. She would get us to his mother's house, where a store of information maybe lay in wait.

But then he called that night while Amy was at a work dinner. I was in her living room, reading about Rose's travels in Europe. When Gregory said, "What are you doing tomorrow?" I knew I was going to lie to her. It was my new pattern, my new survival. No truths for anyone in my life.

"We can get to Corte Madera by ferry or by bus," he said. "I don't have a car here because of parking."

"Boat," I said, and we set a time to meet at the Ferry Building.

Later, when Amy returned, I told her about Sam. I kept my focus on that. About Gregory I said I'd called the library and found out he was off until the weekend. Amy was disappointed but said at least Saturday would be easier for her. She was tired from her evening of forced networking, and when she went to change out of her suit I searched her cable for a movie we could watch instead of talking. *Walk the Line* was on—the kind of movie that was easy to sink into. With that and wine and a lemon-lavender cake I'd bought on the way home from seeing Gregory, I convinced myself that I wasn't doing any real harm. Amy needed to work anyway, and didn't I have some kind of right to pursue, on my own, whatever was to be pursued?

But still I felt guilty the next day when Gregory and I boarded a ferry together. I had to sweep Amy from my mind as, like guided magic, the boat took me and Gregory northward along what seemed to me the majestic bay. All the corny thoughts—the wind in our hair, the swooshing of the water and churning of the motor, the postcard thrill of the Golden Gate Bridge—I kept to myself. We glided past Angel Island, where so many hundreds of thousands of Asian immigrants had waited, leaving poems of loss and homesickness on its walls. Gregory knew more about Angel Island than I did. He'd been there dozens of times, had helped curate an exhibit about its history.

Sitting side by side, heading toward the house where he had grown up, Gregory said he'd started reading about Laura and Rose Wilder. Before that, what he'd known about them came mostly from the TV show reruns he had sometimes watched as a kid.

"Now you know that Michael Landon looked nothing like the real Pa," I said.

"Isn't that always the way."

"The real Pa never cried and never wore his shirts half open to expose his chest hair."

When Gregory laughed, I felt better. "I can't believe I'm doing this," he said. He stretched out, his leg touching mine for a moment. "You with your stolen documents."

He spoke lightly, but the words brought me back to the reason we were there. If Gregory was related to Rose, then he was related to the real Pa too.

"What was your grandfather like?" I asked.

"He was kind. A representative of his generation, you know? World War II veteran. Show little emotion. Keep moving forward. I was in eighth grade when he died."

"Did he talk about *his* parents? Did your mother?"

"She always said they were good, upstanding-citizen types. Civic pride and all that. Californian pride. That was important to my grandparents too. I remember that."

"And you only found out about his being adopted a few years ago."

"My mother didn't even find out until after he died. I remember when she told me, it was after a round of radiation.

She said she wanted me to help her go through her grand-mother's things, and I said I would, but somehow we never got around to it." Gregory turned his face to the sunlight, considering this. "I know we should have talked about it more. But I guess she figured—well, those things would be mine. She figured I would see for myself. She was never as interested in the past as I was. Better to keep things there, you know? History was like trivia. She didn't seem particularly curious to know the circumstances of her father's birth."

I didn't admit to Gregory that I felt suddenly jealous, thinking about all the family history he had right here for the taking. To be looked at or not, ignored or not. It was, at least, there. Possible. It could be pored over and preserved. My own origins were forever vague to me, lost through language and war, maintainable only through Ong Hai's remembered stories that had no documentation. No wonder my mother, and now I, held on to that gold pin.

"Your grandfather and your mother—they didn't move a lot? They weren't wanderers?" I asked.

"No. They stayed here all their lives."

"She was a wanderer. Rose, I mean. She and Laura both were, and Laura's Pa. They were called homesteaders and set-tlers, but really they wanted to keep going, see what else lay beyond the visible horizon."

I didn't say that my family too had wandered and settled,

had sought a home in the Western world that they'd never quite found.

When the ferry docked in Larkspur we got a cab toward the village of Corte Madera a couple miles away. This was part of Marin County, Gregory explained, which a lot of people now considered total yuppieburbia. But it was not like the McMansioning in the Chicago suburbs, bloated with circle driveways and three-stall garages. Here, fancy houses hid themselves in the hills or in conspicuously understated neighborhoods. Shrubbery edged over some of the narrow streets, nearly concealing stone driveways and dirt walking paths, pickup trucks and Volvos, picket fences and chicken coops, in what were apparently multimillion-dollar backyards. It wasn't always this way, Gregory said; his house was the only one he knew of that had stayed in the same family over generations.

It occurred to me that I was following a stranger to his childhood home. What did I really know of Gregory beyond his supposed lineage, his connection to Laura and Rose? I tried to keep track of the street names and told myself to call Amy, even while justifying not calling by telling myself that everything would be fine. In spite of Gregory's hesitation the day before, he was easy to be with, easy to talk to. We were, it seemed, familiar to each other, hadn't suffered a single lull in conversation.

When the cab turned and a gray-shingled bungalow came into view, I didn't need Gregory to tell me that this was the house that had been built for his grandparents over sixty years ago. Though it had the seacoast cottage look of other homes in the neighborhood, I was comforted by its shaggy paint and unmowed yard. I could see families gathering for holidays here, wrapping themselves in blankets to sit on the porch a while longer. They would keep a fire going; they would light candles at dinner and stay up late, talking to each other. It was the kind of place that would look good in any weather, that would appeal even in the dreariest of rains.

Did people actually live this way?

I wondered if I would ever know that for myself, if anyone in my family would. Was it possible my mother and Ong Hai were already there—did they really love wherever they lived? In the *Little House* books, you knew when their house really seemed like home because Ma Ingalls would bring out her delicate china shepherdess figurine, one of the few adornments she owned.

Gregory and I paid the driver. A narrow path, with tassels of grass erupting between flagstones, led to a door at the back of Gregory's family house. Through its square window I could see part of a yellow kitchen.

In 1948 Albert Stellenson had had the house built on several acres. The town was sleepy then, surrounded by hills and orchards. Gregory's mother had slowly sold off parcels of land as wealthier people moved into the area and property taxes spiked. Now the house was Gregory's, and he said he wasn't sure what to do with the responsibility. He didn't want to live there—the commute to the city was too long for him, and the idea of being in that house, just him, was too isolating. He said he should probably rent it out, but that would mean packing up and moving all of his mother's things, and, more than that, relinquishing a hold on the place as he knew it.

He hadn't wanted an inheritance so soon, but now it was his, waiting: this solid structure, this compass point.

Inside, the dusty, locked-in smell of minor neglect. A few withered plants, a stack of mail and magazines on the kitchen table. The living room was in a state of in medias res—blankets bunched up on the sofa, books open on the coffee table and soaking in the light from the large front windows, the sheers pushed back unevenly.

As I looked out at the overgrown greenery in the front yard, I let myself pretend that I was staying here. I imagined myself coming downstairs to the kitchen in the morning, bringing a cup of coffee to the living room or maybe out to the old, vine-tangled pergola in the backyard.

From the kitchen, where Gregory was opening cupboards, he said that his last serious relationship, which had almost turned into an engagement, had ended because of this house. This was too interesting not to pursue.

"What happened?" I asked, going in to take a seat at the scarred wooden table where Gregory and his mother must have sat countless times.

Haley was the woman's name, and she had envisioned the two of them living there together, eventually raising a family. This was before Gregory's mother died, and Gregory couldn't help thinking Haley was counting the days to death so she could move in. It wasn't fair or rational of him; his mother had liked the girl, and wanted the house to remain in the family. But it made Gregory realize that he wanted everything to stay stopped in time a while longer. He wanted a preservation house. He wasn't yet willing to inhabit the place on someone else's terms.

"And what happened to Haley?"

"She's engaged to someone else. A friend of mine from Berkeley. I'm going to their wedding next year."

"So you probably wouldn't have stayed together anyway."

"Probably not."

He was standing in front of the open refrigerator, surveying the door shelves full of condiments. He picked up a jar of olives, looked at the expiration date, and put it back.

"I'm never here on the trash-pickup days," he said apologetically. He filled two glasses with water, handing one to me. "There's also tea and coffee, if you don't mind it straight up."

"This is fine," I said. I told him I liked the kitchen, and I did, even if the counters and cabinets looked like they had last been updated in the eighties. The floor was vinyl-tiled and a lapis-colored light fixture hung over the table. I thought if I squinted I could imagine what the room had looked like in the forties and fifties. Gingham and floral curtains at the windows, enamel stove and oven. I remembered how so many old-timey children's books and cartoons had images of pies cooling on windowsills, and usually a comic character—a dog, a rapscallion, a hobo—was angling to steal them. I had loved these dreamscapes, where neighbors popped by to borrow eggs and sugar. I wasn't much of a baker, but I imagined rolling out a piecrust in Gregory's mother's kitchen, filling it with tart cherries or apple slices. I'd slide the pie into the oven until it turned a perfect golden brown, edges ruffled, then I'd set it on the windowsill, where occasional breezes would lightly stir the poplin curtains. All of this part of a grand tradition, reaching back to Laura Ingalls Wilder and further. If the *Little House* books were to be believed, Ma Ingalls was capable of baking anything; as Pa said, she *could always beat the nation cooking*. Once, she had even concocted a new delicious pie out of green, unripe pumpkin.

"Was your mother a good cook?" I asked as Gregory glanced through a utility drawer. He seemed to be reminding himself of what was there.

"Yeah, actually, she was." He looked up, smiled. "You know how people say that you're either good at cooking or you're good at baking? She was good at both. Just sort of intuitively. I remember the last thing she baked—I know this might sound morbid, but I don't mean it to be. I remember it because she knew it. She baked this lemon cake with fresh fruit in the middle, with lemon curd made from scratch and mixed with mascarpone—it was complex and took a long time, and it completely wore her out. And she said, as we were eating it, that it was probably the last cake she'd ever make."

"I'm really sorry, Gregory."

He picked up a box of tea from the counter and regarded it. "Thanks. I'm sorry too. It's still kind of weird for me to be here. Even though it's been two years, this house is still hers."

I kept forgetting that we'd met only two days before. Maybe he felt the same way, or realized it, because he seemed almost embarrassed as he changed the subject.

"You sure you don't want some tea?" When I said no thanks, he said, "Well, I guess we should start looking through that stuff."

We went upstairs, to a spare bedroom jammed with artifacts from a leftover, unfinished life. There was a mannequin in one corner, with a half-sewn polka-dot dress on it. Filing cabinets and plastic storage bins were stacked against the walls, and bookshelves held everything from photo frames to old board games to zip-locked bags of ribbon.

"Here they are," Gregory said. There were only three boxes, cardboard that had been softened by years of being moved around. We carried them down to the living room.

Gregory brought his book bag over and took out a notebook. "I should be cataloging all of this," he said.

"Is that going to take a long time?" I asked.

219

"Fine, fine," he said. "I'll do it later."

The first box contained photo albums, some of which he said he remembered seeing before. Most of the pictures were stuck to the pages, which made Gregory wince, muttering about having to transfer everything to archival-quality stock. He carefully peeled one off to check the back and found it labeled in that classic slanted old-fashioned cursive that reminded me of Rose's hand, of Mrs. Louis Stellenson's hand. *Louis and Mary, 1912. Honeymoon.* Gregory's great-grandparents were leaning into each other as if bracing against a wind tunnel. Beneath their feet, cobblestones, and a hazy European village in the background.

"They look like they're in love," I said.

"My mom said they always were. Apparently he brought her a cup of tea every morning."

I handed the photo back and he turned the album to another page. "Here's a baby picture of my grandfather," Gregory said.

I leaned in to see a sepia-toned infant draped in the voluminous lace of a christening gown. Albert Stellenson. Could this truly be Rose's child? He had large eyes, dark pools that stared just a little to the side of the camera lens. How old was he here?

"Can you imagine being a woman, alone, in 1918, having to make that kind of decision?" Gregory said.

"Or having it made for you," I said. Then, "Do you wish I

hadn't told you about all this? I know you didn't ask to know any of it."

We were sitting on the living room rug, a dhurrie with a faded diamond print, the photographs between us. Gregory leaned back against the sofa. "I would have wanted to know more at some point. It doesn't change what I think about my family. It's not like I'm going to tell people, *Hey, I might be part of the Ingalls and Wilder clan.* Even if it's true, fundamentally, it doesn't matter."

"Hey, there are *Little House on the Prairie* royalties at stake," I joked.

But Gregory shook his head. "That's actual, serious stuff. People go crazy about shit like that and it ruins them. Anyway, it's not like we can do a DNA test. And I would never go that far anyway."

I admired that, and told him so. In the back of my mind I remembered Alex calling him a Berkeley do-gooder. Alex didn't tend to get all macho-like around other guys, but I had a feeling he wouldn't care for Gregory.

"What about you—what's your real family like?"

"I have a brother who's a year older. That's it. My dad died when I was six, and my mother and grandfather live in a suburb of Chicago." I tried to describe the Lotus Leaf, and how I was helping out there while trying to figure out what to do next. The café sounded more successful than it was, our lives less fragmented than they were. I told him that Sam was in

221

San Francisco but didn't mention how he'd disappeared from our family for over a year, how he'd stolen jewelry and money and run out again.

"I always wanted siblings," Gregory said.

I looked down at the album in my lap, where pictures of the Stellensons gazed up, facing something just past my line of vision. I wanted to see what they were seeing; I didn't want to think about Sam, or anyone in my family.

"So your great-grandparents were Mary and Louis Stellenson. They got married in 1912 and adopted Albert in 1918. Albert grew up. Then what?"

Albert married a woman named Eleanor right after the war, Gregory said. After their daughters Louisa and Margaret were born, Albert had the Corte Madera house built. He worked in insurance—he was good at sales, became one of the top men in the company. Eleanor became an award-winning gardener. Louisa died tragically young, a teenager in a car accident. Margaret went to an all-girls college in Southern California, where she fell in love with one of her professors—Gregory's father.

"I don't even know what my dad is doing now," Gregory said. "Haven't talked to him in years. He probably doesn't even know about my mother."

"Why haven't you talked to him?"

Gregory showed me a picture of his parents' wedding day.

A courthouse ceremony, his mother in a crepe sheath, his father in a suit jacket, shirt open at the collar.

"He had a lot of other women," Gregory said, shrugging. "And then I guess he had some kind of crisis. I think he left teaching too. He was just never interested in being a father."

"Did she ever remarry?"

"Yeah, but it only lasted a couple of years. This was in 1985? It's crazy, but I barely remember him. His name was Hal. He was a lawyer and he was into boating. That's basically what I remember. He always wanted to go boating, and he used that word. *Boating.* They married on a whim. And then he was gone."

I thought of my own father, and how he had existed so long ago that I sometimes forgot he had been a real person in our lives. And when I did remember I felt a wave of shame: How could I forget my own father? What was wrong with me, that I didn't register his absence, the permanent lacuna, which should have marked each day?

How could Gregory's father go so many years without seeing or even speaking to his son? Or was this how time had its way with us, allowing us to believe that absence wasn't just possible but endurable—forgettable? That the more time accumulated, the more it could keep gaining?

We were pretty much done with the first two boxes, and before we started on the last one Gregory got up to find something to eat. I got up too, stretching my legs, and went back to the front window. There was something beckoning about it—a place where I could stay for hours. Surely every member of Gregory's family had stood where I was standing, staring dreamily, watchfully, measuring each shift of light.

At the moment it seemed truly golden, and I wondered what time it was. I remembered that I should call Amy.

Gregory came back into the room and set cups of tea and a package of wheat crackers on the coffee table.

He stood next to me then, and just as I was aware of how close he was he put his hand on my shoulder, letting it slip down my back. He pulled me toward him, almost sharply, and I knew what was going to happen. We were on the sofa first, then the floor, and neither of us said a word. He paused to locate a condom in his book bag, and if it had taken even a few seconds longer we probably wouldn't have been able to go on. But then he was poised above me, his face nearly invisible, silhouetted by that light through the big windows, and we were moving with a kind of urgency, a determination, that I hadn't known with Alex—or anyone else, for that matter. The strangeness of what we were doing made it all the more intoxicating, and when he gripped me tighter I did the same.

When it was done and we both lay there on the dhurrie rug, the embarrassment took over. I sat up first, reached for my clothes. We took care not to look at each other getting dressed.

At last Gregory said, "Should we keep going? That last box, I mean."

It made me feel better to hear him stumble. Yes, I said.

Soon we were sitting across from each other again and Gregory was bringing forth packets of letters. We sorted them by date: correspondence between Albert and Eleanor during their wartime courtship, and correspondence between Eleanor and Margaret when Margaret was in college. They covered everyday events—who had visited and what they had worn, who had married whom, who had moved into or out of the neighborhood. No mention of anything having to do with adoption or family history.

After a while Gregory looked up and said, "I kind of feel like I should apologize."

"It's fine." Then, feeling silly, I amended it to, "It was nice."

"It *was* nice."

"Probably not what either of us expected from the day."

He laughed, so I did too. In the pause that followed, I said, "I'm not seeing any indication that these letters are going to tell us anything about Rose."

Gregory agreed, but we continued reading what his great-grandmother, grandmother, and mother had written and put away for safekeeping. Three generations of gossip and tidings, bound in ribbon and left to neglect.

Then Gregory said, "I've been wondering. Why didn't you tell me all of this Rose Wilder stuff the other day, at the library? When you were with your friend."

I could feel myself blushing under his gaze. "I lost my

nerve, I guess. I didn't know if I had the right to spring this on you. I still don't know. I mean, I've become a thief."

"But if Rose Wilder hadn't given your grandfather that pin, then none of this would have been found."

"Well, she didn't really give him the pin—more like left it."

"Same result though."

"Unless it's all a weird coincidence, a bunch of assumptions. I have a friend, in Iowa, who went to Rocky Ridge with me. He thinks I'm reading Rose into this whole thing, that the letter could just as easily have been something she kept for someone else. Like maybe she was the one who helped someone go through the pregnancy and give the baby up for adoption. And maybe the pin connection isn't legit either. I can't verify it. Can't prove it."

"Yeah, that is possible."

"The biographies say that after the birth of her first child she had complications that rendered her unable to have more children," I admitted. "But she also had a habit, throughout her life, of quote-unquote adopting young men. Like when she traveled to Albania she befriended a young man and eventually paid for him to come to the States and go to college, and there were a few local boys she helped out financially too. And then in Vietnam—maybe she took a liking to my grandfather. Maybe that was all a psychological by-product of the child she lost, or the child she gave up, or both."

"It's circumstantial," Gregory agreed. "But even if I'm not related to her, she probably knew my grandfather's birth mother. Why else would she have that letter?" As I considered this he went on, "I can see how tricky this would be to write about, since so much of it is speculation."

I shook my head. "It's not my field." I told him about Edith Wharton and my stalled job search.

"Is this your next project, then?"

I hadn't yet allowed myself to think of it that way. "I don't know. Maybe that was my mistake with Edith Wharton—putting all my focus on stories and texts in which someone like me could never have figured. My adviser told me outright that the more marketable option would be to go the route of ethnic lit."

"That seems like such a narrow way to think about reading anything."

"In this world reading isn't really reading anymore."

"So what are you doing here?"

I didn't answer, or couldn't, and Gregory didn't press the issue. As I looked through more letters, I thought about that fateful conversation with my adviser, how I'd worried that my decision to stick with Wharton for my dissertation might seem like identity avoidance. Which maybe it was. I used to figure that white people who studied nonwhite people had to have some kind of subconscious fetishizing or cultural appropriation going on. But now that I'd actually barged in on a real person's life without his permission, there was no denying that appropriation went around the other way too.

After several minutes of silence, Gregory said, "All this speculation. Chance occurrence, what gets remembered, and by whom. This is how history happens, right? Like Rose going to Vietnam and meeting your grandfather, if that's what happened. She probably wasn't planning to give that pin away, or leave it behind."

"Do you want to see it?" I asked.

I retrieved my tote bag from the sofa and unswaddled the gold pin from its paper towel. Gregory held it up to the waning light as I had. He took out his phone and found that passage from *These Happy Golden Years*. *"A little house,"* he read out loud, *"and before it along the bar lay a tiny lake, and a spray of grasses and leaves.* Well, there is a house etched here. And these look like grasses and leaves. I don't see a lake, but maybe that got worn off."

"I suppose there were a lot of these kinds of pins made," I said.

"Probably."

Echoing Alex, I said, "Even if it's real, it doesn't mean anything else is."

"That's true. And we might never find out." He sounded, to me, bizarrely okay with that.

"Doesn't it bother you, not to be able to know?"

"The truth is what I already do know," Gregory answered. "This is just background, context."

"The same way history and gossip are, at some level, the same thing?"

"Your words." He handed the pin back to me. As I was opening my bag, he said, "Hey, is that the book where you found the letter? Can I take a look at it?"

I pulled out the stolen copy of *Free Land*. "Help yourself," I said.

Gregory studied the spine and binding and deckling before slowly opening it. He turned a few pages and said, "You haven't looked through this?"

"No. Why?"

Gently he flipped through the chapters. Then he stopped and said, "Here."

He angled the book so I could see the penciled words on the last page of a chapter. A few lines of cursive handwriting that, after my days at the Hoover Library, had come to seem familiar to me.

"There are more," Gregory said. And then, hesitating, he gave the book back to me.

We went page by page. Rose had written only a few notes—a compilation of fragments, dashes of thought, and one longer passage. None were dated. By the glow of lamplight in Gregory's living room, we read them out loud.

The last of the evening light is on the walls.

One pushes for gain and after the gain braces for the reversal. The tide recedes.

Oh yes, if one could be so cavalier!

Here, it is almost as far west as a body can go. This close to the Pacific! This close to such vastness! See there—the Golden Gate opening. It is the end of the rails and the end of the story.

When did she become this old woman, hardened, face darkened?

What else was she to do? How could she not want to know the resolution? Who decides? When does her story become my story?

Never mind the body. The mind is the tyrant.

If someone notices her at all, the glance is brief. He keeps on walking, with no further thoughts given to the woman in the curled-back straw hat, stock-still in front of the gray-shingled house she has come to see.

If she waits long enough she will see a man in the window. He speaks to someone. His wife. Into view come two children, girls, who reach for their mother.

The portrait of a family is complete, and in kind, the garden flourishes with mid-summer blooms. No one here needs to be a wanderer or scavenger.

The afternoon is ending.

The girls tumble into the yard, the ribbons on their dresses are like flags.

In the window, the man and the woman watch their children. What do they see?

The old woman, being old, goes without notice. The fact of her age must be admitted, if nowhere else but beneath her own hands. Years and years and finally this: silence, survival, sunlight, all conspiring, and a little gray house in the West.

THIRTEEN

As Gregory drove us back to San Francisco in his mother's electric-blue Subaru, I called Amy. She was relieved to hear from me at first—she had left a bunch of voice mails and texts on my phone—but when I told her where I was, she said, "You're with *him*?" so loudly I knew Gregory had heard her. We agreed to talk when I got back to her apartment, and I could picture her, wineglass in hand, legs drawn up on the turquoise midcentury sofa I had so admired in her living room. A grown-up life.

Gregory and I didn't speak much. Back at his mother's house we'd taken pictures of each inscription in *Free Land*, and I'd said that it was proof that Rose had wanted to know what happened to Albert.

"It's still third-person," he reminded me. "It's still oblique. There's no way to know if this was about her or someone else."

"Rose knew better than to use the first-person," I argued.

"She wanted to make sure that no one would know absolutely." I wanted to see it as a kind of promise, a family secret coded and hidden, but still written—in order to be found.

Gregory hadn't asked to keep the book or the letter from his great-grandmother and I didn't offer. I kept changing my mind, thinking I should. But I couldn't let go of those pages yet, just as I couldn't let go of the possibility that maybe Rose had gone to that house in Corte Madera before her trip to Vietnam in 1965. What if the sight of my mother, a girl peeking out from the kitchen at the lucky Café 88, had reminded Rose of Gregory's mother—a girl who might have been her own grandchild? What if this was the reason she had spent so much time talking with Ong Hai?

It was past eight by the time Gregory and I crossed the Golden Gate Bridge. The streets dizzied me with their profusion of signs and painted grid lines sloping up and down those vertiginous hills.

When we stopped in front of Amy's building, it suddenly felt like we were at the end of the date, not knowing what to do next. A kiss, a call-you-later, a have-a-nice-life?

I was glad when Gregory reached for my hand. "If you end up writing something about all this, will you let me know?"

"If I ever do, of course. Thank you," I said. "Have I said that yet? You've been incredibly generous."

"I should be thanking you too."

"Do you believe all of this? You believe Rose is your great-grandmother?"

"I may never know what to think. But one way or another, whether it *was* Rose or Rose imagining someone else standing outside that house—my family history has become more interesting. I wish my mother could know all this." He let go of my hand, his voice turning light. "I guess I'll need to read those *Little House on the Prairie* books, just in case."

"And Rose's books."

"Maybe I'll even go check out those archives in Iowa."

"If you do, tell me." Though as I said it, I realized I didn't exactly know where I was going to be in the future. Would I even be in Chicago or the Midwest?

I opened the car door and Gregory held out his hand again. "Good luck." The gesture and words seemed kind of silly after everything we'd done, but I took his hand again anyway. I wanted to ask if he was thinking what I was—how much and how little connected us, after all. Perhaps that was why we had felt compelled to touch each other, looking for a way to acknowledge how strangely our stories had intersected.

How else did any family tree happen, if not for the mistakes and coincidences that brought people together? Just as it happened to be that Laura Ingalls's parents concluded their homesteading search in De Smet, South Dakota, where the nearest major city was Minneapolis, some 260 miles away, so it happened to be that Almanzo Wilder, working his way west, had ended up in that same remote town. Their daughter, Rose Wilder, that solitary figure—or so she seemed to me now, with ribbon-trimmed hats and long skirts—might have shaped my family's trajectory in America. So might have Gregory's mother, bounding out of that little gray house while an old woman stood hidden, watching. Rose, or whoever she was, becoming a contradictory apparition, a remainder, a reminder.

Amy was waiting just as I had pictured her. She turned off the TV as I came in, and set her drink on the glass coffee table. I could tell that she was struggling between being upset and being understanding.

"I'm sorry," I said right away.

"I don't get it."

I kept apologizing, trying to explain that, after arguing with Sam at the coffee shop and then at the house in Pacific Heights the day before, I'd gone on an impulse to the library to see Gregory. I hadn't expected even to say anything to him, and then I hadn't expected him to call me. "We were just carried along," I said. "Caught up in the momentum." Not that I admitted just how much.

Amy sighed. "You have no idea what my job is like. It's so the opposite of exciting. So the opposite of mysterious. There's no discovery, Lee. I was looking forward to this."

"I know. I feel awful." And I did. It was a breach in the very foundation of our friendship. And because of that, I couldn't bring myself to tell her all that had happened between Gregory and me. It seemed shameful, too uncomfortable to joke about, though Amy might have joked, *Little Whore on the Prairie. Gives new meaning to the phrase westward ho.*

So I described, instead, how Gregory and I had turned every page of *Free Land* looking for Rose's scribbles, how he had looked out the living room window as if he could pierce the early evening light and see Rose looking back at him through the arbor that had once framed the walk to the front door.

"It gives me the chills, and I wasn't even there," Amy said. She still firmly believed that Rose was Albert Stellenson's mother. "Think of her standing outside that house, waiting to get a glimpse of the child she'd given up and who'd grown up into someone she couldn't recognize. What if Rose hadn't left that pin in Saigon? What if your mother hadn't brought it to the U.S.?"

I looked at her. "Are you forgiving me, then?"

She thought this over for a second. Taking another sip from her glass, she said, "There's nothing to forgive, Lee. This is your story."

But I didn't know if that could be true. What was mine to tell? How would I tell it, if I ever did? Were all stories up for grabs?

"We've hardly even talked about what you're going to do this fall," Amy said, widening the conversation. I was grateful for that. "You can't keep staying with your mom."

"I know."

"Move here," she said again. "Just stay in that second bedroom. It would be so much fun. You could probably pick up some adjunct teaching, right? Or do something else entirely. Who says you have to stay in academia?"

"Stop being such a good friend," I said. "Besides, what if this is all I know?"

Amy understood that. Sometimes she wondered what she'd missed, she said, stepping off the academic medical track, and sometimes she thought it the best decision she'd made. She knew as well as I did that if I quit now I might not ever get a way back in.

"I do like how faraway this place feels," I said. "You know— *California*, italicized. The dream and all that. I can see why people feel like they can start over here."

"That's right. Time to join the gold rush, girl."

We got up from the sofa and headed to the kitchen. As ever, it provided for us. Leftovers, cheeses, pastries, a found bottle of blanc de blancs. As with all of the meaningful relationships spun throughout the *Little House* books, food drew us back together, gave us a way to keep talking. *West Coast living*, Amy insisted again. Like Rose; like my brother. *This is the place to be.*

But first, I had to go home.

FOURTEEN

Walking through O'Hare, I kept my tote bag close to my side. I glanced at my phone—no messages from anyone. For a moment, in the midst of airport suspension, I could almost pretend that I was just an anonymous traveler, nearly outside my own self, unknown, with no obligations at all. The feeling lasted about ten seconds. The stoic *Welcome to Chicago* sign, with the mayor's name underneath it, stirred up in me a mix of homesickness, pride, bone-tiredness—that letdown of an adventure ended.

For once, I didn't mind how long it took to get from the terminal to the tram to the economy lot where I'd parked. I lengthened the drive back to Franklin, taking alternate turns through neighborhoods of split-level houses. The strange language of the rapid traffic reports on WBEZ—*Lake Cook to the junction, 35; 30 Ike Thorndale*—made me feel a part of the city yet also apart from it, in my own little capsule, unworried about the time it would take to get from one intersection to another.

It was evening, past dinnertime, when I arrived at the house on Durango. I knew I'd be walking in to two televisions playing in different rooms. No way to slip past my mother. Even as I pulled up to the curb I could sense she was looking at me. She liked to keep a close watch on all the cars on our street, liked to know who was coming and going. She was suspicious of new vehicles that appeared overnight, suspicious of neighbors who had visitors.

I hadn't spoken with my mother since the night—had it been less than two weeks ago?—when she had talked about buying a house for Sam. In college, I'd had friends whose mothers called them every day, sometimes more, and sent them e-mails and texts. Their conversations were sweetly casual. *Are you going out tonight? I had sushi for dinner, how about you?* My mother was not that kind of mother and I was not that kind of daughter. Whenever she called, she had a specific purpose in mind. *What day are you driving back here for Christmas? Exactly what time?* She would call repeatedly until I gave her a set answer, and then she would call to remind me. Our conversations were so brief that my roommates sometimes thought I was talking to a telemarketer. It was my mother's tone of voice that managed to unnerve me, keep me in line. That constant undercurrent of disapproval, as though she were always catching me in the middle of getting in trouble.

All the while, of course, she had her own secret life.

After seeing Sam in San Francisco, scenarios had sprung up in my mind: my mother and Hieu carrying on an affair; my mother and Hieu in love. My mother deciding between two men, two loves. Then, my father's death making the decision for her: she would have neither. But maybe she couldn't let go of Hieu, yoked as they were by guilt and blame.

I didn't see my mother as extortionist—tough as she could be, I didn't want to see her that way. I could see Hieu, though, giving her money in the way he'd given packs of gum and Hot Wheels to me and Sam. Unrefusable. They had the pride of old-school Vietnamese, and if this secret arrangement had been going on for twenty years, then it might continue forever.

Unless Sam and I had changed that.

When I stepped into the living room my mother was, as expected, knitting and watching television. She didn't lift her eyes to me. I had the old urge to flee to my room but decided to get things over with: I sat down.

At the next commercial break my mother said, "I guess you think you go wherever you like, here and there."

"I had to do some research."

"Research," she said mockingly. "Only in special libraries. You spend so much time on things that are long ago. Then you call it work."

"Actually it is work," I began tensing up. "But I don't want to talk about that."

243

"You think you can do anything you want?" she said again. "Go here and there, change the menu and change the sign? But guess what—I'm the one who has the say." She was going to stand her ground again, make sure I knew my place.

Ong Hai, no doubt hearing this exchange, came into the living room.

"You're back," he said. "Where'd you end up going?"

He'd known, of course, that I'd lied to him about staying with a school friend in Iowa. "San Francisco."

"No joking? What's going on there?"

"First there was some research," I said. We were talking over the volume of the sitcom my mother was watching, or pretending to. "And I saw Sam."

My mother's knitting needles slowed and she examined my face for a moment, maybe wondering if I was telling the truth.

"He's definitely living there," I continued.

She let out a puff of annoyance. "No, he's not."

"Then why did I see the house he's staying in?"

Gently Ong Hai retrieved the remote control and turned down the volume.

"He's working for some rich friend of his."

"What kind of work?" Ong Hai asked.

"Something to do with medical sales," I hedged. Just as Sam had known I would.

My mother didn't say anything. Ong Hai's forehead was wrinkled with worry.

"It's true," I said, more to her than to him. I thought about telling her that I'd even held out the false promise of money and he hadn't fallen for it. "He's living in a house, a beautiful house, up on a hill. He has no plans to come back."

It was time to tell my mother and grandfather about the gold pin. They had a right to know, even if it was all or partly based on conjecture.

"What I was researching—" I started to say, but at the sound of *research* my mother cut me off, even stopping her knitting to hold up one hand.

"It's enough," she said.

"You might want to know what this is about."

"Be quiet."

Ong Hai spoke over her. "Tell me about it, Lee."

From my book bag I pulled out the wad of paper towel that held Rose's pin. One of the pieces floated to the floor.

"You'll clean that up," she said.

"Here," I said, and handed the pin to my mother.

From her look of surprise I guessed that she had already discovered the theft of the rest of her jewelry.

"It was Sam," I said quickly, in case she was going to start accusing me. "Except he left this behind in my room."

Then I brought out the old photograph I'd swiped from Rose's archives. I gave that to Ong Hai.

He regarded it, squinting at the man that nearly fifty years and thousands of miles had obscured. He said, "Who is this?"

"Don't you know?" The tension rose in my blood—how much I wanted him to know.

"Is that Saigon?"

My mother held out her hand to take it. "Too blurry," she said.

"Is it you?" I finally asked Ong Hai.

"No," my mother said, just as Ong Hai said, "It is!" He was leaning over my mother's shoulder to study the image again. "Maybe. Maybe it is! Where did you get this?"

"That woman in Saigon, all those years ago in 1965. I think her name was Rose Wilder Lane."

Even my mother seemed interested in this. I tried to explain the web search, the "August in Vietnam" article Rose had published in *Woman's Day*, the papers at the Hoover Library. I had never held my mother's attention this long, not with any matter of literature or research, and I found myself talking too fast, stumbling over my words.

"This picture was there and they let you borrow it?" Ong Hai asked.

Instead of answering directly I asked, "Do you remember Rose taking a picture of you?"

"No," Ong Hai admitted. "But she had a camera. I know that."

"There's more," I said. From my room I retrieved my old girlhood copy of *These Happy Golden Years*. Ong Hai muted the television and I read aloud the passage that described Almanzo giving the pin to Laura as a Christmas gift—the same passage I'd read to him and my mother and brother in the car nearly twenty years earlier.

But even as I focused on the page, I could feel the moment slipping from my grasp. My mother looked down at the pin in her lap but didn't react. My grandfather listened, sitting on the arm of the sofa, but didn't exclaim or jump up as I had somehow expected he would this time around.

"Don't you see?" I said. "It all adds up. Rose in Vietnam. The photo. And this book describes the pin. Laura Ingalls Wilder was Rose's mother."

"How can it be?" Ong Hai asked. "Isn't that book just a story?"

"It's a TV show," my mother said.

"The books are based on their real lives and Rose helped write them."

My mother regarded the pin again, safe in her hand. She ran one index finger over the little house that had been engraved into the gold. "I remember she was wearing the pin one day. She was so big and white and the pin looked funny on her. I never forget that—how strange she is, showing up in the middle of Saigon."

"She did like to talk. Asked me so many questions about Vietnam," Ong Hai said.

"Because she was writing an article about it," I said.

He took the pin from my mother, held it out for his far-sighted eyes. "What does it mean, Lee?"

"It means we know who she is now. We know the history of that pin."

"Maybe," my mother said. She picked up her knitting again. She seemed to be making a cable-knit baby sweater, perhaps for a friend's grandchild.

The *Little House* books were American classics, I told them. I wanted to explain that they represented an idealized, old-fashioned landscape of pioneering, making do, and scraping by, no matter how forced the veneer of family life and good cheer. I wanted to tell them that my own concept of American history had been unknowingly shaped just by reading those books, and that they had rooted in me a paradox of pride and resentment—a desire to be included in the American story and a knowledge of the limits of such inclusion. Like the Chinese workers who helped build the transcontinental railroad and yet were left out of pictures and edged out of history.

"All these years," I said, "haven't you wondered who she really was?"

"Didn't think she was anything else," my mother answered.

Ong Hai said, "I don't know if I ever thought about it that way. I didn't know there was a big story. It is very interesting," he added.

"This is huge. This is major. Nobody knows this stuff." My voice was rising.

"So she was the daughter of a famous American lady," Ong Hai said, but it was like he was trying to make me feel better.

Frustrated, I said, "I guess I just thought you guys might want to know this part of your history."

"What are you talking about?" my mother said. She drew forth a length of yarn from its cylindrical knot. "We already knew everything that matters. You should leave that lady alone."

In my mind, Rose and Laura were still arguing with each other, building the *Little House*. They needed each other, called to each other, and drove each other mad. In my mind, Rose was choosing between two lives. But here in Franklin, in the living room with my mother and grandfather, the three of us dumb-mouthed in front of the television, the past had never been mine to challenge.

My mother spoke again. "Did you tell Sam about buying a house here?"

It felt like it took all my energy to reply, "He doesn't care about any of that."

"You didn't tell him," she accused me. "You're supposed to tell him the right way."

I stood up. "I'll send him a long e-mail. Is that what you want to hear? Right now, I'm going to go to sleep."

Ong Hai got up too and headed down the hallway with

me. At my door he handed back the photo that Rose Wilder had snapped in Saigon.

"I think it could be me," he said, still sounding like he was trying to cheer me up.

"But is that what Café 88 looked like, the street?"

"Sure, it did look like that," he agreed, though it was probably true that it could have been one of hundreds of streets in the city.

"I want to figure this out."

"I know you do." He patted my shoulder and said, "Until then, it's good to have you back here."

Sometime in the night I woke up. A sound—a garage door grating open. I peeked through the blinds and saw the husband of the couple who lived across the street. The guy was dragging out a lawn chair from around their Buick. He set it at the fender and sat down, clasping his hands together, sticking his feet out like it was just another leisurely afternoon. I couldn't read his expression.

I couldn't go back to sleep knowing he was sitting out there. I kept checking on him. I'd hardly ever talked to him and his wife but I knew that Ong Hai occasionally brought them some Vietnamese food and they in return had given him some potted plants. When their grandchildren visited in the summer, they brought out an inflatable pool and a Slip 'N Slide.

It was past one in the morning. I'd fallen asleep with everything from the past weeks—Rocky Ridge, Gregory Stellenson—vaporizing into mere circumstance. I hadn't mentioned those names to my mother and grandfather and I knew then that I probably never would.

Now, alone again, stilled again, I went back to my books and notes. I opened my computer. I thought about e-mailing Gregory but wasn't sure what to say. Would he have to remain my secret? Would we just be social media friends, peeking at each other's photos? Rose would have been a master of the online persona, wielding it as it was meant to be, a way to shape and project a voice. I wondered if Gregory was going to tell anyone what had happened to him. *This girl walked into the library and told me I was related to Laura Ingalls Wilder.*

No matter what Amy said, I knew that the story I'd tracked down was only slightly, peripherally, mine. It was Gregory's, possibly; it was Rose's, possibly. Me, I was a bystander. A finder. Was this to be the rest of my future, trailing other people's lives, whether they were real or fiction, then turning them inside out, looking for critical nodes to explore and exploit? Was I always going to be the go-between, the one translating one text to another, one person to another, conveying interpretation?

Another window showed a new e-mail from Alex, with a series of question marks in the subject line. Alex, who had read all the *Little House* books. Who had driven with me to Missouri, had kept watch while I sneaked into the storage room at Rocky Ridge; who had been my accomplice. We'd made no promises to each other, but I knew I couldn't keep ignoring his texts. Hey, I started to type in reply, then, hating the look of it, hit delete.

I closed all the windows on the computer. I checked on the old man in the garage; he was still sitting in the same position. I wondered if he had fallen asleep.

I stared at the blank screen for a minute before clicking on the Word document that held my dissertation. The last time I'd worked on it, over two months before, I'd stopped in mid-sentence while revising one of my chapters on *The Age of Innocence*. I'd first read that book in ninth grade, captivated by the wealth porn—opulent Gilded New York, strict social structures, hothouse blooms and Roman punch, and all the longing that had to be repressed. It was hard to recall what it was like to read a book just for fun, to become absorbed in the world of it. That was probably why, I realized, I had returned to the *Little House*, wanting escape from the escape of Edith Wharton—as if the literature of childhood wouldn't be so fettered with critical complications.

My hands were on the keyboard, each index finger resting on the little raised dashes that signified the placement of the *f* and *j* keys, or what my computer teacher in high school had called *home*. On the screen, I read a sentence I had started about Ellen Olenska sitting in the Public Garden in Boston, a portrait of her being painted without her knowledge. I pressed command-N: new window. New blankness. I closed my eyes for a moment, and started writing.

The sunlight got me out of bed by seven, though I'd collapsed there only a couple of hours before. For the first time in years I had sat at my computer until I'd nearly fallen asleep, the words blurring on the screen. The achiness I felt seemed almost akin to accomplishment. Outside, the old man across the street was gone, the garage closed.

I was surprised to see Ong Hai at the dining table. He had his box of cereal bars in front of him again, and as I made some tea he unwrapped a bar for me.

"Can she handle the morning rush on her own?" I asked.

"Ah, well. People won't get coffee as fast."

"She's going to be mad."

"She's mad at me, that's okay. I wish *you* and your ma don't fight so much. It's not good. Not healthy for anyone. You have to try and get along better, Lee." He'd said this so many times before, and I'd always agreed and said that I would. Usually I meant it, and sometimes I did make an effort; my mother, I sometimes thought, did too. But it never lasted.

"I tried just last night," I pointed out. "I was trying."

"Okay," Ong Hai said. "But what about Sam? That's what she's thinking about all the time. She doesn't have to worry about you."

"It's always Sam, even though he took her jewelry and even though he's staying in California. I don't know what you guys expect me to do."

I considered telling him the truth—the booming marijuana business, even what Sam had said about Hieu and our mother. Over the years Ong Hai and I had been able to talk about most everything from dinner plans to Oscar nominations to the extinction of the dinosaurs. Prepping meals together, we had agreed about Sam's irresponsibility and my mother's irascibility; we had complained about Chicago weather; we had brainstormed ways to pretty up, on a budget, the restaurants he and my mother ran. I had always thought we were on the same side.

But I had come to understand, more now, the burden that came with knowing what could change someone else's life. No matter what he said, I *had* altered Gregory's perception of his family and his family's past—and perhaps, as an extension, altered what he thought of himself. With Sam, knowing his whereabouts, his plans, and his role as the son who wasn't going to be returning anytime soon, made me not just the same old messenger but the decision maker. It would have been easier if Sam had sworn me to secrecy. But he didn't really care.

He wasn't going to be around to see our mother's reaction. I was the one who had to decide what she and Ong Hai should, or had a right to, know.

Ong Hai said, "I just mean you have to give her some understanding. She's very upset about Sam. You know, I wonder too why things go wrong. Your ma, I think she doesn't know who to blame."

"For what's happened with Sam?"

"For what happened to your ba."

He so rarely mentioned my father's death that I was taken aback. "She blames herself, and that's why she's always spoiled Sam—I get it. But I lost ba too. We all did."

"You're the daughter, so it's different."

"It shouldn't be like that."

"But it is. Anyway, I want to tell you something else. While you were gone your ma made some decisions," Ong Hai revealed. "She met with Hieu about some, what do you call it—financing."

He dropped Hieu's name as though the guy had always been around, as if Ong Hai himself hadn't fallen silent often enough, refusing to say anything about him.

"Hieu," I repeated. "We're talking about Hieu now."

My grandfather didn't blink at that. "Here's a possible fix," he said. Hieu had offered to invest money in the Lotus Leaf as a business partner. He would be part owner but my mother and Ong Hai would continue to run the place as usual.

"Where'd he get all this money?"

"Real estate." It turned out that Hieu had not only done well in the Florida house-flipping market, he had gotten out before it all went to crap. "Even before that, he made money here too. He's more than a millionaire by now."

"And what about the money he's been giving Mom over the years?"

"Does it really bother you, Lee? This is your ma's business. You know that. Did you ask her?"

I laughed at that. "Sam is so angry about it. He still wants the money. Is it true there were college accounts set up for us?"

"I don't know that. But you went to college. You had good scholarships. You didn't need any college accounts."

I had said as much to myself, told myself that I had no claim to Hieu's money anyway.

"You're more independent," Ong Hai said. "And now it's all in the past. Right?" When I didn't acquiesce, he went on, "Hieu's a good man. He would be a good business partner."

"So this is how everything is going to be," I said. "The whole past remade."

"You know how your ma is. She needs things her way— her terms." Ong Hai rose from the table and tucked another cereal bar into his shirt pocket. "You coming over to the café soon?"

I had no desire to, but at my hesitation he said, "Come on and help, okay?"

So then I couldn't say no. When I agreed to be there in time for lunch he smiled and gave a little salute as he headed out the door.

Alone again, I stood in the kitchen and drank another cup of tea. Beneath my bare feet the worn linoleum floor seemed gritty and I thought about sweeping it. I noticed the dishes sitting in the sink and a few stray apple peels on the counter. The whole house, in fact, looked neglected. My mother and Ong Hai might not have had much interest in home décor but they'd always insisted on keeping our rooms wiped and clean. They'd seen enough restaurant vermin to make sure of that. Once, when Sam and I were kids, our mother had brought home a pair of dead cockroaches, wrapped in napkins, and left them on our beds. I had screamed and screamed, and my mother, not telling me that the roach was dead, forced me to pick it up and flush it down the toilet. *See what happens when you slob everywhere*, she'd said. She talked about how clever the cockroaches were, how they could live in my pillowcase and crawl over me in the night, and how they could lay eggs under my bed and climb up through drains in the sink. Every now and then the memory would cause me to throw my sheets back and check every wrinkle. Sometimes I felt phantom critters skittering across the bed or heard them whispering up the walls. When I once mentioned this to my mother she had laughed, proud to know that she had taught me well.

In spite of this, and the fear of what a fallen crumb could

invite, I brought a cereal bar to my room to read what I'd started the night before. It was a relief to look at the screen and feel the need to rearrange things, to shape the sentences into something better. I glanced at the clock. I had two hours, maybe two and a half, all to myself.

FIFTEEN

A week later, I saw Hieu.

It was midmorning at the Lotus Leaf, my mother and Ong Hai working on summer rolls and pho, me back at the cash register. I wasn't very good at it—I usually forgot to smile and ask people how they were doing—but my mother believed that whoever had the best English was obligated to deal with customers.

We were in that lull before the lunch-seekers arrived, so I was staring out the windows when a silver Mercedes convertible rolled into the parking lot and stopped in front of the café. The man behind the wheel was tall for an Asian guy, and starting to go bald. I didn't recognize him exactly, but when he walked into the café I knew it had to be Hieu. Chu Hieu, my mother's benefactor and, perhaps, something more. I hadn't seen him since my father's funeral.

"Hello, Lee," he said. With his spread-collared shirt and

cordovan shoes he was a lifetime away from the laughing young man in threadbare Hanes tees and flip-flops splitting a six-pack of Miller with my father. He spoke in Vietnamese, "Remember me?"

I nodded. "I didn't know you lived around here."

I could feel my mother listening from the kitchen.

"I live in Florida half the time," he said, following my cue and switching to English. "I hear you're a big success in school. PhD and everything. Your family is very proud."

"How do you know?" I asked. My words surprised me, and him too.

"Your ma," he said simply, though of course I already knew the answer.

She appeared then. Her face and voice were unreadable as she offered him some tea. I had forgotten to ask if he wanted to order anything. Hieu declined but my mother told me to prepare a pot of jasmine tea anyway. They went outside and sat down at one of the rickety-looking metal tables Ong Hai had set out on the sidewalk in front of the parking lot.

I brought them a teapot with two ceramic cups, along with a plate of miniature red-bean pastries. Hieu thanked me as I set down the tray. Back at the cash register, I watched as they resumed talking, leaving the food untouched.

A customer came in then, looking for a chai latte and a few summer rolls to go. As I finished pulling together the order, I glanced at my mother and Hieu again and saw him start to put his hand on hers. She drew quickly away. The customer left with her summer rolls and I pretended to clean up the pastry display.

At last they stood. My mother was picking up the tray and bringing it into the kitchen before Hieu had even gotten into his Mercedes. He gave me a slight wave as he backed out, and I wondered: Did he wear a ring? Was he married or had he been? Twenty years ago Hieu had lived in an apartment that had a pool table in the living room instead of furniture. On weekends and at holidays he brought over bags of gummy candy, boxes of Whitman Samplers, tubs of ice cream, and new games for the Nintendo he'd given me and Sam. He and my father laughed and joked for hours, late into the nights, drinking beer and then whiskey, playing card games and smoking cigarettes.

My mother chose that day not to run errands or go out for more supplies. We ended up practically driving home together, Ong Hai having gone ahead to get takeout for dinner. Back at the house, neither of us spoke as we stepped around each other in the kitchen, she steeping tea and washing dishes while I searched the refrigerator for a piece of fruit to snack on. She had changed into flowy pants and a T-shirt—she always changed the minute she got home—and they made her look so much younger, like one of those undergrads who go to class in pajamas. At the same time, she still managed to employ the full power of her don't-approach-me stance, the one that kept almost everyone, from store clerks to panhandlers, at bay. It had always worked on me too, and it dawned on me that maybe she counted on that.

I understood—and it had taken me the whole day to figure it out—that Hieu's visit to the café had been no coincidence. It would have been arranged by my mother. It would have been at the call of my mother. In her own way, she was letting me know what I'd been too afraid to ask.

I shouldn't have been so nervous, then, to ask her why Hieu was at the café, but I couldn't even look at her when I spoke the question.

She rinsed dishes and set them in the drainer. "Eh," she said dismissively. "Business."

"What about the money?" I dared to say. "The college accounts. Did all of that go into the Lotus Leaf?"

"You went to college," she said indignantly.

"I could have used some help. I could have gone to a different school."

"That's stupid."

"It's not fair."

"Why do you think anything belongs to you?" My mother was scrubbing at the calcium deposits around the faucet. "The Lotus Leaf is the whole family's."

For once her voice didn't rise into the sharp tones of anger, and the effect it had on me was silence. Foolish, to think I'd ever had a claim. That was how she won again, leaving me to weigh my next attack, locate the next angle.

Then Ong Hai opened the kitchen door, bringing in an early summer gust and the sound of someone starting to mow a lawn down the street. He held out a paper bag. "Tacos for dinner."

This seemed to annoy my mother more than my questions about Hieu. "What happened to the Thai food?"

"There's this new Mexican place next to the Thai place. Looks good, so why not try it?"

I brought the bag of tacos, burritos, chips, and guacamole to the table while Ong Hai removed his shoes, washed his hands, and grabbed a couple of beers. My mother started toward the living room but Ong Hai called her back. "Tran, oi. Come sit down."

To my surprise, she did. Reluctantly she refreshed her cup of tea. I set out plates and forks and Ong Hai brought out the Sriracha.

So the three of us sat down together for dinner.

I was on my second carnitas taco, thinking of ways to bring up the subject of Hieu again, when Ong Hai did it for me. "Hieu's buying the café?" he asked outright, as casually as if he were asking about a new show on TV.

"Maybe," was all my mother said.

I spoke up. "There are three new banh mi places in the city. It's having a moment."

My mother, who had only picked at the chips and guacamole, stood up. I thought she was going to strike down the idea, but she said, "Is it perfect? When it's perfect, we can try it."

She rinsed out her teacup, set it near the sink, and headed to the living room.

"You see?" Ong Hai said to me. "There's always progress. Tiny bit by tiny bit."

I waited until I heard the sound of the television before asking him if Hieu was married, if he had a family.

He shook his head. "Never married."

"Why hasn't he been around before now?"

"Out of respect," Ong Hai said quietly.

But I wasn't sure now what that meant. Had my grandfather known all along about my mother and Hieu, about whatever relationship or agreement they'd had? Had he too kept it carefully hidden from Sam and me?

"Hey," he said, switching topics, "they're showing that *Bourne Ultimatum* movie again."

Ong Hai and I—and Sam, when we were all together—had often watched action movies, especially repeats, because then we could discuss the various plot points and logistical gaps. We were fascinated by the scope of such films, and marveled at how much money and energy and bodily effort went into their production. How money could make the make-believe real. Even though Ong Hai owned plenty of DVDs, he preferred watching movies when they appeared on TV, commercials and all, because they seemed, that way, like an unexpected gift.

Usually I looked forward to such moments, retreating to a

cavern of someone else's tumult and adventure. This time, I told Ong Hai that I needed to get back to work.

"Your research?" he asked.

"I really think it could be you in that photograph."

"You want it to be so," he said, and I nodded. "Well, it could be. No doubt it maybe could be."

"How many times did you tell us that story about meeting Rose and how she spent time in your café?"

Ong Hai smiled in recollection. "You know what word fits for her? Generous. Not too many people around like her back then. Not American ladies either."

"That's where it all began, right? Well, here's another part of the story."

"True, maybe that's true. But whose story?"

I felt the unintended sharpness of that question. "Yeah," I said. "No wonder Mom thinks I need to leave it all alone."

"Your ma doesn't like those kinds of questions because she thinks it makes trouble."

"That's only because she wants to be in control."

"The person who controls the story is the person in control," Ong Hai said. He meant it as a joke, I think, but it was more real to me than he could have known.

His movie was starting, so Ong Hai went to watch and I went to my desk. In my e-mail inbox there was a new message, from a name I didn't recognize. It was a professor at one of the schools where I'd applied for a postdoc. The e-mail said that the recipient of the fellowship had withdrawn in order to accept a tenure-track teaching job, and that I was the runner-up: it was a one-year fellowship and it was mine if I wanted it. I needed to let them know within the week, since fall semester would be starting in less than two months.

The school was near Philadelphia, on a train line that Alex had called the Eastern Corridor, a term I'd often heard and kind of loved, picturing old-fashioned passenger cars racing through neatly structured halls. Something cozy, close, and dependable; something out of Cheever, waiting on a platform for a train ride home.

I had never lived anywhere beyond the Midwest and barely remembered applying for the postdoc. I didn't know anyone who lived around Philadelphia. Still, I didn't hesitate to answer the e-mail immediately. *Thank you*, I typed. *I accept.* I thought about it for a second, then backspaced. *I happily accept.*

SIXTEEN

I didn't tell my mother and Ong Hai about the fellowship right away. I worked at the café through morning and lunch and spent the afternoons writing. My adviser, congratulating me about the postdoc, made sure to emphasize that it was a lucky strike, and she hoped that it would motivate me to get my chapters revised and articles sent. I understood: I had been granted an academic miracle, saved for a year from the slushes of adjuncting. I supposed she knew without my ever admitting it how close I had come, and how often, to walking away. I still couldn't say what the point of it all was for me, or what I was in it to achieve. All I knew was that this reprieve was a buying of time. A possibility. A whole new city.

But I couldn't exactly say *that* to my mother and Ong Hai. They had come to believe that I'd be staying at home indefinitely and the past week at the Lotus Leaf could only confirm that: I might become a decent daughter after all. I might even find myself a moneymaking Asian husband, at which point I could leave with permission, ribbons and bows taped to the getaway wedding car. By then, my mother no doubt hoped, Sam would have come to his senses and returned. After all, he knew it was the son's obligation to care for the older generation. I remembered learning this idiom from friends in college: *A daughter is a daughter all her life; a son is a son until he takes a wife.* Whoever came up with that wasn't Vietnamese.

It had been nearly two weeks since I'd returned from San Francisco and told my mother and Ong Hai about Sam, and Rose, and the pin. But it felt like I'd never said anything at all.

I had no idea what my mother, in the privacy of her thoughts, her room, her shower, planned and imagined. I could see her seizing the idea to move to San Francisco herself, or finding a way to lure Sam back with money, fulfilling the lie that I'd told and that Sam had seen right through. I wondered if she even had his new phone number, if she called him or left messages. Or perhaps she'd resolved to ride it out, figuring he would need her again one of these days.

On Saturday nights she and Ong Hai stayed up later than usual because the café opened at ten on Sundays. I waited until then to tell them about the postdoc. My mother was settling into a new Hallmark Channel movie and I asked Ong Hai to come sit with us for a while. He'd just finished another batch of pickled vegetables for the four different kinds of banh mi—chicken, pork, shrimp, and tofu—he kept practicing.

"Is this a job?" Ong Hai asked, and when I said pretty much, he said, "Well, that deserves congratulations!"

"Is it a real job?" my mother asked.

"It's only for a year. But it gives me time to find something else in the meantime."

"What kind of job only lasts for a year?"

"Philadelphia's not that far," Ong Hai said, as though it were just another suburb. "Sounds like a good opportunity."

"It is," I said.

"What if you don't get a job after that?" my mother asked.

"Then I'll keep looking, I guess. Same as everyone else."

It crossed my mind for a moment how differently this news might have gone over in another household. I had a fleeting fantasy of a family rallying around with cheers and hugs. It was the kind of life that someone like Alex might know. But it had never been my family. If the postdoc was an accomplishment— a lucky strike, a miraculous reprieve—it was also, in my mother's eyes, a sign of structure gone wrong. When I lived in Madison, it had been easy enough to drive back to Franklin, so it had been easy for my mother and Ong Hai to believe that I was just an extension away from home. Now I really was going to leave, just as Sam had done. And there was no telling when either of us would be back.

Of course I thought of Rose and Laura again, and how they too had left their homes and families, their known structures. For what? Laura, her sisters, and her parents had filled up a covered wagon and driven away from the comforts of grandparents and aunts and uncles and cousins, had floated across seasons and rivers and rattled over hundreds of miles of prairie, searching. They knew the risks: injury, death, failure, loneliness, never seeing their families again. Letters would take months if they arrived at all. And Rose had hurried away from home while still a teenager, eager for the dramas she believed only a bigger city might provide; even when she came home she never could call it her own.

"Everyone has to leave," I said, feeling like I needed, in some way, to defend myself. "You left too. You both did. And we've moved a dozen times since."

"We had no choice to leave Vietnam," my mother countered.

But Ong Hai overrode her. "We did choose," he insisted. "Maybe it didn't seem like it, but we did."

And that's where we stayed, those words, at least that night. My mother turned up the volume on the television, which was now in the midst of a movie about a city girl in stilettos finding romance in a Texas ranch town. Ong Hai headed back to the kitchen to finish the banh mi. And I returned to the blinking cursor on my computer. I was learning, more and more, to obey it. To stay in my chair and see where the words I typed would take me.

When I called Alex about the postdoc—we'd talked only once since my return from San Francisco—he asked me to come up to Iowa City. He said that every time he saw a piece of bacon he thought of salt pork and the *Little House* books and thus he thought of me. We could spend what was left of the summer writing, me revising the diss and him finishing a draft of his story collection, and meet up for evening dinners and movies. The idea was tempting: a pretend life, a pretend relationship. But soon, e-mails about meetings and readings would start, letting us know that the fall was upon us. I was moving and, next year, Alex would be too. We could only ever end up in the same place through sheer coincidence or through one of us jettisoning plans, tying one boat to the other's, and trailing along.

"You know that's how it is," I said.

"I do know." There was a pause, then, "I just don't know where this leaves us."

"Nowhere," I answered, and then, because the word sounded so harsh, "Which is where you and I have always been, right?"

"The undefined space?"

"Liminal, academics call it."

"Of course they do."

"If you're going to be in D.C. sometime, Philly isn't too far away."

"Maybe one day we'll take that dream trip to De Smet," Alex said.

I had told him the rest of the Rose Wilder story, or where it had ended so far—her notes buried in the pages of *Free Land*, the image of a woman standing outside that gray house in northern California, trying to recognize something of herself, trying to know if the people in it had ties to her. Was it really Rose? he asked, and I wished I could answer. I wasn't even sure if I could hope that it was, to wish that kind of fate, that kind of hunger, on a woman I had come to know and respect.

Of course, I never said what had happened between me and Gregory, and Alex, if he wondered, didn't ask.

In the olden days, courtship hadn't been any easier. Whether in *These Happy Golden Years* or *The Age of Innocence*, so much had had to be left unspoken. A girl could never state her feelings or be so bold as to show she even had them, not until her suitor made his intentions clear. For months, Almanzo walked Laura home from church and drove her miles in his sleigh, to and from her teaching school, and still she did not think of him as a beau. It would take many more months, and more buggy rides, and the force of habit and routine—people in the town getting used to seeing them together—to make their courtship something real. Rose, coming of age in the new 1900s, hadn't bothered waiting for marriage. She wanted great glamorous love and got it, for a while, until she saw into Gillette Lane's smile and found nothing on the other side, realizing she could do better on her own. Meanwhile, Laura and Almanzo's marriage lasted sixty-four years, until his death at the age of ninety-two. It had seen them from deep debt to royalty riches, from a two-room house to a sprawling farm. Still, late in life Almanzo was quoted in an interview as saying, "My life has been mostly disappointments."

As for me, the sad fact was that I had yet to have a great relationship, yet to feel the flurry and fury of obsessive love, and I was far from the slow calm of settling down into a domestic life. No one in my family ever spoke of such things. The very prospect of a kissing scene on TV used to prompt my mother to change the channel. In high school, I had overheard Sam talking to a couple of girls on the phone but, except for that one ill-fated prom, he made sure any romantic dealings were concealed. I'd hardly ever heard Ong Hai say anything about his wife, my grandmother. And my mother rarely mentioned my father. I had never brought a guy home to meet the family, had never even mentioned the existence of a boyfriend. My mother and Ong Hai would never have inquired about my love life, and the idea of asking them about relationships seemed laughable, impossible, and far too private. In such matters, I was always on my own too.

———

Over the next week I helped Ong Hai finalize the banh mi, adjusting the spice level down just slightly, and trying baguettes from different bakeries. A wine shop had opened a few doors down in the same strip mall that housed the Lotus Leaf, and Ong Hai was friendly with the florist shop next door, so he brought both places a sampling of banh mi as part of a trial run. They asked for more, and Ong Hai returned to the café with two free bottles of wine and a bucket of fresh ranunculus. I went ahead then and finished redesigning the take-out menu, finally ditching the Oriental-looking font for modern, cleaner lines. For the website I used the same saturated persimmon color I'd chosen for the café's new decal sign. It had arrived while I was in San Francisco, and on the day Hieu returned to the café, Ong Hai helped me take down the old sign and apply the new one.

Ong Hai had already told me what my mother never would have—that in agreeing to a business partnership, she'd conceded that focusing more on take-out sandwiches and spring rolls might be a good idea. She would not have admitted that she didn't really have a choice, that her other best option was to shut down the café and start over somewhere else. I couldn't imagine her going back to the buffet life, its grease and odors weighing down her hair, and maybe neither could she.

I was bringing in some napkin refills from the storage

cabinet when Hieu came up to the counter and handed a cream-colored envelope to my mother. She waved him toward one of the tables. Ong Hai put together a late lunch of banh mi, summer rolls, and a bowl of pho, more food than one person could eat. When I brought it all to Hieu's table he invited me to share the meal with him. I glanced back at my mother, who was rearranging the pastries in the glass case. The envelope was still on the counter and she didn't look back at me, so I sat down.

"I hear you're moving to Philadelphia," he said.

I guessed he already knew too that I was headed there that weekend to find an apartment.

He zigzagged Sriracha over the pho. "I remember you and Sam singing songs to us, over and over, until your ma got mad. I still know those words for 'Puff the Magic Dragon,' and the one that goes, 'Oh beautiful for spacious sky, and amber waves of grain.'"

"Yeah, we liked to pretend we were a famous singing duo."

"You were good kids."

"And then what happened?" I said jokingly.

Hieu smiled but said, "I always wanted children of my own."

It was uncomfortable to hear this kind of statement. It was one thing to comment on someone's weight or height—that was an Asian thing to do—but this was getting downright confessional.

I dared myself to ask, "Why didn't you?"

He gave a small, easy laugh. "No one knows why some things happen or not." He pushed the banh mi and summer rolls toward me, but I shook my head.

"It's the same with La Porte," Hieu said, his voice turning pensive. "I think about it. I wish I had never convinced your ba to move there."

I asked him what he meant. Ong Hai had always said that Hieu had followed us to La Porte, that he had relied on my father for jobs and advice.

"Oh, well, your Ong Hai—you know he tells the stories."

"So you were the one who got us to La Porte? What about after that?"

"Well, after that you went to Naperville, remember? That's where my friend Lan was."

"I don't remember. I was only six. What about all those community college classes my dad paid for?" But even as I spoke, I realized the truth. My father had never paid for any classes. How could he even have afforded any for himself?

Hieu was looking uneasy now. I could tell he was about to clam up, so I said, "It's fine. I get it. You were the one who got us to La Porte and then got us out of there too, right? And the other places?"

"Your ba—well, he didn't like to stay in one job," Hieu said. "He was all the time looking. But what difference is it? He was a good father. He was a good man."

Just then a group of hipsters walked in, so I had to get up.

Hieu said, "You're a good daughter, Lee. Don't worry—we will take care of this place."

While I waited on the hipsters, who talked among themselves about the banh mi they'd had from some food truck in New York and how amazing it was, my mother took my place at Hieu's table. I could hear them speaking softly in Vietnamese but couldn't discern any of the words. My mother had the envelope in her hand and she drew from it a piece of paper that might have been a check. No paperwork, no legal documents to designate a business deal. Of course. This was always going to be the terms of their partnership—classic, old-school, old-fashioned Viet-style. A deal made and sealed not with a handshake but with a promise of loyalty. My mother put the paper back in the envelope, folded it, and stuck it in her shirt pocket. Then she slid the plate of goi cuon summer rolls toward Hieu, telling him to eat.

That night Ong Hai opened the free bottle of prosecco from the wine shop. It had been another placid day, rare, absent of the bickering and passive-aggressive jabs that my mother and I so often exchanged, and we lingered at the table. My mother was clearly relieved to be able to keep the café going, and Ong Hai was happy that he had heard the hipsters comparing the banh mi favorably to New York.

But I had been thinking of little else but my father and Hieu and Ong Hai. Had it really always been Hieu who had taken care of us, who had found future jobs, who had moved us from place to place? All these years, had my grandfather been bending the stories about my father, shaping him into a man that his children could admire?

If Ong Hai had any sense of what had been changed for me, he didn't show it. He wanted to talk about ways to promote the Lotus Leaf through social media. "I been paying attention to the news," he said. When the café had first opened I'd created a Facebook page for it, but almost nothing had been posted there since.

"Eh, focus on the food. It's more important," my mother said.

When I looked at my grandfather he seemed lost in his plans. There were some people who seemed to wear a smile even when they weren't smiling, and he was one of those. Other people looked pissed even when they weren't, and probably that described my mother and me.

Ong Hai, I imagined saying. *What is the truth about ba?* But I knew I wasn't going to say that to him. Not at that moment—maybe not ever.

My mother picked through the mail on the table, setting aside the thick fall catalogs for gardening gear and furniture. Then her hand froze for a second, reaching for a plain envelope, and I saw why: Sam's distinctive artsy handwriting, spelling out Durango Road in Franklin, Illinois. There was no return address.

She turned it over and tore it open with her thumb. Inside, wrapped in three pieces of blank white paper, were ten one-hundred-dollar bills. That was it. No note. No apology. I had never asked how much he'd stolen from the café or how much he'd gotten for my mother's gold jewelry.

The money, its crispness, its crudeness in the way it lay there on the table, tilted the whole evening. The juice glasses we'd been using for the prosecco seemed pathetic, and the three of us sitting together, plotting the future of the café, became ridiculous, incomplete. Leave it to Sam to disrupt everything again, to make a mess and do it obliquely, to deliver a slap without a word of explanation, and to do it all without ever having to make an answer to any of us.

My mother left the money on the table. She said, "I was thinking before that I don't like that new sign. It's too orange. Lotus leaves aren't orange."

I didn't answer. She walked out of the kitchen.

I couldn't feel any anger toward her. Ong Hai and I left the money there too, soon retreating to our separate spaces.

Later, I was rewriting a paragraph when my mother came into my room. She stood in the doorway, looking around, perhaps noting the bag I'd already packed, gauging what I might be taking when I moved. It was almost midnight; usually she was asleep by then.

"Sam's phone number," she said quietly. It wasn't a question, but it was.

I picked up my phone, located his number, and wrote it down on a half sheet of notebook paper. When I handed it to my mother she folded it into a smaller square without even looking at it.

"He's happy in California," she said, another statement that doubled as a question.

"He seems to be," I said.

We regarded each other, my mother and I, and I had to wonder if I appeared to her as she appeared to me: at some measure lost, irretrievable. I could not name the last time we had deliberately hugged or even touched. I thought of Hieu trying to take her hand and my mother pulling away. She had always known the stories Ong Hai had told about my father. She had neither demurred nor agreed. Her silence had allowed the stories to perpetuate, to take the place of the actual man— whoever he was.

She reached into her pocket and pulled out the hundred-dollar bills Sam had sent. She held them out to me, saying, "Here." When I didn't move, she shook the bills a little, impatiently, and said, "Take."

I went to her and took the money. "What for?" I asked.

"You're moving soon. Probably need this."

"Okay." The bills were folded; they felt like Post-it notes in my palm. I imagined Sam collecting the money from Judson, then going back to his barely furnished room in that cantaloupe-colored Victorian. I saw him taking sheets of paper from the printer tray, wrapping them around the money, and maybe hesitating a minute, wondering if he should write something. What could he say? *I'm sorry?* That was no more likely of Sam than it was of my mother. Quickly, Sam would have put the money into an envelope and addressed it to our rental house in Illinois. Then he would have carried the envelope around for days while he remembered to get a stamp—the Liberty Bell in mid-ring—before sliding it into a corner mailbox somewhere in San Francisco.

"Thanks," I said. My mother turned to leave and, in a burst of sadness, with those bills in my hand, I said, "He's sorry, you know. That's what he's trying to say."

My mother paused her step. She said, "You don't remember what it was like. When you and Sam were kids. We worked hard—Ong Hai and I worked hard. Sometimes it wasn't enough."

She was acknowledging, perhaps for the only time, what Hieu's money had signified. When she left a moment later she closed the door.

A thousand dollars. I was grateful for the gesture, and needed the money. *Now, take this for the monetary value it's worth*, I told myself, *and nothing more*. But, critic that I was supposed to be, I knew it would haunt me for a long, long time. As an allowance I'd never before been given. As a transfer, a payback, a slight reversal of the favor my mother had always shown one child over the other, a handing down from my mother to Sam to me. I would think of it as blood money. I would think of it as my mother's offering—if not of love, exactly, then something in its general vicinity, something having to do with protecting and, equally, relenting. Since I'd told her about the postdoc she hadn't made any remarks about how all the Vietnamese kids she knew stayed at home and understood that their first priority was family. She hadn't rolled her eyes at the idea of a doctorate in literature or talked about how so-and-so's son or daughter had just opened up his or her own dentistry practice. I wouldn't have gone so far as to say she'd accepted my decisions. Maybe she had just given up fighting them. Maybe she had learned something from Sam, and didn't, after all, want to risk losing contact with both of her children. Though if it was that, then she didn't know how impossible that would have been for me—to leave as Sam had done, to escape without looking back. For that was one of my biggest problems: I looked back all the time, too much, too often. Like Rose, I would be circling my mother the rest of my life.

SEVENTEEN

In my new college town I found a studio apartment overlooking a park where kids and moms and strollers hang out by day and skateboarders clatter by night. I set up my desk so I could watch these people come and go, waiting for the first hints of autumn, and later snow, and later green, to stain the big-branched trees. I had an inflatable bed that doubled as my sofa and a blanket-covered box that worked well enough as a nightstand. From Craigslist I scored a TV for twenty bucks. Only the desk, a back-to-school special from Target, was new.

I didn't have much to unpack. Still, it took me two weeks to find Rose's gold pin. My mother had wrapped it in layers of tissue and tucked it into one of my garbage bags of clothes. Looking in the bathroom mirror, I affixed the pin to my T-shirt, trying it on for the very first time. Laura and Rose had worn it at the base of their throats, to set off the high-necked, lacy frills that were the style then. In the mirror, from any distance, the pin reminded me of something a flight attendant would have to wear. Only up close could the jewelry offer its surprise, that little lone house coming to life in just the right light, at just the right angle. I didn't know what to do with it, so I folded it back in the tissues and kept it in my desk.

Each day I walked to campus, usually to the office that came with my fellowship, sometimes to the library, where students stared at computers in the quiet of the great reading room. Some days I wrote. Some days I read about Homesteading Acts of the late 1800s. In the evenings I cooked in my little kitchen while watching eighties reruns. Whenever I was invited to gatherings with professors and grad students in my department, I went.

At the end of September I flew back to Chicago for a friend's wedding. I spent an extra night in Franklin because Ong Hai wanted to have a dinner out—a real dinner, he said, because we'd never actually celebrated my degree or my postdoc. So we went to a seafood restaurant in Downers Grove, with entrées that hovered in the thirty-dollar range. We never ate at places like that; when I graduated from Illinois and when Sam and I graduated from high school we had gone no fancier than Ong Hai's choice of P. F. Chang's. It was strange to see my grandfather in a new button-down shirt, sitting at a table with cloth on it instead of paper.

My mother was running late, held up over a disputed bill

with the guy who had come to fix one of the café's refrigerators. Ong Hai and I ordered crudo appetizers and helped ourselves to the heaping bread basket. He said he'd been wanting to try the restaurant for years. He buttered the heel end of a baguette and chewed away.

There were many moments when I could have asked him about my father and Hieu. It wouldn't have been difficult but it wouldn't have been assuring, either. If I knew Ong Hai, I knew he would answer vaguely, more or less sticking to his story, then shift the subject.

I had come to accept, if not his version, then his belief in it, or at least his insistence on that belief. I couldn't blame him for wanting me and Sam to see our father in a better light, to keep him in our minds as someone who would have done so much if only he'd had the time. In Ong Hai's version of events, the wars in Vietnam needn't be dwelled upon. In his version, his old Café 88 had been a welcome haven for neighbors and tourists alike, even a mysterious American woman who had taken a liking to him, who had left him with a part of her history.

At the moment, Ong Hai's story was about the reinvigorated Lotus Leaf. Business had improved since the banh mi, and there were almost more orders than he could handle. It was a trifecta of banh mi, pho, and summer rolls, and now a Chicago magazine wanted to include the café in a feature titled "The Best Sandwiches in Chicagoland Right Now."

"They're going to take a picture," Ong Hai said. "I wish you could be in it."

"You're the better representative," I said. I asked if Hieu was still in town. I suspected that with his backing the café might stay open regardless of how it did.

He had started to come by the café more, Ong Hai said, and stayed for lunch or tea a couple of times a week.

"That's good for her, then," I said.

"So we'll see."

What about Sam, I asked—had my mother spoken to him?

Ong Hai didn't know. There'd been no mention of Sam since that day the thousand dollars had arrived in the mail, and Ong Hai's stance, as usual, was to be patient. He was certain Sam would return, certain that anything could be mended. As for me, there'd been no communication with my brother since that morning in San Francisco. Not even a text. Some days I felt resigned about the silence—what was there to say? Other days I insisted to myself that he would have to contact me first.

When my mother arrived at the restaurant, irritated from arguing with the repair guy, she didn't look like someone whose business worries had been allayed. And if she did have a suitor at her doorstep, then she wasn't showing it: as ever, her clothes, this time faded floral blouse and corduroys, looked bound for Goodwill or retrieved from there, hard to tell which.

Sitting down, she exclaimed at the prices on the menu and

refused to get anything more than a shrimp appetizer and a glass of water. When the shrimp arrived she loudly pointed out that there were only two on the plate.

Ong Hai insisted we both try some of the miso-glazed black cod he'd ordered. She ate one forkful reluctantly, refusing to admit that it was good. But I saw her glance back at his plate.

"You coming back home for Christmas?" my mother asked.

"I guess so." I'd never had another or better place to go during the holiday break.

"Sam too," she replied, offhand. Ong Hai and I stared at her. She bit into a piece of bread and went on, "If he doesn't have to work. I talked to him yesterday."

"What did he say?" I asked.

"I just told you."

"Is he still in the pharmaceutical industry?" I couldn't resist.

"That's a big money business right there," my mother said.

"Did you tell him I moved?"

"I don't remember."

"So you talk to him now," I said.

"Well, geez, tell him to give me a call sometime too," Ong Hai said. He laughed, diverting the tension of the moment.

I let it drop. I had wanted to leave my mother in a way that wouldn't nag at me for the next few weeks and months. I didn't want to fly back to my studio apartment thinking of all the things I could have batted back to her, the rejoinders left unsaid.

I didn't want to be pressed to her will and words like that. But I should have known that I didn't have any such power to change that feeling of anticipated regret, at least not just yet.

We paid for the expensive seafood and went back home to the rental house in Franklin, and we watched television and drank more tea, and I slept again in the bedroom where I had spent much of the past summer. Later, when my mother and grandfather were asleep I got up to see my father's altar again, still decorated with extra candles from the memorial of his death in August. The only fruit in the house was a half bunch of bananas, so I set that in front of him, feeling how visibly they seemed to represent diminishment, a coming up short. What would my father have done with the rest of his days— where would we have all ended up? Would we have been together? When I closed my eyes I asked him to look out for us, if indeed he was a spirit, if indeed he could do such things. I'd been asking him some variation of that since I was six years old.

In the morning my mother left for the café before I even got up, and Ong Hai drove me to O'Hare. Then I was on a plane back to Philadelphia, looking down at the clouds and fields that separated us, stretching away like so many silences.

Since the fall semester of my postdoc was supposed to be devoted to writing, it was assumed that I would be revising parts of my dissertation and submitting them as articles to various journals, as well as doing preliminary research for my Next Project. I was an Americanist after all, my field and degree stamped and filed, and when the job market list appeared I dutifully sent out applications for two dozen different assistant professorships. I knew I didn't stand much of a chance, but figured it was better than doing nothing. *Those jobs have to go to* somebody, my adviser always said, her version of a pep talk. Amy and I still talked about living together in San Francisco and I kept that offer safe—a backup plan. Whatever happened, I wouldn't be going back to Franklin.

I might have easily driven up to the Mount, Edith Wharton's estate in Lenox, Massachusetts, a pilgrimage many of my colleagues had already made. I might have, but more and more my thoughts were turned instead to Danbury, Connecticut, four and a half hours away, where Rose Wilder had finally bought a house in 1938, at the age of fifty-one. She'd settled there, more or less, for the rest of her life, keeping it her home base through the next thirty years of traveling. By the time Laura died, in 1957, Rose had become only an infrequent visitor to Rocky Ridge. The fateful copy of *Free Land*, if indeed she'd inscribed those words on its pages when I thought she had, would have found its way into the farmhouse well after she'd stopped calling it home. Another mystery, another crux.

I made the drive to Danbury at the height of the fall colors, taking in the blaze of sugar maples and oaks as I stood outside the white colonial that had once belonged to Rose. It was

289

someone else's now, a private residence, and I didn't see any marker or sign to indicate the history held there. Most people, driving past, would not have guessed that several of the *Little House* books had been shaped, rewritten, and edited within those walls. It reminded me to send a long-overdue e-mail to Gregory, telling him I was thinking, after all, of writing about what we had discovered, even if it was half or even wholly speculation. He wrote me back, then called, talking about his family, and mine, and the Ingallses and Wilders who had brought us together. By then Gregory was well into the secondary texts. By Thanksgiving we were exchanging notes and documents, starting to collaborate on a family history that seemed to belong, in a sense, to both of us.

True to my mother's word, Sam was in Chicago when I went back for Christmas. He told me he was still bunking in Judson's house, and though he would soon be able to afford his own place, what was the rush. Like me, he stayed in Franklin only a few days. We watched movies together; we pretended we had never argued. Whatever deal he and my mother had worked out, I didn't pursue. I knew that she and Ong Hai had already forgiven him every theft and transgression. My mother would let him go to ensure that he would return. In that way, Sam had won. In another way, my mother had. While the two of them shopped the holiday sales, Ong Hai and I cooked banh xeo, spring rolls, and lemongrass beef noodles. When he told his stories about Saigon I listened, then started, finally, to ask more questions. *Did you plan on having Café 88 forever?* (Never.) *Did anyone else in our family cook?* (His mother, who could tell the quality of a dish by its scent alone.)

Later, Hieu showed up for dinner, surprising me and Sam into near-meekness, all of us working to keep the conversation on food, or celebrities, or people who had nothing to do with us.

In this way I could imagine the future washing the past, not negating it exactly, but nonetheless polishing it, wearing down the stones.

Across the street, the old man had died. The kids were moving their mother away right after the holidays.

In early spring, after a last-minute Skype interview for a visiting teaching gig at a small college in southern Colorado, I received word that the job was mine. It was another temporary reprieve, another chance. In spite of all doubts, I didn't know any other track. Gregory was the first person I told, and the second thing we talked about was the school's proximity to Independence, Kansas, and the former "Indian Territory" site of the original *Little House on the Prairie*. We made summer plans to meet there, and to travel to the Hoover Library, where Gregory could read Rose's journals, and to drive to De Smet and Mansfield and perhaps even Burr Oak, Iowa, and Walnut Grove, Minnesota, and finally Pepin, Wisconsin, where Laura Ingalls had been born in the winter of 1867.

And now it is May, the month of my father's birthday, and

291

I am packing up again. Whatever will fit in my car. The rest to sell, give away, leave at the curb.

Whenever the Ingalls family moved, Ma took extra care with her china shepherdess figurine and a decorative wooden bracket that Pa had carved for her. That these were objects of design, for pleasure rather than utility, has always stayed with me. And so I take particular care of the gold pin that I have, in whatever sense, inherited from Rose. Whichever Rose that was. Whoever she turns out to be. I take my computer full of notes and pages: my writing, whatever that will turn out to be. I retain, always, in the back of my mind, the twinges and fringes of guilt, about Alex, about Amy, about my family, and about Sam—more unfinished pages. Maybe it's my chronic, lifetime second-generation problem. Looking forward and looking back, trying to locate the just-right space in between. Always translating, and often getting the words wrong. Trying to figure out the clearest line of narrative, only to find more knots, more clouds. So far I have spent almost half of my life studying and thinking about American literature, and the landscape has seemed one of incredible, enduring, relentless longing. Everyone is always leaving each other, chasing down the next seeming opportunity—home or body. Where does it stop? Does it ever? I want to believe it all leads to something grander than the imagination, grander than the end-stop of the Pacific. Or is that it: You get to the place where you land; you are tired now; you settle. You settle. You build a home and raise a family. There are years of eating and arguing, working and waking. There are years of dying. No one knows what the last image will be. Rose might have stood in front of the Stellensons' house in her old age and wondered, guessed, ached. Or maybe she had not. Maybe she had sworn she wouldn't. Maybe she had thought, *Too late, too old, too late.*

Or maybe she, an independent woman who would die in her sleep the night before a planned trip around the world, did return to that little gray house, only instead of regretting, she simply watched, gauging a family she did not know and remembering the one she had—all long gone now. She was a sole survivor. And yet maybe she was not.

So who gets to say the secrets? Who gets to keep the stolen goods? I will load up my car with the pin, the poem, the photograph of a man who might be my grandfather, the copy of *Free Land* marked by Rose's hand. Like millions before me, I will try a new town, no doubt moving again in a year or two, on the lookout for work and for the next better place to be.

I will gather my belongings. I will worry about what I've forgotten. I will check my maps, my phone, check for my sunglasses and water. I will never feel ready for anything. I will start driving because I have to, because it's eleven hours to Chicago and fifteen hours after that, an indirect route through the Midwest that is my family's home, toward the prairies, and the hoped-for landscape that always lies just beyond to the west.

ACKNOWLEDGMENTS

Though this novel draws on some real-life events and characters, it is firmly rooted in fiction and takes liberties with historical facts. It grew out of that great old question "What if?" and out of wondering how two seemingly opposite cultures might have so much in common. I have read, admired, and fretted over the *Little House* books since I was eight years old; I owe part of my love of reading (and reading about food) to Laura Ingalls Wilder and Rose Wilder Lane.

I am so grateful to Liz Van Hoose and Nicole Aragi for their incredible guidance and support. Many thanks also to Ramona Demme, Duvall Osteen, Christie Hauser, Carolyn Coleburn, Rebecca Lang, Barbara Campo, Dave Cole, Amanda Brower, Gina Anderson, Tsuyako Uehara, and everyone at Viking Penguin.

I also thank Donald Platt, John Duvall, Liz Han, Nush Powell, Derek Pacheco, Kera Lovell, Purdue University, the

ACKNOWLEDGMENTS

University of San Francisco, the Laura Ingalls Wilder Historic Home and Museum and the Laura Ingalls Wilder–Rose Wilder Lane Museum in Mansfield, Missouri, the Laura Ingalls Wilder Memorial Society in De Smet, South Dakota, the Rose Wilder Lane Papers at the Herbert Hoover Presidential Library and Museum in West Branch, Iowa, and everyone who's ever indulged me in conversations about the *Little House* books.

As part of my research for this novel I read and appreciated Rose Wilder Lane's *Diverging Roads, Free Land*, and *Let the Hurricane Roar*, among other works, William Holtz's *The Ghost in the Little House*, John E. Miller's *Becoming Laura Ingalls Wilder*, William Anderson's *Laura Ingalls Wilder: A Biography*, and Anita Clair Fellman's *Little House, Long Shadow: Laura Ingalls Wilder's Impact on American Culture*.

And as always I thank Po, wise reader and constant support, who understands my *Little House* obsession and has been to De Smet to prove it.